THE MUSK *and Other Stories*

THE MUSK *and* Other Stories

Arupa Patangia Kalita

THORNBIRD

NIYOGI BOOKS

The Musk and Other Stories: English translation of selected Assamese stories by Arupa Patangia Kalita; Niyogi Books, New Delhi 2017.

Published by
NIYOGI BOOKS
Block D, Building No. 77,
Okhla Industrial Area, Phase-I,
New Delhi-110 020, INDIA
Tel: 91-11-26816301, 26818960
Email: niyogibooks@gmail.com
Website: www.niyogibooksindia.com

Editor: Manali Das
Design: Shashi Bhushan Prasad
Cover image: Rahdhola Pothar, an well-known paddy field of Golaghat, during an autumnal evening. © Achintadu, own work, Wikimedia Commons / CC-BY-SA-3.0.

ISBN: 978-81-933935-8-1
Publication: 2017

Printed at: Niyogi Offset Pvt. Ltd., New Delhi, India

Contents

Foreword

As a young, budding writer of the Little Magazines of Assam during the seventies, Arupa Patangia Kalita (born in 1956) soon made a mark in Assamese literature. The Little Magazines in the seventies of Assam formed a hotbed for the second wave of the Progressive Movement in Assamese literature. Arupa Patangia Kalita, imbued with progressive ideas of the time, shows in her short stories and novels an unabated and unwavering sympathy for the hapless, suffering humanity. And yet, her fiction never smacks of propaganda born out of a political agenda.

In fact, her novels and short stories are always pleasantly saturated with fine artistic qualities. It is this combination of thought and art that has distinguished Arupa Patangia Kalita in today's Assamese literature as a writer of the front rank. Her sympathy for the oppressed and exploited class has also added another dimension to her oeuvre—the feminist dimension. Of course, her feminist leaning always gets revealed as a part of her broader humanist outlook. Her first novel (rather a novelette) *Mriganabhi*, which appears in this collection with the title *The Musk,* is a pointer to this fact. Her most valuable and most popular novel *Felanee,* a very fine example of the subaltern novel in Assamese, is another instance of the same. These novels showcase Arupa's two bright aspects as a fiction writer: the aspect of potential social themes unfolding, as if naturally, and the aspect of her rich craftsmanship with a poetic quality, though she is not known as a poet—a quality which we see in Anita Desai's *Cry, The Peacock*.

Whatever qualities and characteristics we find in Arupa's novels are also reflected equally well in her short stories. It is, therefore, in the fitness of things that this collection of her fiction contains not only some of her short stories, but also two of her short novels, or more precisely a novelette (*Mriganabhi*) and a long story (*Alekjaan Bano's Love*). The readers who do not have access to Assamese will get a taste of her short stories and novels, both. The contents here are, of course, not critically selected with an eye on seriousness of theme and a matching richness in art. The pieces here are the translators' choices, which may itself be a rewarding cause of interest for the common reader. Translators, after all, are the good readers. And yet, it is found that these stories together present an overall view of Arupa Patangia Kalita—the fiction writer, one of the topmost of her generation of writers that appeared in the seventies and is continuing to write with increasing richness, much to the delight of all.

Another positive aspect of this collection is its comprehensiveness; it covers most of the aspects of the author's themes of short stories. Arupa Patangia Kalita, being a persistent socially conscious writer, the stories in this volume show the aspects of the society around her with which she is most concerned. The society in Assam, since her youth, has seen political turmoil. The decade-long Assam Agitation to free the state from illegal migrants turned violent by taking on a fascist character, and thus, bringing in its trail inhuman suffering for many. She also witnessed the subsequent violent extremist movement for an Independent Assam that let loose a parallel reign of terror, causing nightmare to many. Against the background of these, she was witnessing the unrelieved suffering of the poor, the weak and the homeless.

Arupa had to live through a period, which as if, made her wield the pen by whispering to herself—'time is out of joint…'. In such a time, she, with her wounded consciousness witnessed the economic-and gender-based oppression of the weak and the dislocated, and also the loss of social moorings of a section of humanity. Arupa Patangia Kalita, a product of the Progressive Movement, makes her readers see this history in the making, and also feel and think for themselves.

Prof. Gobinda Prasad Sarma

Retired professor, Department of English, Gauhati University

Former dean, Faculty of Arts, Gauhati University

Eminent critic and writer

Two Days from Phantom's Diary

Last night was extremely hot, but in the early morning there was a light shower. It brought down the temperature. The passengers in the early morning bus were all dozing. Suddenly, the brakes were applied, followed by a screeching sound. The passengers jolted as if they were water inside a closed vessel. There was no time for them to grasp the situation. Four young boys, from among the passengers, were already brandishing their guns: one was pointing the gun at the driver, the second positioned himself near the door and the other two were threatening the passengers. Being soaked in the drizzle, the jeans worn by the boys which have never seen water, emanated a nauseating odour.

It was the Friday bus that carried passengers comprising traders who brought merchandise from the small town to the capital situated a hundred kilometres away. Just within five minutes, the boys extorted a fat sum of money. They approached the bespectacled man; he had ₹1,000, which he handed over to them without the least protest. The boy grabbed the money like a kite. The man experienced a pain in his heart. How much could he have accomplished with this sum? The boy stank, making the man nauseous.

'Give whatever else you have,' demanded the boy in a rough tone.

The man laid down his specs and closed his eyes, losing himself in his own world of fantasy. It was thick darkness, only layers and layers of thick darkness ...

The slightly built man felt a strange power flowing through his veins. With extreme swiftness, he seemed to tug the stained collar of the boy and growled like a tiger, 'Miscreants, gang of criminals! Making an effort to earn is tedious. In the name of rescuing the nation, you are extorting easy money.' The other boy who was extorting money at the rear end of the bus came pointing his gun. The man inflicted a severe blow to the boy and he fell on his face. As if having touched a spiteful object, the man pushed the gun away with his foot. Then, like a cat charging at a mouse, he bumped the heads of the two boys together, leaving them unconscious. Like doves struck by pellets from a shotgun, they remained on the ground. The other two boys who came near the man also received severe blows which made them fall down. The man dragged all four of them to the centre of the bus, and shouted, 'Miscreants, gang of criminals, sucking the blood of men has become an obsession.' He spat on the face of one of them ...

When the man opened his eyes, the bus was moving. The passengers suddenly became aware that they will have to go to the police station. It seemed they were pushed from the tiger's mouth to the lion's jaw. The bus stopped. The passengers alighted. The man also got down. When the driver and the handyman returned from their tea break, they found the bus deserted. They decided to go to the police station and return.

The man boarded a different bus. At least he escaped from the harassment of the gang. The bus jerked a lot. That particular stretch of the road was devastated by flood three years back. The flood came, dried up, but the road was never repaired. The bus, which was packed with passengers stacked together like betel leaves, swayed from side to side. The man could not move his foot. Initially when he started his career in the small town, which was 30 kms from the highway, it took him half-an-hour to 45 minutes to cover the distance. After 20 years, now it took him two to three hours. The whole road was dotted with big potholes. It was extremely hot inside the swaying bus that now moved at a snail's pace. Another man was trying to make room for a woman who was covering her mouth with her hand and making an awful sound; a gesture in order to allow her to be near the window. The passengers looked like sugar crystals in a container. A baby let out a shrill cry as the belt of someone's bag got stuck round its neck. An old lady was harshly rebuking the boy standing next to her as he treaded upon her toes. The woman making that awful sound suddenly threw up. The stinking vomit soaked the shirt of the man standing near her. The scorching heat, the commotion, the rancid odour of the vomit, the severe pain from the immobilised foot—everything added to the man's misery. He shut his eyes …

Layers and layers of darkness enveloped his consciousness. His distress and agony were soon immersed in this darkness, amidst which a pen glowed like the fire from the will-o'-the-wisp. He picked up the pen and started writing for the national dailies—emphatic language, fluent English, intense reflection. What caption should be given to the article? It was the crucial time for king-making, so who would give ear to the condition of the ramshackle roads of a state like ours? *The Bananas are Devoured by the Bats* would be a suitable caption. His report would come up for discussion in the Rajya Sabha and would subsequently, be published. There would be editorials on that fatal portion of the road. The Central Government would question the State

Government, files would be probed, the mismanagement of loans sanctioned by The World Bank would come to light, and all leading to newspaper headlines … investigations … public wrath. The road would be repaired on a war footing.

The bus was finally moving at a steady pace now. It reached the highway. He changed into a clean shirt and put the soiled one in the bag. A cup of tea refreshed him.

Having arrived at Guwahati, the man hesitated to get down from the bus; wherever he tried to step, it was soggy. As soon as he stepped down, he found his foot in the pulpy mud. The entire bus-stand was ploughed by buses. Perhaps there had been a heavy shower last night. Most of the roads were covered with red soil sliding down the hills. By the time he reached his aunt's house, after having completed his office chores, he looked like a man coming from the paddy field, covered all over in red mud.

The compound of his aunt's house was immersed in knee-deep water. As he waded through the water, he found the house to be waterlogged, too. His aunt was preparing dinner; the gas stove on a bed.

On seeing him, she started to moan, 'Oh! Where will you sit? What will you eat? I cannot even offer you a cup of tea in this house.'

His uncle had died a long time ago and his aunt had to bring up her son single-handedly. She managed the village property until he was employed in Guwahati. She sold away the village property and purchased a plot of land in Guwahati, complying with her son's wish. The house was built and a daughter-in-law soon joined the family. It was her time to enjoy, but she was crying instead.

The man attempted to lighten the situation by humouring her, 'It is only a trickle of water. Why should you cry?'

His aunt had toiled her whole life, but he had never seen her shed a tear.

'I am not scared of water, but this is not just water; a slight drizzle is enough to bring all hell inside my house,' she cried.

In a little while, some more water carrying a lot of garbage—lumps of excreta, a rotten crow—entered the house. The man felt nauseous. He was served a cup of tea and two rotis.

'This is the type of danger that we fail to confront,' his aunt's face bore clear signs of dejection.

He could not swallow; something choked him. He reclined on the wall, sitting on the bed raised by bricks. His eyes were drooping shut. Darkness was spreading like sand and he seemed to be rolling in it. There was darkness in his eyes; his whole being was enveloped in darkness, even the roots of his nails ...

He had become the editor of a newspaper. There was growing public opinion against the digging of hills. A photo of his aunt was splashed in the front page. His aunt, who had courageously struggled throughout her whole life, was now declaring herself a failure against the danger of mud immersing her house. There was a mass rebellion led by his paper. The tilling of hills was stopped and they were mended. Seated in the verandah, his aunt was enjoying the rainfall. The roses, ashokas and togors, brought from her village, were sprouting beautifully. The flood could not perish them. Even the smile of his aunt was printed in the front page of the newspaper. There was no pile of red mud sliding down the hills after a shower—the hills were covered with green foliage ...

'Eat, eat this,' said his aunt, serving him some food in a dish.

Taking a handful to his mouth, he put it back; a foul odour, like that of raw fish, emanated from it. He got ready to depart. Folding his pants, he got down from the bed. He caught sight of some sprigs in the verandah. They were kept piled near the dustbin for some time. Now the water had brought them in. He made his way through the garbage.

When he boarded the homeward evening bus, he felt an itching in his legs. Would his hands and legs become like that of his aunt who had patches of scars all over? His legs went on itching. There was some space in the evening bus due to the slackness of passengers, allowing him to stretch his legs. Crossing the highway, the bus entered the dilapidated portion of the road. After covering the distance, the bus came to a halt. It would proceed no further. The roadside shopkeeper passed on the information that the bridge ahead had a hole in it. All the passengers got down from the bus. Two mini-buses, a few taxis and a couple of rickshaws together ferried the passengers to and fro.

The man, along with four others, booked a taxi. They started crossing the bridge on foot. Half way through, they saw that a piece of iron sheet had come off from the centre of the bridge.

'These bridges are from the time of the British. How long will they last after all?' This statement was made by Jeevan Saikia, the head clerk who worked in the tea estate two kilometres away from the small town.

'Has your garden received the letter from the British Government?' asked Nabin Sharma, a pharmacist working in another tea estate.

'All 14 tea estates have received it,' remarked another senior clerk who worked in a garden a little further away from Sharma's.

'I don't understand what letter from the British Government you are talking about,' said the man who was cautiously crossing the broken bridge.

Once they crossed the bridge, all of them sat in the car. It started bouncing over the potholes in the road.

The man asked once again, 'What letter were you talking of?'

Nabin Sharma replied, 'The British Government has informed that the bridges constructed for communication while establishing the 14 tea estates in the area have crossed their prescribed period of durability. They have urged strongly to rebuild those bridges.'

'Sharma! Do you have a copy of the letter in your office?' asked the man eagerly.

'Why not? Of course, there is,' replied all of them in unison.

The man reclined in his car seat. The breeze was blowing through the lowered window-panes. The heated body was gradually starting to cool down. The eyelids were becoming heavy. The car reached the portion of the road that was damaged by the flood. The passengers swayed inside the small car, as if being carried through the waves of the flood. The heavy eyelids invited darkness—thick like velvet—his face was soon engulfed in it. The darkness spread out to form an enchanting carpet that carried him instantly to some distant place ...

He was leading a small group to Delhi with the letter in his hand. He had been able to knock at the right places. The British Government's duty consciousness was being compared with the indifference of the Indian Government and a copy of the letter was printed in the newspapers. He returned from Delhi after extracting a hefty amount as grant. Work was progressing on a war footing, bridges were being reconstructed. The public hailed him as a hero; there were press conferences, he was being eulogised all over the TV and radio.

It was past 10 at night by the time he reached home. The children were asleep. His wife was waiting. There was no electricity; a lamp was lit. She quietly took his soiled clothes and arranged water, towels and sandals for him near the bathroom. He slipped his feet carefully into his sandals, as the straps were on the verge of breaking. But he found his feet encased in sturdy straps. His wife suppressed a smile and lowered the lamp to his feet; a new pair of sandals with blue straps shone in the darkness.

The man rubbed his hair, and asked, 'What is this?'

She answered softly, as she desperately wanted to spend some time alone with her husband without awakening any of the children. With a gesture, she asked whether he would take dinner then or later.

The man also answered in a hushed tone, 'Not just now I am feeling tired, so let us sit for some time.'

Actually, he wanted to have a cup of tea, but did not want to send her back to the kitchen.

Wearing the new sandals, he went slowly to the back verandah. Before sitting down, he placed a stool near him. The woman came out with a cup of tea, as if reading his mind. She sat on the stool near him and stared at the jaded face of her husband. It was only a single day, yet she felt as if she was sitting near her husband after a long time. The man ran his fingers through her tresses; the slippery hair came off her loosely tied bun and covered her face like the light cloud over the moon. In the pale moonlight, he went on staring at her enchanting face.

'Why did you purchase the sandals? I told you to buy clothes,' he said in a soft voice.

'Yes, I bought my clothes, dresses for the children, and also your sandals,' she whispered.

'So many things you have purchased. After all, how much money did you have?' He looked curiously at her.

She replied, 'Do we buy things like you? We buy only after carefully checking and bargaining … I forgot to tell you something. I have plucked the coconuts from the newly planted tree; the kernel is so white. Tomorrow I will make laddus. And another thing—today at noon while I was cooking, the papaya tree bent down. Why wouldn't it? The papayas are so big. I gave it a prop, but tomorrow you will have to fix it properly.'

'Hazarika!' His neighbour Sarma called out. 'Today we have guard duty.'

The man immediately rose to his feet.

This has been going on for the last one year. The military had started this. Although not on a daily basis, but once a week, they checked the record; there were no chances for deceit. If someone was caught yawning at work, he would be asked, 'Did you have guard duty?' Informing Hazarika that he would soon follow, he told his wife to serve him dinner.

After finishing his dinner, he asked his wife, 'Is there any letter for me today?'

'Yes, I had forgotten! A boy delivered a letter.'

'Anybody familiar?' He was curious.

'No! Wait, I'll fetch it,' she said, getting up.

He opened the letter, only to find an AK 47 inside. The gun bumped into him heavily.

'Give ₹50,000, or else …' read the letter.

The second bump made him roll down.

From where can I give ₹50,000? I have to worry even before buying a pair of hawai sandals.

'You must give. If you don't …'

The gun came up again. Even before a sound could be heard, he rolled down in pools of blood; he fell down on the road, just like the boss of their office, Mr Saikia. Like Saikia, his feet, too, turned yellow from the profuse bleeding. His wife stuck her head to his yellow feet. The man felt his head spinning. Saikia was heavily insured: his elder son was a doctor and the younger one had the requisite qualification needed to be employed in the office, he owned his house, and even rented one out. But what did he own? He wanted to fold the letter and put it aside, but was unable to do so. It was as if a letter bomb had blasted in the centre of his house; his beloved wife, children and house had all turned into debris. Someone covering the mouth carried lumps of flesh in a cart. The man was unnerved.

His wife let out a yawn.

'Whose letter is it?' she asked, yawning again.

'Ah! It is an official letter. You go to sleep. I shall lock the house from outside and open it myself,' he said, stepping outside.

After going a few paces, he read the letter again under the streetlight. Checking the date, he realised that they wanted to meet him the next day; the name of the place was completely unfamiliar. Even after working for 17 years, he had never heard of that place. Nevertheless, he would have to go. Once again, he visualised the soles turning yellow from the profuse bleeding. The enchanting face of a senseless woman pressed against those soles. Saikia had held a high post; he had connections with the police, the military and politicians. What happened? That did not change anything. He decided to go the next day, as he had no choice. He looked at his house—the bedroom light was still on—his wife was awake. Whenever he had vigilance duty, she would not sleep.

Sarma, Dowerah and Hazarika—all three were headed in his direction. Dowerah once handed them ₹10,000—borrowed money—and made an agreement for another ₹10,000. Dowerah even borrowed ₹2,000 from him once. During Dowerah's time, even if it would come to the knowledge of the police and the army, there was no problem. Everything passed off smoothly. There was even rumour of money being shared. But now, it would come out in the newspapers and new dangers would crop up. Recently, Chandan Saikia was arrested from the office itself. A quiet man, his crime was that he paid money to the terrorists.

One arrested terrorist had a list of names who paid money and Saikia's name figured in it. The police, the army, the legal proceedings—all joined hands in harassing the man. Even now the case was pending. Although the thought of sharing the news about the letter crossed his mind, he stopped short of it. He was unsure of the outcome.

All of them used their sticks to strike at light posts, telephone posts and gates of residences while loitering around for a while. Then they stopped near the river bank; cautious not to step on the bridge, as they could not see the potholes in the dark.

A heap of stones, brought either to repair the road or to fill up the potholes on the bridge, lay there. They sat on that pile of stones. The calm breeze comforted their bodies. Two army vehicles passed them by. Gradually, the night deepened. Large mosquitoes surrounded them. The river bank was covered with jungle.

The man suggested, 'Let us sit in Dowerah's house and have a cup of tea.'

They would often have tea breaks at each other's house during these night patrols. While they were having tea in Dowerah's verandah, two army vehicles halted near the bridge. The frequency of army vehicles had increased recently. It was the 14th of August. Many terrorist organisations had declared a bandh the next day. Violence was rampant all around. Perhaps due to this, army vehicles were seen more frequently. Seeing no one near the bridge, the military men came hurriedly towards them and started abusing them. The four men were being severely rebuked for relaxing and sipping tea instead of guarding the area.

The man wanted to say something but suddenly something choked him. In a split second, a slap resounded on his cheek, followed by an abusive slander, 'All of you are supporters of terrorists, helping them to blow up the bridge.' Leaving behind a strong stench of liquor, the military personnel marched to their jeep.

Once again, the men made their way towards the bridge. The vehicles tore through the darkness. Striking mosquitoes with one hand, Dowerah murmured, 'Why should they slap us? We are not their bonded slaves!'

The man who was slapped, dozed off on the heap of stones. Pressed by tiredness, he went on swaying. The man jumped into the enchanting darkness which shrouded his consciousness …

Gradually, he immersed himself in the whirlpool of darkness; darkness that penetrated his ears and nose. With a gulping sound, he drank that darkness; his parched throat drank it. He emerged from the darkness with a strange power flowing through his veins. He protested, 'Are we bonded slaves? Why will you slap me? Who are you to interfere with my human rights?' Facing a raised gun, he snatched a pistol from someone's waist. They could not even grasp the situation. With his sharp aim, he threw away the weapons of the three men. The rest also met with the same fate. They scattered, with wounded hands. He initiated a mass protest against the persecution which was carried out by the state machinery in the name of security; first in his locality and then in other places. It was as if something was obstructing a river from flowing; he removed a couple of clods that served as barricade and the water rushed turbulently. Amidst fervent protest, he was being convened into an uncommon personality. People breathed freely …

'Wake up! Those hornets and wasps are coming.' Dowerah shook the man. He woke up instantly.

An army vehicle halted. An officer came out and shook hands with all of them. He said very politely, 'The public must extend full support to the army in combating the terrorists.'

Expressing his sympathy for the trouble caused to the men earlier, he drove away.

'All army officers are not bad, some are good,' the man uttered to himself.

At around 3 am, all the men left for their respective homes.

The man slept lightly towards early morning. He had a dream; a big boil had erupted on his cheek, the headless hardened boil caused tremendous pain. The man went on groaning.

He woke up in the morning, had a cup of tea and went out in search of that unknown place. After asking around, he reached that particular road. It was not exactly a road, but rather a ploughed paddy field. While trying to cover the distance, tagging his bicycle along, he fell down twice. He stopped at the junction as directed in the letter. Whom to ask? Where to go? It was beyond his capacity to pay the amount they demanded. He could at the most arrange for ₹20,000–₹25,000, and that too borrowed from someone. Would they agree? What if they disagreed? He had a job here. He had a roof over his head. Where would he go? Where would he escape? The man sweated profusely.

He caught sight of a towel-clad boy, gesturing to follow him. Following the boy, he stepped onto the front yard of a straw hut. It was a rural family hut. An old woman was spreading grains on the floor. The house had two rooms; entering the first room, he looked around and sat down on a chair with a broken handle. His throat was parched. He asked the old woman for some water.

She came out with a glass of water, and looking around, she enquired, 'Have you come to pay money? These fellows are making life unbearable; they neither study nor plough the field nor go to the market. They only do this! For fear of the military and the police, we cannot even gather our crops.'

The boy whom he followed, came with two other lads; one was wearing a towel and the other one was in a pair of jeans and a loose-fitted striped shirt. The man noticed a gun tucked under the striped shirt. The one with the towel also had a bulge in the shirt near the waist.

The boy in the white towel demanded, 'Give us what you have brought.'

'I received the letter only yesterday.'

'When will you give? We can't give much time,' the lad said.

'It will take 15–20 days.'

'No,' the other towel-clad lad said.

'I cannot give you so much. After all, I am not worth so much.'

'Not a single paise less,' the boy in the jeans said.

'Somehow 20 …' The man's throat went dry, he licked his lips.

'Not a single paise less than 40.' The voice of the jeans-clad lad had a metallic coolness.

The old woman came running through the front yard. She said something in her dialect. The trio jumped up.

'Don't come out of here, careful, if you tell something …' said the jeans-clad lad as he went out biting his lips.

The man remained sitting in the broken chair inside the hut. He clutched the only intact handle of the broken chair. Closing his eyes, he invited the soft mud-like clouds of darkness. Like an ostrich, he stuck his face into the mud. His consciousness was immersed in the darkness. Like the lush grass of the rainy season, the man inside him grew luxuriantly …

He was tied to a tree in an open field by the three boys. He vehemently declared again, 'I will never give you anything, not even single paise.'

'What have you said? You are not giving us money,' the white towel-clad lad said.

'No. I will not give you the money that I have earned by turning my bones into soil and blood into water,' retorted the man.

With one single tug, he freed himself. He threw all three to the ground with the swiftness of a jungle cat. Growling like a tiger, he said 'Call, call your fathers.'

He dragged the trio like dead rats to a berry tree with a hornet nest hanging from the main branch. 'I'll throw you into the hornet's nest. You are growing fat by sucking the blood of human beings. Let the hornets also get a share.'

The trio clutched his feet, 'Let us go free.'

He spat on their faces and on their blood-thirsty weapons. Pelting a couple of kicks at them, he gave the trembling trio their arms. 'Take these! Don't think that you can dominate us with the aid of these for long. Time is not always the same.'

He reassured the terror-stricken people of the city. The weak and the feeble were huddled together. His initiative resulted in the establishment of relations between the people and various anti-terrorist groups. The suppressed people were now like a river that had broken all barriers. A large anti-terrorist procession was led by him. The procession grew in number; people came out like rats to the Pied Piper's pipe.

The sound of firing in the vicinity made him stagger. A spark came flying and made a dent in the wall of his eyes. He could not comprehend what happened in that split second. He tightly grasped the broken handle of the chair. He simply remembered the quiet woman asking him to give a support to the papaya tree which was bending under the weight of the large papayas.

That woman was supposed to make laddus. She might have already filled the dish with white laddus. The children were perhaps being rebuked for snatching the laddus, 'Don't eat them all. Spare some for your father as well.'

The sound of crackers bursting surrounded them. A spark penetrated the left side of his chest. He felt as if someone had pushed him into a deep well. There were a series of thudding sounds for a while. Then everything went silent!

The eyelids that never winked out of fear, now seemed to be staring out of amazement. He took off his specs and placed them in his lap. He gazed down at his own pool of blood.

The Bhogi of the Bogamati Shrine

One could not really call it a road; it was just an uneven and pot-holed narrow opening through the trees created by the movement of men and animals. It was a very bumpy ride on the jeep. The dust carried by the strong winds made the whole place seem hazy. The month of Bohag had begun; still there was no sign of rain. There were clouds in the sky, but the winds did not allow them to descend to the parched earth. Even the sunlight was dulled by the intervening clouds. Under the heavy brooding sky, the dry and angry winds were roaring about in the forest—a forest completely devastated and stripped bare by heavy felling. At times the winds would rise up a cloud of dust from the heaps of dried leaves, lowering them again at other times. The forest had been cleared on all sides—there were only the bare stumps of the trees as far as the eyes could see and at places, merely heaps of cut branches. One could imagine that this must have been a dense jungle once, full of insects, birds and beasts. This forest has been finished off within a very short time—the stumps of the trees still seemed alive; there was green still to be seen at places on the leaves of the cut branches lying in heaps.

In this devastated forest, buried completely in dust, some scantily clad people were roaming about, lost like motherless chicks. These were the children of the forest: those dark-skinned young men who were chopping the wood; those people who were trying to cut the few remaining trees; those boys who were carrying the planks of wood from one place to another. On each of their faces, one could see the torment and pain of cutting down a tree. Those people did not look towards our jeep—they had got used to seeing vehicles like this.

The road was gradually getting more and more winding. On the right were the mountains and on the left was the red river. The soil of the hills was strangely white. But the colour of the river was very dark. Oh, that was not water! Those were wooden planks floating in the water. The river was filled with dark cut pieces from the trees. It was difficult to transport these heavy logs from this height using vehicles. This hill river would carry the wood to the plains, from where they would be loaded into trucks.

On the side of the meandering hilly road were some small huts, the insides of which could be clearly seen. They seemed more like nests built out of straw and sticks. There was almost nothing inside—one or two aluminum utensils, a wooden bench and a couple of sacks. The big-bellied, runny-nosed kids with spidery hands and feet had no clothes on them. The adults did not have much either. How far had we come from the city? Maybe 30–35 kilometres ... But it seemed as if we had arrived in the midst of primitive men from the Stone Age.

Why did the king set up this shrine, called the Bogamati Than, in the middle of this dense and inhospitable jungle? What was the royal intention in setting up this temple to the Goddess Kesaikhati at the top of this hillock? Maybe its out-of-the-way, remote location made it a suitable site for offering human sacrifices. Sacrifices were made for the welfare of the royal family, the country and its people. But did the king think only about the welfare of his people? The prince of the Barua clan was sacrificed here because of political self-interest. Who knows what else had happened in the name of human sacrifice at the Bogamati Than?

The turns of the road were getting sharper. The driver stopped the car. That strange river was in front of us. It lay silent; the depth of its shallow waters not enough to submerge a person's feet completely. In its bosom lay multi-coloured stones and pebbles of various shapes and sizes. Suddenly tides arise on this dry river, the strong waves carrying away with them whatever they found on their way. A little while later, again the calm, placid and lifeless river ... The car went over the dry river. A forest official, trying to cross the river in his car, was swept away by the tide and he never made his way back.

There were some trees left on the top of the hill. Still, it would not be long before the axes reached that far even. One could see the tall steeple of the Bogamati Than. On the left was the red river; on the right were the hills; and on the hillock, a forest of teak trees. All along the way this far, all we heard were the sounds of trucks, saws, axes and the felling of trees. Now, we could also hear the twittering of birds. The wind was also calming down. In the breeze, one could smell the fragrance of some wild flowers.

Suddenly, the peace of the jungle was shattered by the loud, piercing blare of rap-music floating towards us. Our driver, Aditya stopped the jeep. A red van was standing right in the middle of the road. On the banks of the river, some young men were dancing to the rhythm of loud, blaring music—a wild, frenzied dance. They were wearing colourful loose shorts and had long hair tied with rubber bands. They looked towards us. Their eyes were drunk; their legs trembled. They began to argue with our driver. He and Dr Barua got out of the jeep.

Have the boys come here for a picnic? No, they have been there for quite a few days now. There, in their tents, one could see a generator and a gas stove. Behind them was a heap of empty bottles. On the left was a pile of garbage: shapeless blue plastic bottles of mineral water, used cans and tins of sauces, pickles, butter and cheese. We could also see clearly many small packets of contraceptives. A cold shiver ran down my spine. A couple of them came forward on seeing Aditya and Dr Barua. What if they did something to Aditya, Dr Barua or even me? Those packets seemed to lay there baring their teeth, grinning at me.

My throat was dry. Everywhere around was the all-pervading stillness of the jungle. Aditya and Dr Barua were coming back. One of the men in baggy trousers moved the van from the road. Our driver made a quick salute of relief to God when he put his hand on the steering wheel. Dr Barua was cracking his knuckles; one could see two veins bulging on Aditya's temple. On that lonely road, the sound of shallow English music chased us a long way.

The car stopped. We were at the *than*. The afternoon sunlight fell on the steep green hillock below the fields, along the meandering path of the red river. The silvery red river snatched away our heavy burdened thoughts. It was as part of my research work, after many days and weeks of planning and arranging, that we had come to visit the shrine at Bogamati. But now I did not feel like taking out my notebook or my camera. A sort of sluggishness seemed to engulf me, and make me weak, slowly. I just wanted to spread the end of my sari on the ground and go to sleep under the gigantic mangrove tree. My world, my job, my studies, my responsibilities—all those chains fell off from my feet, one by one. I wanted to sleep, just sleep. I let out a yawn.

Dr Barua and Aditya made their way to the little house near the temple. A silver-haired old man came out. All of them started walking back towards me. Dr Barua's lips looked parched. The man, who asked for three cups of tea during an-hour visit to our place, was without a single cup of tea all this while. He had taken all this trouble only for me. He was from this area, knew the roads and pathways well. He was a reporter for two newspapers. Besides, he had visited these places earlier while he was doing his research on dialects.

The old man was relishing a cup of tea, two slices of bread, a piece of cake and a sweet. One could not understand him very clearly—it was difficult to pronounce words distinctly with a toothless mouth. He had been the caretaker of the shrine for the last 30 years. His father and grandfather had also been caretakers of the same temple before him.

The man was bent over with age; his shaggy eyebrows trembled as he spoke, his indistinct words seemed to drown in some strange sadness. 'Ma, don't ask me about such things. In this temple there were many human sacrifices made in the name of Kesaikhati Devi. In the valley of the hill lived the Sar clan. Each year, *bhogis* were brought from the Sar clan ...'

The history that I had sought out in books and papers in the libraries and archives for so long had suddenly come to life in the middle of the ruins of the lonely, lifeless shrine.

On the north of the temple were the extensive fields bequeathed to the Sars by the king. Who was that in the field? Was he the young man I had been looking for all this while in the moth-eaten books, in the yellowed paper of texts, in the stone sculptures of the temple ruins? His long hair was blowing in the wind. He had a very fit and healthy figure. He was neither sick nor stunted. He was not a bastard. There were no pockmarks or cuts or blemishes on his body. Even his ears had not been pierced. He had never been bitten by snakes or dogs or foxes. No bird or kite had ever dirtied him. He did not eat what was unpalatable; he had never put leftovers into his mouth. His jingling anklets spoke of his youth and youthful energy. He bore no marks of labour on his arms and feet. He was running about like a child, among the people working in the fields, gathering their love and affection. There, he tripped a girl and ran away; there, he snatched the bundle of rice saplings from the man's hand and threw them upwards; there, he let loose the two oxen from the harness of the boy's plough … How irresponsible and carefree was his rippling laughter!

But did he really laugh? Or did his long mane, soaked with his tears, get glued to his face? He was tied to the pillar in the south of the temple, below the big peepul tree. A few links of the chain, still smeared with oil and vermilion, lay near the pillar. Was it really just vermilion or was it the blood stains of that healthy young man? This chain, used to tie elephants, was now used to tie him. Why does he try to break the chain? The chain cuts into his crazed body; his fine silk dress and golden ornaments are drenched in blood. Does he want to run away?

A Sar prince from his dynasty had run away into the hills, where he married a hill maiden. That is how the Kharkong clan had grown in the hills. Do the hills beckon to him too? Does he not remember the story of that Sar prince who escaped? Why else was this oil- and vermilion-stained, snake-like chain still lying at the feet of this iron pillar? Did his parents, brothers and sisters not come to look for him? Did no one come running to this desolate hilltop where he was crying his heart out? Royal decree! Was it just a royal decree?

The tax-exempt golden harvest of the fields, the many royal facilities, the bed chamber of the elder brother of the Sar prince illuminated by the presence of a royal princess—these were people of the Sar clan. They were given whatever they wished for. The storm created by the dishevelled hair of the golden anklet-wearing Sar prince raised tides in the red river; his cries seared through the hills, slicing through the trees, scratching them deeply.

He became a *bhogi*. He would sit on this rock and eat his favourite things. The coldness of the tortoise shell-like rock was like the cold touch of his stony heart. His tears had coagulated making his heart as hard as the rock. He had risen to the top of the society, people, even life. Since he was beyond the reach of the law and justice, he had become uncontrollable. The fear of imminent death had made him frightening. The breeze from his hair created havoc in all directions. He had dragged that same round-cheeked young girl, who he had tripped and let fall in the fields, even after she had become the mother of two, from her own kitchen and raped her in her own bed. Her husband, father-in-law, mother-in-law, brother-in-law, sister-in-law—everyone looked on. But he was a *bhogi*, a royal *bhogi*. As the time of his death grew closer, the more horrifying became his dance of destruction. Unlimited food and sexual excitement had made him extremely dangerous.

That is him, with his blood-shot eyes, soft silk clothes on his body, golden anklets presented to him by the king on his feet. He is running about in the limitless fields given to his family by the king, letting his hair, which had never been touched by razor or scissor, blow in the wind. His anklets jingle. He carries a bow and arrows on his shoulder, a sharp sword bared in his hand. People bow before him to pay their respects.

Suddenly, he jumps up with a scream—with his own hands he has imprisoned a pregnant peasant woman. She is crying like a female deer. What could she do? What would he do? The people in the fields watch holding their breaths, as if turned to stone. He cuts open her stomach with his sword; his young hands are drenched in the blood of a human foetus.

Before he was sacrificed, he was made to stand on the fern-covered mound, so that people could see him. Gold ornaments, expensive clothes, adorned with sandalwood, everyone paid their obeisance to him. The husband of that round-cheeked woman who he had dragged out of her kitchen, the family of the woman whose stomach he had slit open—everyone had come to see him. The king washed away all the crimes, the wrongs, the injustices that he had done by giving compensation. He was going to die for the king and for the people.

Pointing to a few rough, uneven stones lying on the fern bed, the old caretaker said, 'These are the *bhogi*'s footsteps.'

This was the way, through this dark tunnel, he was taken to the banks of the *kunda* The damp tunnel reeked. A few bats flew past, flapping their wings near our ears. The bent old caretaker had no trouble crossing the tunnel, but our backs were beginning to ache with having to stoop so much. The cold impact of the slippery stone steps on our bare feet sent shivers down our spine. This was the water of the *kunda*; he was stripped bare on its banks. In the unsteady hands of the feeble, old caretaker, we saw a huge crescent-shaped knife, the Chandrahans Da, blackened with rust. The old man was not able to lift it. He knelt down in respect. In the dark temple, the huge curved form of the knife could clearly be seen in the momentary flicker of light ensuing from the flash of the camera.

This was the sacrificial altar. It was as wide as a human neck, and was adorned with flowers, oil and vermilion. That concave block of wood also came to life in the flashlight. From the oil-smeared block ran a little drain towards the *kunda*. Dark and deep, this spring was supposed to meet the red river underground. Its water never dried up. The caretaker chanted some mantras and asked us to take some water from the *kunda* in our palms and raise it to our foreheads. My body trembled as I bent forward to touch the water. What were those smooth-bodied things slithering about in the water? Many long thin snakes! They circled around in the water, went down at times and then came up again. The slimy water slipped between my fingers. His neck was placed on this very block of wood; the head caretaker cut his body into two with one blow of the knife. The body fell into the *kunda*; the head fell at the feet of the Goddess.

What is it that slipped out through my fingers? Was it slimy water or blood? In the light of the little mustard-oil lamp that was burning at the feet of the Goddess, I could flickeringly see the body float up in the *kunda*. The dark waters of the spring turned crimson; the snakes crawled all over his headless body, slithering around it, encircling it. As we watched, his headless naked body began to sink in the dense waters of the *kunda*. His head lay at the Devi's feet; his long hair soaked in blood, his eyes wide open. A little stream of blood from his neck ran through the drain towards the spring. There will be good times. There will be welfare for everyone. The king will become invincible. When the altar had been reddened by his blood, there was a gun salute. Crackers were burst, conches were sounded. The head caretaker who had severed the head in one stroke remained ostracised for seven days.

Bending over almost twice as much, we came out of the dark tunnel into the temple. Outside there is light, there are people, a little further away is a modern world. That lively young man who disappeared in the waters of the *kunda* is a past, a frightening past. Aditya and Dr Barua were taking photos of the temple. Someday, this temple would collapse, be reduced to ruins, and in it will be buried its gruesome past.

Outside, the driver of our car was waiting impatiently. He came running towards us; his forehead beaded with sweat, 'Sir, please hurry up! There is trouble in the reserve.'

These days, the word "trouble" chased people everywhere, every moment of their lives.

'There has been a murder down below,' the driver pointed to the plains.

There were extensive fields around the hillock, on the peak of which stood the Bogamati Than, as also the winding red river.

We almost ran down the stone steps. The driver started driving his car silently. On one side was the red river, on the other side the hills. After driving for a while, we were forced to stop. We reached the tents from where we had heard the garish English music earlier; on all sides were wooden planks and logs hewn out of the felled trees. One dark-skinned thin man, wearing just a loin-cloth, was lying in the sand on the banks of the red river. Blood from his chest was flowing into the water. A large number of scantily clad men were standing in groups, from the road right up to the camp. All the young men we had seen dancing on our way up were holding guns in their hands. The men in loin-cloth were standing a little away from them. There was no question of our being able to move our car forward, the group of men would not move away from the road. In their eyes one could see the fire; the fire of the dry leaves that were burning everywhere.

The boys had ordered an ancient simul cotton tree with extensive stilt roots; even four men could not encircle the tree completely to cut it down. It was the royal command; they had the necessary official papers. But the people refused to cut that tree. That tree had been their God for very long; they had cleaned the area around its base regularly and lit a lamp there every day; they had tied threads around it and prayed to it for their wishes to be fulfilled. They would not cut that tree, no matter what. But how could the boys let such a big catch slip out of their hands?

The driver was trembling. 'Sir, we must go quickly. God knows what might happen at any moment. The people are very agitated, and the boys …' The man spat out his disgust.

One of the boys, wearing slippers and a pair of colourful loose shorts, came towards us; one of the same sort that were to be found everywhere these days. They were all built in the same mould: the same sunken eyes, dark lips, a body wasted with drinks and drugs, and the usual absolutely indifferent brash behaviour.

'All of you please go now and make sure that this news does not get out,' he said looking at Dr Barua. In his voice was a metallic calmness.

One could distinctly hear bullet shots by the river, and also the frenzy of people screaming and shouting; as if a snake had entered a crow nest. Various cries and shrieks chased us. The driver stopped the car again.

'What happened?' Maybe I sounded very frightened.

The driver laughed a little. 'No, Baideo, the water is rising in the river.'

The tides would come to the strange river now. The driver belonged to this area. Besides, till the other day, he had driven a mini-truck, which had transported wood from here to the city, by day or by night. It was not even a week since he had started working on his own, having brought this old jeep and plying it as a taxi. Dr Barua had also arranged for us to travel with him for the same reason—the driver knew the ways of the crazy river.

But where? There was no sign of the waters rising anywhere! The same flow of crystal-clear shallow water continued over the stones. The sun was about to set. The loud cries of a flock of woodpeckers were shattering the peace of the skies. One of the old banyan trees, on which a very large family of woodpeckers lived, lay flat on its face on the sandy river bank. Probably that tree had been cut only that afternoon. The birds were agitated to find their shelter gone, when they returned in the evening. The birds circled around the fallen tree, shredding the orange-hued sunset sky.

'It's coming, it's coming, the water is coming,' we screamed out in unison.

Unbelievable! There were waves in the dry river. Like the raised hood of a snake, the waves rose and rose and filled the river with water. Who was that dancing in the same rhythm as the waves? Who was that going towards the flock of woodpeckers? He was trying to chase away the flock of birds with a clapper. Whose long hair was it creating a storm in the air?

I had left that young man at the Bogamati Than. His body had been cut up into two, the head at the Devi's feet, his body into the *kunda*. I had touched the snakes. His anklets jingle as he chases away the birds. He rapes that round-cheeked girl after dragging her from her own kitchen; he takes out the foetus from the pregnant woman and plays ball with it in the wind. The king has paid compensation for all his crimes and wrong-doings. All his wishes have been fulfilled. With the royal decree on his head, he has gone completely wild. His family had brought him and offered him as a sacrifice to the Devi. Golden harvests grew in their tax-exempt fields and the radiance of a royal princess illuminated their home. Beyond the reach of the society, the family, rules and regulations and justice, he had run amuck. For he was a *bhogi*, the king would sacrifice him for the welfare of the kingdom and for the removal of all dangers from the royal throne …

Naren Balina Devi Sahasrang paribatsaran. Vidhi datateyena sakrati tripting lakhayng trivintare.

[With one sacrifice, the Devi was content for a thousand years, with three she was content for a hundred thousand. The consecrated blood would turn into nectar …]

The Goddess

The very first day I was in for a shock. We had rented a new house. I pushed open the window of the bedroom and oh! What do I see Three or four feet away from the window stood a life-size image of Goddess Kali: the mouth agape, the red tongue lolling out, a garland of human heads around the neck, pitch-black hair unfurled, blood dripping from the *dao* held menacingly, a head hanging from the other hand soaked with blood and the fierce nakedness. The image on the glittering altar was surrounded by incense sticks, flowers and offerings. The sight was slightly unnerving for me and I closed the window as a reflex.

With time, I got over the initial jitters. I saw the image day in and day out and gradually became accustomed to it.

Every morning, I was awakened by a hoarse howl. Even at early dawn, the devotee of Kali, who was the master of the house, a corpulent sight, would prostrate himself at the feet of Kali without drying his just-bathed body and give out three thundering yells, 'Ma! Ma! Ma!' I would spring up from my bed at the very sound.

I would then take up my morning cup of tea, but the aroma of the piping hot tea was drowned in the sharp scent of incense and my ears would be filled by the sound of the small bells and drums. The master of the house would then go out. His mother's and sister's prayers soon followed.

The whole day, the altar of Kali would smell of flowers, incense and sandalwood. The copper dish, where offerings were kept, would be overflowing with sandesh, batacha, grams and pieces of various fruits, even before the noon.

At noon, when the noisy household grew silent, a living skeleton was almost always seen stealing its way, taking the fruits in the folds of its sari and hiding itself behind the bakul tree. The very sight of the woman would send a chill down my spine. Could a human being live that way? The woman was as thin as a dried bamboo stick; the worn-out sari wrapped haphazardly around her body, the wild look in her eyes hidden in the sockets, the hair cut in a curious fashion, *kadam sat* as it was called.

Having gulped down the offerings, she would sit on the altar and pour out curses on Goddess Kali. She would not stop her avalanche of curses, which would be combined with various gestures, until someone, getting up from the siesta, arrived and beat her away with a stick. The more they tried to drag her away from the altar, the more they beat her, the louder her abuses became.

Slapping her thighs, she would let off an endless train of curses, 'Ah, you see, what an amount of food, ornaments of gold … Ah … Ah … don't you see …'

Being beaten up and kicked around, she would scream most piteously, 'My belly is burning … burning with hunger.'

The stout servant ragged her out like a rope. However, before he could do so, she managed to lick the copper plate clean, and even the tiniest bit of morsel being drawn away by the ants, could not escape her tongue.

The household was the stage of a play, as it were. The lesser characters revolved round the two main characters, helping the action of the play gain momentum. One of the two principal characters was inanimate, earthen, made of tradition and faith, while the other was of flesh and blood. The different scenes of the play would rush into my room through the window every day; sometimes with the moonlight, sometimes with the morning sunlight, sometimes with the silence of noon and sometimes with the dark midnight.

I shivered under the quilt dampened by the wintry drizzle. I didn't look through the window, but I knew that she was not being dragged like a rope by the servant; it was the master who was kicking her.

She was crying loudly, 'O Baba, how cold it is! O Ma, how cold it is!'

Her cry was getting louder still. Were they going to kill her?

It was a strange sight; the woman, almost naked, was holding a bright piece of cloth to her breast like a baby. I knew, just seeing the dangling corner of the cloth, that it was the canopy made of blue silk and velvet, studded with bright glass beads. The servant was trying to snatch it away from her. She was being pushed all around, but she refused to let go of the canopy.

Intermittently she cried out, 'O my Baba, how cold it is! O my Ma, how cold it is!'

The corpulent one ultimately snatched it away from her and placed it over the Goddess. Prostrating himself at the feet of Kali, he asked forgiveness in a repentant tone, 'Ma! Ma! Ma!'

Where has the woman gone? Oh!

She was lying still under the bakul tree. Was she dead? She was lying on her back in the rain, the frayed sari somehow wrapped around her waist. Raindrops were falling on her bizarre, emaciated, naked breasts. What happened? Why was she not getting up? Was she dead?

The altar of the Goddess was housed inside beautiful ornamental grilles. The door always remained locked. The woman inserted her thin hand through the beautifully decorated grille, laughing insanely. She wailed when she could not reach the plate of offerings, cursed the Goddess occasionally, giving out a cry while slapping her brow. 'Ha! Ha! How much food!'

The corpulent one was coming. Oh! Was he going to land a kick on her back? Didn't she see him? She did, and hid herself behind the trunk of the bakul tree. He unlocked the door and brought out the plate of offerings kept in front of the Goddess; some eatables, perhaps rice pudding. The man didn't notice her. He threw the pudding towards the bakul tree. Oh! How, crouching like a dog, she was licking the pudding thrown on the grass! The copper plate was now full of fresh offerings—sandesh, grams, banana, batacha and other delicacies.

A time had come when the woman gave up her habit of stealing the plate through the grille at noon. She spent the time loitering in the streets. Just in front of my house was a tree of shaddock. The green fruits were without any juice or taste, infested by worms. The rotten fruits piled up under the tree. The fruits didn't attract any one, except a few children who would sometimes collect them and use them as balls. The woman stealthily came for the fruits. What did she do with those rotten fruits?

It was a holiday and I had prepared the midday meal with some relish. In the morning, the fisherwoman had come with a big catch. After a hearty meal, I was relaxing on my bed, browsing through a book. But the loud barking of dogs startled me. It was coming from the direction of the shaddock tree. She was gathering the relatively less rotten fruits in the folds of her sari. Obviously, she was scared. A mangy and skinny dog was barking at her. That scraggy dog with maggot-infested ulcers could also sense that she had long ceased to be a human being.

She broke into a smile when I drove the dog away with a stone. The smile brightened her pale, white face for that moment.

She was still waiting …

'What are you going to do with these fruits?' I asked.

She pressed the fruits to her chest. The radiance of the smile in her eyes melted away, giving way to the same old terrible emptiness.

'Would you like some rice?' I asked.

She nodded in consent.

She would take a handful of rice, then like a child suck at the piece of fish—a witch-like apparition, as if one had carelessly wrapped a skin over a skeleton. Having eaten the food, she smiled at me. She fell asleep on the floor of the verandah. In her sleep, she mumbled something. Was she dreaming? What could she dream of: A plateful of rice? The copper plate placed before the Goddess? The canopy?

When she woke up, she smoothed down her dishevelled sari; the blush of bashfulness on the face of a witch? She was also coy once. The orphan girl from a village, who came as the third wife, took care of the large family of the corpulent one who was a rich businessman. Both his wives had been long dead. Jona's granny said that she was very cheerful and looked divine. What had happened to her? Apparently, she was possessed for not performing the rituals of the worship to the Goddess properly. What were the lapses of the 17-year-old girl?

Kamala's mother, who helped me in my household chores, had a different story to tell. One day, her husband had beaten her mercilessly for a little delay in the arrangements of the prayers. That caused an abortion. The baby, her first, was killed in the womb. She survived, but her mind was mauled irreparably.

She went away.

Elaborate preparations at the corpulent one's house was under way. I was also invited to the annual Kali Puja festival. The expensive, but gaudy decorations of the house pointed towards the recent prosperity of the corpulent one. Ornaments of pure gold glittered on the Goddess under the bright light. The canopy was new. Certainly, the former one had become impure. The corpulent one was reciting the incantations in unison with the priest. The altar was covered with offerings—kheer, sweets, fruits and various other delicacies. Amidst the great din, my ears were trying to grasp the sound of her footsteps. She was certainly locked up somewhere.

Suddenly, all hell broke loose. She appeared from nowhere, and got up on the altar. Then, she began gobbling up the offerings placed before the Goddess, raising a storm of abuses. 'Ah! Ah! Gold ornaments!'

Fighting the reach of the men with great alacrity, she went on swallowing the food ravenously.

'What an affair! Bah! Bah!! Don't you see! What an affair with a clay woman!' She laughed sinisterly.

Trying to retrieve the banana that fell from her mouth, she cried out, 'How hungry I am!' She sobbed.

A kick from the corpulent one threw her to the ground. Her delirium continued, 'What an affair with a clay woman! Bah! What love!'

The stout servant dragged her away like a rope. But she did not let go of the bowl of kheer that she picked up in the melee.

The ritual continued through the night and so did the beating of the drum. A short spell of silence and the sound of her smothered weeping would fall on my ears. Was she wounded? Did she not fall on the sharp corner of the altar? Through the sleepless night, the incessant beating of the drum and the suppressed weeping of the poor woman ran through my agitated nerves. Perhaps through time, continuum ran the parallel soundtracks of the festive drums and the weeping … the weeping and the drums … the drums and the weeping … the weeping …

A Precarious Link

One

Manohar's fruit stall is at a very convenient place; it is right between the market and the bus-stand. He had started this small coop near the main road about 20 years ago. He had migrated to this small town in Assam to help out his uncle in his business of selling onions and potatoes. He started his own business of fruits once he grew up into a young man. The mangoes in his shop are full of flavour and sweetness, the apples are fresh and juicy, the pears are like rasogollas, the nashpatis melt in the mouth, and the grapes burst juicily against the tongue. The sales in his shop are quite substantial. The fruits would never rot; rather it sometimes become difficult for him to meet the demands of the customers. His voice is as sweet as the fruits in his stall. His son has also grown up to be just like him; his words also dipped in the sweetness of the pint-sized bhutia oranges.

Manohar always remained neat and clean; he would always wear starched dhotis and ghee-coloured half-sleeved banyans. One could always get the fragrance of incense emanating from his small shop. A small idol of Ganesha rests inside a wooden box, and an earthen lamp burns day in and day out. His son had once installed a red-coloured blinking light in front of Lord Ganesha, but infuriated, Manohar had it removed.

There are two framed colour photographs in the shop; both of Manohar. In one of them, Manohar is dressed in a checked shirt, a silk handkerchief tied around his neck and a bunch of red ripe apples placed in front of him. The other photo has Manohar wearing a dhoti and a kurta, and posing with a heap of mangoes. Both of them have their designated places in the shop which has over a period been painted with black oil. The shop would always be filled with a kind of effusive redolence: the smile-filled conversations of Manohar; the mild fragrance of the apples and oranges; the catch-me-if-you-can aroma of incense and cotton wicks dipped in mustard oil; and the sharp perfume worn by the vivacious son.

The man of my house is someone who likes to take care of his health. He stays seven leagues away from paan, alcohol and smoking; he practices yoga every day and has a bookshelf filled with books on nutrition. Our son is also growing in his father's footsteps. Both of them often have serious discussions on the nutritious elements of different types of food. After reading many books on nutrition and calculating the calories and vitamins, they have come to the conclusion that seasonal fruits and vegetables are the best. It is, therefore, no surprise that a commendable ratio of our monthly food budget is earmarked for Manohar.

His shop lies right on the road to our workplace and it has almost become a regular routine for us to stop by. Most of the well-to-do people in the town are his permanent customers. People would sometimes get together and start a conversation right there on their scooters and cars: Dr Baruah would answer the queries made by lawyer Hazarika on the ongoing viral fever; Professor Vijay Chaliha would ask Executive Engineer Ramen

Kalita regarding the completion date of the bridge on the Kulsi river, which is on the way to Guwahati; businessman Ramen Nath would treat everyone to a sweet Kashmiri apple from Manohar's shop on the occasion of him buying a new car.

Manohar would smile and ask, 'What are you going to treat me with, Babu?'

All of them would start their cars and scooters; the packets of fruits tied beautifully by the skilful hands of Manohar with them.

The man of our house has been researching on mangoes these days; he has been waxing eloquent on the ability of the fruit to help the body store vitamin A. I have also been reading up a little on mangoes. We would often have a little talk on mangoes with Manohar while on our way back from work. Manohar would describe with relish the famed sweetness of himsagar and surma-fazli mangoes. I try to take part in the conversation, armed with my bookish knowledge, and narrate how the langda mango got its name—*langda* meaning crippled fakir.

Manohar would jump with excitement, 'I will treat you to langdas, Baideo. I will bring such special langdas this time for you that you will not forget in your life. *Kya Khusboo, kya mithaas*' (Such fragrance, such sweetness).

He would resort to his mother tongue Hindi when he became too excited. But that doesn't happen with his son. He would actually speak in fluent Assamese when he would get excited.

The black bull would gobble up a mango in the blink of an eye, and Manohar's son would give chase, '*bopai aah anekoi aam khuam je mahadebak pithit dekhi jabi*' (Come here, my son. I will feed you mangoes in such a way that you will be reminded of Lord Shiva on your back). Looking at the retreating bull who had deftly avoided the blow of his stick, he would say again in fluent Assamese, '*Xi eta Xaat ghaatot sengeli*' (He is a slippery old eel).

We had once visited Manohar's house which is situated towards the end of the town. His thatch and bamboo cottage lay serenely under the cool shade of six mango trees. He has been able to grow these mangoes, even in the soil of Assam, without letting a single insect invade the fruits. He has gifted us mangoes from these trees quite a few times, but he never took a single penny in return. Manohar drew our attention towards those trees and said that a number of fruit-sellers had their eyes on them. But he wouldn't mint money by selling mangoes off those trees, even if his life was on the line. His children would eat them, he distributed them among his neighbours or he would gift them to his kith and kin.

Manohar's first grandchild had turned a month old on the day we paid him a visit. I had taken a pair of new clothes for the baby. I was surprised to find a weaving loom in the verandah. Manohar introduced us to his daughter-in-law who was wearing a hand-woven pair of *mekhela-chador*. It was white in colour and embroidered with red and yellow flowers. I forwarded the pair of clothes I had brought.

The girl with a charming face brought forward the *bota* with betel nuts on it, 'What was the need to bring these things? It is our fortune that someone like you has come to our humble abode.' She becomes comfortable with me after some time.

Manohar's son had brought her home with the society's sanction after "playing love" with her for three years. Manohar's family didn't resist much; his elder daughter had also been married off to an Assamese boy. I asked her if she faced any problems marrying an outsider, a "foreigner". Manohar's son had come in to take something. She looked at him once, and let go of a giggle as an answer to my query. Indeed, it was a question that would make someone giggle. I had to echo her laughter when I saw

Manohar's son clad in a big *gamosa*, busy stoking up a hay-fire to chase away mosquitoes from the cow-shed.

We had a wonderful meal consisting of sweet mangoes served in a shiny bell-metal plate, along with a bowl of *akhoi*. We returned home by sunset. His son had cleaned off the dust that had settled on our scooter from the pebbled road that leads to their house. The scooter was sparkling clean now. My husband was indignant. 'What was the need for you to do this?' he said.

The fair, gentle-faced boy simply smiled, with his head bowed down. There was a nice bond, a link, which was being built between Manohar and us by the sweet mangoes, apples, juicy oranges, naspatis, pears, pineapples and grapes. These are the links that make our lives colourful, embroidered with beautiful, big and bright flowers.

Two

Jackfruits haven't flowered much this year; instead mangoes filled up the trees. Manohar's business was flourishing as usual. The buying and selling of his mangoes increased as the heat of July ripened. He used to get his stuff from the traders in Guwahati's Fancy Bazaar on credit earlier, but then he would have to pay a couple of rupees extra per kilogram. But he was now getting his stuff with cash.

The town has its weekly closing day on Saturday. He would get around ₹30,000–35,000 worth of mangoes together. But the mangoes wouldn't even last till that next Saturday; they would all be gone by Friday. He would earn a little extra that way, as he got them in cash.

His son would go to Guwahati on a working day and get the other fruits such as naspati, pineapple and grapes. But Manohar insisted on going himself to get the mangoes. He would carefully choose the himsagar, surma-fazli, langda, chaucha and such other varieties of mangoes. He would then load these carefully chosen mangoes onto the 4-pm government bus and bring them under his own supervision.

His son would wait at the bus-stand with a hand-cart. Father and son would then very carefully bring down the crates of mangoes, as if they were bringing down a baby, and load them onto the hand-cart. Manohar's son would be atop the bus, while Manohar would be waiting below with the cart-pullers. The cart-pullers knew that they would be in hot water if they weren't careful while de-loading Manohar's consignments.

Manohar would always tell the cart-pullers on his way to the shop from the bus-stand, 'Mango is not just a fruit; it's heavenly manna, none less than amrit. These are stuff that belong to the gods in heaven. They should be taken care of with a loving hand.'

The cart pullers would also buy half-a-kilogram of mangoes each after de-boarding the crates. Manohar would give them the mangoes at a low price, without making any profit.

'Let them eat. They are hard-working people. Let them eat something good,' he would say.

His daughter-in-law had woven a *gamosa* for him this Bihu. He was shaking the dust off the mangoes with that *gamosa,* while counting something in his head. The fruit-sellers from the nearby places and villages also take their supply from Manohar nowadays. Manohar is hoping to accumulate some money this mango season. He was initially hesitant to invest his entire capital, but that fear is no longer there now. The entire money comes back in terms of profit and the original capital. It has to happen. He never brings cheap, gas-ripened, sour, immature mangoes.

He is thinking of building another room in the house. He is also thinking of getting an electricity connection. His daughter-in-law is in the family way. The grandmother is hoping for a girl, but Manohar is rooting for a boy. He would send both his grandchildren to school. He has not been able to give even a single piece of gold jewellery to his daughter-in-law. She would always use that same old scarf in winters; it's time to get her a new one. She has had to make do with so much of hardship in her life. The dreams buzz in his heart, just like the buzzing of the bees in his shop.

Three

The town is inhabited by people of all creeds and languages, and hence, there would be some festival or the other being celebrated at any given time of the year. There is Bipadnashini Puja this Sunday; the prasad or offerings require 13 varieties of fruits. Sales will march right from early morning in Manohar's stall.

He put together all his capital, down to the last penny. It amounted to ₹38,000 after putting in the money saved by his wife. She approached him as he was counting the money, and asked him how he was going to carry it all. She was a bit scared. There are reasons for being so; it was only recently, on a Saturday, that dacoits looted ₹2,00,000–₹3,00,000 at gunpoint from a government bus going to Guwahati. It is on this bus that all the traders, small and big, go to Guwahati to get their goods; the town remains closed on this particular day. Everybody would be carrying money, in various amounts. Manohar is also harbouring the same fear as his wife. What would he do? He has to go. He has to carry on his business as long as there is hunger in the stomach. He has to take his money this way; he has to bring back his supplies.

Manohar used to carry his money in his shopping bag earlier; this time he has asked his daughter-in-law to sew two pockets in his banyan, near his chest. There is no guarantee of the heart that lies in the chest nowadays, where is the guarantee of money? How can Manohar narrate his tales of woe to his wife?

He smiled at his wife standing by his side, holding a cup of tea. 'Gautam's mother, relax. Has this Manohar ever committed any sin? Has he ever cheated or committed any crime? God will always be there for good people like Manohar.'

Manohar folded his hands at the portrait of Mahadeva hanging on the wall. When he opened his eyes, he saw his daughter-in-law waiting with chopped betel nut on the *bota*. Manohar's teeth were still strong, but he preferred the chopped betel nut. So, she started giving him that every day. It felt good, Manohar felt good. His heart filled with joy when his betel nut was served with such care by his daughter-in-law. He went out after putting the *paan-tamul* in his mouth.

It was hot as blazes that day. Manohar had a tough time in the rotten, sultry heat of Guwahati. It started drizzling once they left Mangaldoi; the breeze began to cool down. Manohar had dozed off a bit. Suddenly, he found out that the bus isn't going any further from Sitalmari. It was about 12 kilometres before they could reach Manohar's town. What has happened is that 12–13 kilometres south of the town, in Rowmari, some extremists had detonated a remote-controlled bomb. Seven army men were killed instantly; one of them being a high-ranked officer. Not a single extremist has been captured, and in order to ensure that no extremist escapes the town, they had stopped the coming or going of any vehicles, into and from the town.

The bus, indeed, stopped once it reached Sitalmari; it wouldn't move any further. Manohar missed the government bus today; he had to catch a private one, instead. There were about 20 buses lined up there, along with the one Manohar was on. Gun-wielding military personnel were frisking the people after forcing them to get down from the buses and making them stand in a row. Some bloodcurdling, terrible rumours started circulating among the people, who were by now drenched in rain and perspiration. Someone said that the bomb has reduced the young soldiers to what looked like pieces of pig meat, butchered and kept ready for sale in the market.

Rowmari had become like a graveyard in broad daylight; not a single soul to be seen in the village. Four farmers, who were ploughing in the fields, now lay dead; killed by the bullets of the military. Two sowing girls also lay dead in the field; molested before being killed. The mud in the fields is now red with blood. The people who were supposed to reach home by six in the evening had to stay back, hungry and thirsty, till about 11 in the night.

Only three buses were allowed to go to the town after 11 pm. It created a state of absolute chaos as passengers of all the 20 buses piled onto the three vehicles. Manohar, too, boarded onto the roof of a bus. He turned around to look at the bus that he had boarded from Guwahati; parked right under the streetlight, it was loaded only with Manohar's supplies—supplies worth ₹36,000. It was his entire life's savings. Two drops of tears hung from his eyes.

A lot of people decided to stay back with their consignments. Naren sells readymade clothes on a plastic sheet on the footpath near Manohar's stall. He is staying back; he has brought a few more clothes for the next market day. Subodh Pal, an assistant in Musica is also staying back. He has brought three colour TV sets. Jivan, who works in Hazarika Press, will also stay, as he has brought quite a lot of paper. And ...

Manohar wanted to come down from the bus, but was pushed back by a crowd hustling onto the roof. The crowd was an agitated lot. After the blast in Rowmari, the military didn't just stop at crushing the village, they also smashed the town. The town was in the grip of an unannounced curfew. Many shops have been damaged; many shopkeepers have been admitted to the hospital. One of the shopkeepers tried arguing with the army, but was so badly beaten up that he was battling for life. Manohar, about to de-board, decided against it and once again took his seat on the roof. Who might be the boy who argued with the army? These rumours clawed into the hearts of the people.

When Manohar got down from the bus at around midnight, he couldn't recognise the beautiful, green town that he had always known since his childhood. Every corner of the roads was filled with army men; the streets were strewn with broken glass, *gamosas* and torn slippers. He immediately ran to his stall after getting down from the bus. The door of the coop was still open, the dislodged planks of wood still snarling. The fruits have been trampled to a pulp. The bull was merrily eating them up, shaking its head and ears. Manohar tried closing the door, only to discover that it had come off its hinges. A few nashpatis, still intact, lay scatterred. He thought of picking them up, but didn't. He started his lonely walk back home at midnight through the gravelled, unpaved path.

He silently paused after reaching the front of his house, holding on to the gateway. Is it still there—his home comforted by the shade of the mango trees, or has it been smashed just like his shop? Has the roof collapsed? Is the door broken? What if his house also lies crumbled like his photos of smiles amidst red apples, and green and yellow mangoes?

The sleepless and hungry body started trembling; he was being surrounded by the pieces of broken photographs. A weak light from a wick lamp emerged from the house. His wife and his daughter-in-law escorted him inside. He calmed down a bit after drinking a glass of water and pouring a tumbler-full on his head. He looked at the vermilion mark that adorned his daughter-in-law's forehead, and cried, 'Gautam, my son Gautam!'

A groaning sound came from the inside of the house. He went and stood near his son, one of his shoulders was severly swollen. It was tied up with a turmeric pack. Gautam's eyes filled up on seeing his father.

The shops remain shut on Saturday mornings, but they open towards the evening. He had just sold goods worth ₹30, when it happened. There was pandemonium everywhere. Someone was loading some chicken onto a bus, two of them were found dead; the army recovered revolvers inside the dead ones. Then they charged at the congregated onlookers to disperse them. Manohar's son was hit right on his shoulder when he was trying to see what was going on. He just stared with utter disbelief, from Bidhu's shop, as their stall was being smashed to smithereens by the army.

Four

The town was brought to a standstill by an unofficial curfew. All the buses continued to stand near the Sitalmari market. The other buses that would regularly run from the town also stood parked in their owner's houses. The markets and shops remained shut, and so were the schools and colleges. The hawkers and the traders, who thronged the streets, disappeared. The evening markets also stopped opening. In the blistering, sultry July heat, without a drop of rain or the drop of a leaf, the town turned blighted, just like rotting mangoes.

Rowmari is an affluent village. It is never affected by any natural disasters such as floods or draughts. Every household in the village would have plenty of valuable antiques. As it was not touched by floods, the soil remained very fertile, and the hard-working people grew a variety of crops on it. The small oranges, lemons, vegetables and greens, *koli-joha* rice, the newly grown kidney beans and the green cauliflowers had a taste that was different from all others. However, the extremists chose this village for their operation, as they could easily escape to Bhutan through the forest reserves that bordered the village.

It was peak time for cultivation, and the people of Rowmari were finding it very inconvenient to spend their time lying around in the town railway station. There was fierce gun-fighting going on in the Rowmari reserve forest. All the houses decorated with jali fences, and garden croton plants and kharikajai flowers have been transformed into graveyards. The people of Rowmari were now spending their nights in the station, along with beggars and destitutes. Frustrated with what was going on, they would crack their fingers and curse the boys who had placed the bomb as well as the swarming military.

Girish Baruah, the teacher of the local higher secondary school, was returning home. He would often go on his scooter with his wife and kid to spend a night at his ancestral birthplace, some 20 kilometres away, on holidays. He was returning to the town, like always, that Sunday. He had heard some information about the Rowmari incident, but he didn't give much heed to it. He saw the military camp in the open field as soon as he entered the town. It was a common sight; it has been there for years now.

Baruah continued on the well-known road without any thought. But he didn't see the square cement post lying on the road which served as a speed-breaker; it wasn't painted in white, so people couldn't see it at night. Baruah was a very careful driver, but he couldn't stop the lower portion of the scooter from disintegrating. He, and his wife and son, were flung a long way.

The town was once again in an uproar over the seriously injured family of three. This isn't a city where the neighbours wouldn't know what's happening next door. The people in this small town would rush with help at the slightest problem faced by any household. The buses are not running, the cars won't go. How are they to be taken to Guwahati now? The boy was still bleeding; the two doctors checking his pulse frowned. Finally, the family was taken by train to Rangia; they would catch a different train to Guwahati from there.

Five armed boys escaped from Rowmari into the town through the reserves. The boys lay dead, right near the college, after being shot by the army. The town was again thrown into the clutches of pandemonium. The extremist organisation announced a bandh in the town for 48 hours.

The only road that takes the town outside had a bomb blast under one of its bridges; the explosion couldn't cause much damage due to some technical glitch, but it was enough to shake the hearts of the townspeople, to the core.

The town that was as sweet, fresh, fragrant and colourful like a himsagar mango turned totally putrid; suffocated and stifled by the severe, overwhelming heat of the last four days.

Five

A stinking smell, that of decaying mangoes infested by buzzing flies, seemed to hover over Manohar all of these four days. He couldn't sleep or eat.

The town opened after a full four days. Manohar went out at dawn to find out about his mangoes which were still languishing on the roof of the bus. A few buses were plying, but they would go straight to Guwahati. It would be dark by the time those buses returned to Sitalmari.

Manohar managed to arrange for two hand-carts, after moving around for quite some time. The sun was shining down in flames. Manohar didn't care. He decided to walk all the way down to the Sitalmari market, along with the hand-carts.

His son was groaning in agony; the doctor said that he was to be taken to the Medical College in Guwahati. The bone near his neck has been fractured and he had to be operated upon. The entire effort of his life was stifling on the rooftop of that bus. He had to wade through mud, dirt and heat to put these mangoes there. He didn't even feel the sun burning on his bald head. He got the crates of mangoes de-boarded in the Sitalmari market chowk. The stench of rotten mangoes wrapped around Manohar like a thousand pythons. He actually fell down, gasping for breath. He opened his eyes after the cart-pullers poured some water on his head. They showered a lot of care and affection towards the "old" man.

Manohar felt as if he, indeed, has grown into an old man. Other than the fazlis, which were comparatively harder and unripe, all other mangoes had turned into pulp. He put the chausa, himsagar and fazli mangoes on the hand-cart and threw away the rest in a nearby swamp. He sat down in exhaustion on the roadside. The cart-pullers helped the old man get onto a truck headed in the direction of the town. Manohar just sat quietly on the truck.

It reminded him of a similar incident, years back. Manohar had a headful of thick hair then. A political group announced a bandh for 172 hours. It was winter; Manohar had bought apples worth ₹15,000 on credit just a day before the bandh started. He kept changing the position of the apples, so that they wouldn't end up getting stifled. He would ignore the extreme cold and spend the nights in the coop itself. He would keep the door of his shop just a wee bit open, ignoring the threats of the party boys, and would let air and sunshine fall on the apples. The apples didn't decay, indeed. Manohar could pay back his credit within a week. He was absolutely helpless this time though. There is a huge difference between the times, just like it is between apples and mangoes, December and July. Indeed, the times seen by the bald Manohar were dancing to a completely different drummer compared to the old era.

Manohar started afresh by first repairing his stall. He put together the little money he had and added the price of his watch to it. When he set out to arrange the mangoes, he found them to be ripe and yellow. One can't forget the taste of ripe fazli mangoes, but they would be inedible if they ripen any further. He sat in his shop the entire day with the mangoes in front of him; it was the market day in the town. The nooks and corners were peppered by groups of army men.

The character of the town changes completely on the market day when people from all the nearby villages and the surrounding 13 tea estates converge in the town. Manohar and his son would be all done selling their fruits those days. Someone or the other would sit under the tree eating a mango, an apple or an orange. They might not buy in bulk like the usual permanent customers, but the people who came to the market to buy or sell different things would finish off Manohar's fruits—half a kilo, a quarter of a kilo at a time.

The market didn't even start that day; it looked like midnight, even when it was just getting dark. The next day remained the same. Manohar threw away the remaining mangoes in the swamp behind his shop. He simply sat back in the bus-stand, which had gone dead quiet by dusk, for a long, long time. He would have continued sitting there with his head between his knees but for a group of army men who prodded him with a baton, 'Oi, buddha.'

Manohar's son was groaning in pain. The painkillers would reduce his pain for a while, but once the medicine wore off, the pain would cripple the young boy. Manohar sold the mangoes in his garden to the traders. They plucked all the mangoes from the trees, raw and ripe, right in front of their eyes. Seeing the mangoes being taken away, Manohar's grandson started crying in such a wretched, heartbreaking manner that Manohar's eyes, too, filled up with tears.

When he returned after admitting his son in the medical college, Manohar, who was planning to gift a new piece of jewellery to his daughter-in-law, instead had to sell the chain that was gifted to her by her father. Her face turned ashen when she handed the chain to her mother-in-law, just like the child's face when the mangoes were being taken away.

When she forwarded the chopped betel nut and leaf to Manohar, she said, 'These things can come back later. May he come back soon hale and hearty!'

Manohar went out without even touching the betel nut and leaf.

His son came back from the medical college hospital, his daughter-in-law also had a healthy and pretty baby. His son's in-laws came on the day the baby was introduced to the society, many of his neighbours turned up. The last of the ₹7,000 that he had taken on loan, just before taking his son to the hospital, ended in expenses that day.

The town returned to normalcy very soon, just as it is day after night, just as the sun comes out after the rain, just as a baby grows up.

Six

Manohar bought a basket of cheap mangoes on credit and reopened his hitherto shut shop on the market day. The market looked like a carnival again, after many days. The ones who came in groups from the nearby tea estates, clad in colourful clothes and the ones who came from the surrounding villages filled up the town to its brim. A few sour and cheap mangoes, dark green in colour, lay in front of Manohar in his shop. It was just like this when Manohar started his business with a few cheap and sour mangoes. But it was not in his shop, he used to sit on the footpath with the mangoes in a basket.

The Manohar who sat on the footpath had thick hair on his head; nobody bothered if he went to sleep empty stomach. Indeed, there were many a nights when Manohar slept on his cot in the rented room behind the railway station, without eating a single grain, so that he could retain his money to buy fruits the next day. Can Manohar do the same with the entire family, make them skip a meal? He looked by force of habit towards the blank spaces where his two photographs hung; that of a young Manohar standing amidst luscious mangoes and apples. Will his son be able to take a similar photo and hang it on the same space?

A customer had bought a kilo of mangoes in the morning. He brought back those mangoes and poured them before Manohar, just as if he was throwing the mangoes back.

'Why did you sell me such inedible and sour mangoes? Give me quality products; take a few rupees more instead,' he yelled.

Manohar returned the customer's money without a word. He sat for some time with his head between his knees. He opened his cash box. He saw two 10 paisa coins lying there. He got up with a start. Will there not be money even for a kilo of rice today?

He immediately loaded the mangoes into a basket and raised it onto his head. He closed his shop and trekked towards the same old spot on the footpath under the banyan tree, where he used to sit as a young man. Various shops and stalls have mushroomed in that area. He sat down with the basket at a spot which had no cover from the fiery sun. Customers on a lookout for cheaper stuff started buying his mangoes, half a kilo or a quarter kilo at a time.

Seven

Our college had also unofficially closed down during those days, just like any other organisation. We decided, on the very first day of the bus strike, to go to my sister-in-law's place in Tezpur by train. She had been inviting us for quite some time now; we had not been able to go. The sudden holidays were enjoyed by all. It felt very refreshing to be away from the usual routine, despite the hullaballoo and the feasts and the travelling. We could also stay away from the veiled terror that had taken over our town. The classes have now resumed properly again.

We stopped in front of Manohar's shop, like every other day, while on our way back from college. It was the time when most offices close for the day. Dr Baruah, lawyer Hazarika and engineer Kalita were all there in front of Manohar's shop. Nobody was here in the town in those trouble-ridden days. Baruah spent a few days in the cool climes of Shillong. He said that it was a great experience to be away from the heat and the sick, both. Hazarika had a gala time in his in-law's place. Kalita flew to Ooty by plane. Everybody now wanted to have a good homely meal after shopping for the required goods. Kalita wanted to have a glass of mango shake made by his wife. Mrs Hazarika was to offer a *xorai* at the *naamghar*; she was in need of some mangoes, nashpatis and pineapples. Baruah wanted some sweet mangoes to have with his pudding. We also wanted a few mangoes.

Manohar's shop was closed, so we decided to wait for him.

Manohar was coming from the market with a basket, the perspiring man stood in front of his shop. We were taken aback by his changed appearance; he seemed to have aged a couple of years more in these days. His clothes were dirty; his hair was all strewn. He simply smiled weakly at our overlapping questions:

'Are you not going to sell us mangoes, Manohar?'

'You were supposed to treat us with langdas, remember?'

Manohar leaned against his shop, as if the tiredness of a hundred years has possessed him.

He answered slowly, one word at a time, 'I won't be able to give you any more the kind of fruits you want. A raging fire has caught hold of my fate.'

Manohar started leaving us without a word, without a look towards us.

'Mahohar,' my husband called out once.

He kept on walking; no answer came back from him.

Just as we were looking at Manohar's closed shop, a sudden crowd started running towards us in panic. The brimming crowd turned into an anthill that has been brought down. Nobody could know who went where, who lost what, who fell, who ran. Olive-clad army men were in hot pursuit of the crowd. What had happened? Was there a bomb explosion? Did people die? Was some dead body discovered? Anything of this sort might happen in this valley of death. The cars of the lawyer, the doctor and the engineer fled from the spot immediately. It was just us now with our scooter. Where could we go and how?

Roma Das was going very fast with the shopping bag hanging from his cycle. He stopped on seeing us. 'What are you doing here? Why are you waiting? Why don't you go home?'

We got to know the facts from him. The dead bodies of four young men, peppered with bullets, were kept on the verandah of the police station located right next to the market. A few people from the market entered the station yard to have a look as to what was happening. The army and the police started lathi-charging everybody in the market.

A sound that resembled guns being fired seemed to float over the din. Someone was telling somebody else in an agitated tone that there was definite information of the boys from the organisation having entered the marketplace to get back the dead bodies. Somebody was shouting that bombs have been found near the fish market. Somebody was saying with his hands raised, 'There will be firing now, any moment.' A woman was crying on the road, her clothes dishevelled, 'Mini *re* Mini, where are you, Mini?' An old woman collapsed then and there; a chorus of 'water, water' glided in. Some were carrying an injured person who was bleeding profusely from his head. The crowd was like crows whose nests were on fire; their cawing filled up the streets, the houses, the fields. They turned the sky and the air into one black mass.

The fire that had caught hold of Manohar's fate had swollen into a blazing, all-encompassing inferno.

Aai, the Mother

A rickety wall made of reeds is the only thing that stands between the poultry and ducks' cage and the bamboo cot where Pomeela Bengi sleeps; chicken and duck waste fall under her bed through the fissures in the wall. Every morning, she sweeps the place with her broom made of betel nut leaves, and the area that was beyond her reach had taken a whitish hue caused by layers of fungus accumulating over time. The whole hut reeks of a dank odour.

A clay stove lies a little away from her bamboo cot, a few utensils and some containers lie on a flat wooden plank fixed to the wall. On the right side of the stove are two vessels of water; one is made of brass, the other from clay. On the left lies a big bundle of wood.

Her son Mohan sleeps in the front room—the "room" being an area covered by palings made of slit bamboo, just big enough for a wooden plank to fit in. Last time, a water-gourd plant climbed onto the palings and bore fruits luxuriantly. The poor paling withered under the combined weight of the gourds and the people who climbed on it to pluck them. Even the walls are in a poor state; the black mongrel, while going out and coming in, has created a number of holes in it. Usually, it sleeps under Mohan's bed. Whenever needed, it breaks through the wall to go out.

A couple of Pomeela Bengi's chickens do not enter the cage at night; they spend it on the branch of the adjoining papaya tree. The rooster on the papaya tree, and the one inside the cage, started crowing at the same time. Pomeela Bengi got up with a start. As always, she opened the door and looked outside. The outside world looked hazy, a blend of darkness and light. The whole world has been a blur for Bengi for the last few years. In this hazy world, some black objects crawled around and Pomeela Bengi walked among them with careful footsteps.

The world had already turned bright by the time she returns after attending to nature's call. Darkness was giving way to light, even in her blurred world. She started shifting the husk after taking some rice grains on a bamboo tray. The ducks and the chickens surrounded her immediately. A couple of daring birds were pricking on the tray itself. She shoos them away, but they gather around again.

Bengi would have ceaselessly continued her exercise of cleaning the rice grains and chasing the birds, but for her son Mohan coming in, who chased away the ducks and the chickens. He lit up the clay stove and put the rice vessel with water inside it on the fire. Mohan took the tray from his mother and poured the grains of rice into a bamboo container.

'Put on the rice fast, I need to go early today.'

She jumped up, startled by the voice of her son. She got herself busy right away, increasing the flame, initiating the process of cooking rice.

She has been doing just this for the past several years. She would be glued on to a task till somebody called her off it. That day, she had accompanied Manobai to the rice mill, just like the other times. Manobai and her group would work on daily wages in the rice mill, threshing and winnowing the paddy, in the months when they were not required as gleaners. Manobai and her friends would usually keep Bengi near them somewhere.

However, one day, one of the workers in the mill took Bengi aside to winnow some *joha* rice which was kept separately. She kept on cleaning the rice again and again and again. Evening turned into dusk, Bengi was oblivious to the turn of time. The rice and the paddy dancing on the cleaning bamboo tray started shaking like a dark shadow. The husk turned hazy like fog. Pomeela Bengi's hair, even her eyelashes were coated with husk, it was all white.

Someone from the mill, on some work to that part, noticed the woman and was taken aback. 'What happened, Bengi? Why are you still here?'

Bengi stood up with a start. She looked around and smiled that childlike smile of hers. Manobai and her group had left long back. It was not their fault though. Someone from the mill had informed them that Bengi's son had come and taken her home.

Actually, the workers knew that the entire stock of rice grains would be winnowed and cleaned in a single day if Bengi could be somehow put to that task.

Pomeela Bengi looked around aimlessly, tied the money in a corner of her *mekhela* and tucked it inside. She was actually paid five rupees less that day, but she was oblivious to that, too. She tied her loose hair in a bun and gingerly stepped out of the mill. By then, the floppy, light darkness had coagulated into a thick black night. Bengi felt as if she was wading through some dark waters. She stumbled on, but somehow managed to reach the bamboo bridge over the rivulet. She tried to find her way that would take her on to the narrow bridge. But she ultimately decided to stop below the jujube berry tree. The sky, the water, the bridge, everything had dissolved into a thick blackness by then. She let herself down on the bush of German grass under the berry tree. A mixed odour of sweat and husk wafted across the underwood, below the berry tree. Mohan and Manobai finally reached the river bank searching for Pomeela Bengi. Bengi was dozing away, her head bent over her knees.

When he brought his mother out from the German grass bushes, he decided that he would have to finish the pending work on his house. Renumai has given her word to him; she is ready to come with him whenever he wants her to. She is actually ready to come right away, but where is he going to keep her? He must raise the house. His mother cannot be sent to the mill like this any more. But who would he leave her with, even if at home? Somebody would trick her into doing some work. Everyone knew that once some work is assigned to Pomeela Bengi, she would be on it till somebody asks her to stop, and all that, without any of the usual scrambles regarding money.

Once, Dhonai the shopkeeper tricked her into coating with mud a wall made out of raw bamboo, all for a mere ₹10. When Mohan returned from his daily-wage work in the town and saw blood trickling down his mother's lacerated hands, he decided to send her to the mill with Manobai and her friends. Let her spend her days in the mill with Manobai till he brings Renumai into his home.

After his bath, Mohan found his mother waiting, the rice already served on the plate. Bengi had left her hair open after her bath. The dark orange colour of the *mekhela* matched her fair complexion. She smiled at him as he entered; the same smile a nanny flashes to tease an infant. Mohan's heart ached every time he saw this smile. He couldn't bear to look at his mother for long.

Seated with his head bowed down before the served rice, Mohan almost admonished his mother in his rough, sonorous voice, 'Don't loiter around aimlessly. Go with Manobai and come back with her.'

Bengi served another helping of rice onto her son's plate. She also took out the jackfruit seeds from inside the embers of the clay stove, mashed them up, added a little salt and mustard oil, and placed it on the side of her son's plate of rice. She smiled again like a baby, looking at her son.

Mohan, as always, entered Manobai's house before starting for the town. As always, he repeated the same sentence, 'Bai! Take mother to the mill. Bring her back too.'

Manobai was also getting ready to head out. She plopped a *paan-tamul* into her mouth and replied with a smirk, looking at Mohan, 'Lad's all dressed up today! What's the idea? Planning to bring her in today itself?'

The fair boy blushed, turning as red as a tomato, and walked away, scratching his head.

Manobai kept on looking at Bengi's son. He was wearing a hand-woven shirt, probably made by Renumai, along with the banyan. The shirt hugged the brawny frame of Mohan snuggly. He was wearing the green *gamosa* upto his knee. His muscular calves shook with each step. Mohan's father was just the same. That strapping man with the complexion of a ripe guava had made her go weak in the knees.

But he ended up giving his heart to Pomeela. And how could he not? During their youth, the presence of Pomeela would soften the voices of the people—from the thread shop to the wool merchant. Has Bengi lost all her charms now, even after what she had to go through? The son of that couple had to turn out like this. It would actually be a surprise if he didn't.

Manobai saw Pomeela Bengi entering through the wicker gate. She made her sit down and arranged her hair. That thick cascade of hair that once crossed her waist wasn't there any more. Manobai had once applied salt on this flowing mane of hair out of sheer jealousy. But her tresses kept dancing in the wind; tresses that even salt couldn't ruin. And she danced all the way to his heart and his home, breaking Manobai's heart, once and for all. Pomeela gave birth to three robust boys. Manobai's own daughter looked like a weasel in front of Pomeela's boys. When her own sman stood near Pomeela's beefy partner, it looked as if an old, emaciated cow was standing next to a slick buffalo. She had always envied Pomeela. Most probably, it was her evil eye that fell on the poor girl.

Manobai let go of a sigh and tied Pomeela's salt-and-pepper hair into a bun. She went inside and brought a new pair of *mekhela-chador* and offered it to Bengi, 'Wear it.'

The *mekhela* is deep green in colour; a row of yellow flowers lined the garment. The violet-coloured blouse is also hand woven. Renumai didn't stitch buttons on the blouse; instead, she tied some cords there. The woman isn't right in her mind, who knows, she might pull the buttons apart. Renumai had handed the *mekhela-chador* to Manobai three days back.

Renumai was very worried about her future mother-in-law, even from now. An old wound, buried somewhere inside, ached once again.

'Let her have some happiness, even if in her old age,' Manobai said aloud and tied the new *mekhela* around Pomeela.

The light, curly hair around Bengi's forehead that touched her eyebrows was still intact. Once, an enormous vermilion mark adorned the space between these curls. She rubbed off that mark the day Mohan's father went to the weekly market with a cart-load of home-grown cabbages and returned as a sack of flesh tied in a rucksack. Pomeela couldn't comprehend why and who would bomb the market to kill innocent people; all she knew was that her man who carried a breastful of love for her, just like a hive of ripe honey, was no more.

She just kept staring at the group of people who carried the bloody sack to the cemetery. Mohan was by her side. She just kept looking at that direction, holding Mohan close to herself. Mohan was crying, everybody called out to her again and again. Somebody took away her son who she had held onto so far, but she just kept on looking at the street, without even batting an eyelid. After some time, she fell down on the ground with a thud.

Since then, something snapped inside her. She still remained Pomeela with her three sons beside her. The eldest son was a school dropout. He spent his time fishing and playing football with the other boys of the village. He also went out to work for daily wages a couple of days or so. Once or twice, he went to the town to appear in interviews for posts in the police force, but everything was to no avail. Once he put his heart and soul into potato cultivation, but untimely rains ruined the leaves of the potato plants, turning them black.

On another occasion, he raised cabbages successfully, even earned some money, and bought clothes for himself as well for his brothers. One day, he went away to the mountains, joined the jungle party with a gun on his shoulder, in the quest for their own home state. He came home a couple of times after that in the night, armed like a military personnel. Pomeela spent the first year, waiting for and wailing her son's absence, every night.

One day, somebody came and told her that her eldest had shot down old Agarwala, the white-haired owner of the garments store in the town. He had also shot school master Deka on the road, apparently for no reason at all. Pomeela knew both of them. They used to often visit Agarwala's store to buy wool and thread. And who in this zone didn't know the master? The school master visited their village every day that year during the malaria outbreak. Her son killed them? Pomeela waited no more for her son since. She never got to know anything about her eldest son, ever after.

The second son also left for the mountains one day, with a gun over his shoulder. Pomeela, however, didn't await his return this time. Even though she didn't wait for him, he did come back one fine night; he came back and played with his kid brother. He was sleeping after dinner; the members of the other party came and shot him in his sleep. After the villagers took the body to the cemetery, Pomeela took the blood-soaked bedclothes to the river and kept on washing them, over and over again. Mohan brought his mother home, holding her by her hand. The transformation from Pomeela to Pomeela Bengi (Pomeela the Halfwit) was complete.

Manobai made a cup of black tea with a pinch of salt for Pomeela, and then both went out to the mill. They met Tileshwari and Putali on the paved road that goes towards the town. All of them were walking, chewing on a mixture of *paan-tamul*.

A bit ahead along the road, they saw Mohan returning homewards with a cartful of bamboo palings. He stopped seeing his mother and the rest.

'What is it that you bring, Mohan?' Manobai asked with a shout.

'Some bamboo palings,' Mohan replied, a shy smile hidden under his bowed head.

'Oi Pomeela! Do you know that your son's going to bring in your daughter-in-law soon?' Putali guffawed.

Pomeela Bengi smiled her usual baby smile.

Mohan's sight lingered onto his mother's smile for a few moments. He then told Manobai, softly, 'Please bring back Ma.'

And then he immediately started pushing the hand-cart towards his home. Manobai and her friends went ahead, only to discover Bengi staring at her retreating son, her hand on her waist.

'Bengi, let's go,' Manobai said, pulling Pomeela back by her hand.

All of them were going ahead, their laughter and gaiety filling up the air. It was the day of the weekly market.

Meghuwa, going to the market with a pig tied on the shaft between the wheels in the middle of his cycle, hollered at the group of women, 'The sun has climbed over your heads; it is now that you come?'

Manobai teased Ahina who was carrying chickens in two woven baskets. 'You are going to earn a few extra today.'

Another laughed out heartily, 'Do not finish them off on *lau-pani*.'

Suddenly, they came to a halt. The people who had gone towards the town to the market were hurrying back. Mainao's red *dokhona* was all gashed and shredded; she, too, was all decked up today, out to buy wool and thread from the market. Rina, who had come with her, had lost her *aarnai*; God knows where. Sombari used to set up a stall every market day, where she used to sell freshly made *tekeli-pitha*s. She had no idea where she left or lost her *pitha*-making pots, wood, sesame seeds and the rice flour.

They were all shouting and screaming at Manobai and her group, 'Go back. 'Don't go towards the town! Go back to your village! Five military men have been killed in a bomb blast over the bridge at the entrance of the town.'

Gandhai had also taken a loadful of brinjals on his shoulders to the market. Scampering back, he said, while trying to catch his breath, '*Meltaries* have spread all over the place. Run for your life.'

The group of women gathered together on one side of the road. It is true that the villagers heard a bang around midnight. But these kinds of sounds were common these days. It was just the other day that the two jungle parties had a long gunfire, right on the front yards of Sombari and Gandhai. They had also seen two young men being chased and shot down by the army right in the front yard of the *naamghar*.

The people were scurrying back like deers being chased by a tiger. The words "bomb", "blood", "army" and "bridge" were ricocheting around like pebbles being flung around under the impact of people running. The people started running helter-skelter when they heard the sound of the army trucks' convoy approaching. Manobai held on tightly to Pomeela.

They started running towards the jungle, following everybody else through the fields. Gandhai, Ahina, Meghuwa and Sombari were all sitting silently in the light woods of the reserve forest. Ahina had taken his entire stock of chickens to the market just before planting the cauliflower and cabbage saplings. He was now sitting with a dejected look on his face, his hands on his head. He had no idea where the entire basket of chickens went in the frenzy. Ratna's white pig had also fallen off his cycle and fled somewhere.

Gandhai snapped at them, 'We are all thinking about our lives, and these two are now being greedy about money.'

From the reserve forest, they could see rows of vehicles loaded with military personnel thundering towards their village.

The huddled masses came out from the reserve forest after sunset. They all froze the moment they set foot on the path to their village; raised barrels of guns enveloped them. No one could go into the village; no one could come out either, so were the orders. The hungry and tired men and women kept on milling around in the same place, just like fish that have been kept alive in a small bucket of water.

As night crept in, they saw an open jeep hemmed in between two military trucks. It was carrying a dead body covered with a blood-stained shroud. The group of people was thunderstruck once again. They wondered if it was somebody from their own village. Who could it be?

Pomeela Bengi also kept on staring at the direction of the jeep, just like everybody else, but she continued doing so even after the others got back to their old positions.

'Get down, Bengi,' Manobai forced her to sit down. 'There is no knowing whether we ourselves live or die, what do I do with this halfwit?' she mumbled to herself.

Pomeela Bengi could just look meekly at Manobai after being chastised, and smile at her, just like a baby.

The slumbering people were allowed to go to their respective homes at the pink of dawn. Pomeela Bengi also started homewards, holding onto the hands of Manobai. Everybody found out about it a while later. Mohan, who was fencing up his home, was summoned and ordered to run. A stunned Mohan started running and was shot from behind. The army had surrounded Pomela Bengi's house as an identified terrorist's house. Everybody was looking at Pomeela when they heard the news. She flashed her baby smile again and again, seeing all the people looking at her.

Manobai stopped Pomeela from going home that day; instead, she had kept Pomeela in her own house after entering the village. Pomeela had a cup of tea and then started insisting on going home. She repeatedly said that her son was waiting for her, that she would need to cook for him. Manobai, Sombari and the others gathered around her.

Bengi was growing angry, her face flushing. What if she turns hysterical? Sombari placed a tray of rice before Pomeela and mixed some paddy in it.

'Bengi, please sort out the rice,' she said, handing her the tray.

Pomeela Bengi calmed down and started sorting the rice from the paddy. It was then that Mileshwar came back and informed them about Mohan's dead body lying in the police station. It needed to be identified and brought back.

All hearths of the village remained cold that day, the cows remained tethered in the cow-shed. Army personnel were swarming all around. People would drop in between to see Pomeela Bengi, separating rice grains from the husk; some looked at the half- fastened bamboo panels, some looked at the tilted roof, some looked at the droplets of blood.

Bengi finally went off to sleep, tired, right over her tray of rice grains. Nobody dared to wake her up for dinner; What if she asks for her son?

Teele the old lady said, 'Let her fast today, her son has died after all.'

A couple of villagers decided to accompany Mileshwar to the police station. How could they let crows and vultures feed on the dead body of the innocent boy? Mileshwar himself brought up the topic; some kin of his had to identify the body. Who does he have other than his mother? After a round of discussion, they decided to take Bengi along. After all, it was an official matter involving the administration, who knew what problems would creep up.

Pomeela Bengi also entered the police station, closely following the group of men. She was a bit short of breath. She rested her head on Manobai's shoulder. She was feeling dizzy, probably because of her fast the previous night. The men clad in khaki, the unknown room, the chairs and the tables—everything seemed to be trembling. The world before her was moving ever so slightly, just like the top of a murky, fuzzy pond worried by the tiny drops of a drizzle.

'Oi Bengi, why don't you reply to Sahib? Don't you hear him asking something?'

Bengi lifted her face; somebody had just thrown a rock into her rippling, dusky pond. The dark waters kept rising and falling for some time. Bengi simply stared at the face of the police officer.

He looked at her and asked again, 'Is the dead body that of your son, or not?'

Bengi just looked at him like a dazed dear.

He barked back this time, 'What are you looking at? Don't you hear what I just said?'

Mileshwar decided to reply on her behalf, 'She is a retarded woman, Sir. What can she say? Yes indeed, the dead body is her son.'

'If so, then sign on the papers and take away the dead body.'

The man rang a bell, a constable came and informed, 'The bodies of the dead terrorists had been sent to the headquarters.'

Another constable came and saluted, 'It was sent back, as nobody had come forward to claim the body.'

The two policemen went out marching, their boots stomping loudly.

Bengi was now looking towards that direction. Her son's voice was rising and lowering in her muddled senses. He was bringing her back from the river bank ... holding onto her hands ... she serves rice to him ... he asks her to roast a brinjal in the fire ... he asks for a pinch of salt, oil and a green chilly. The clay stove is alight with a red fire in her muddled mind; the water is boiling in the pot, she is cooking for her son.

'What do we do now, Sir?' Mileshwar asked with folded hands.

'Get the body from the headquarters,' ordered the officer.

All of them went silent hearing the words.

A constable said, 'One would need at least ₹4,000–₹5,000 to bring back a dead body.'

The group of men, attired in *gamosas*, had never met anybody in the high offices. All they could do was just stand with their mouths wide open.

The man sitting on the chair looked at the face of Pomeela Bengi, 'There is a solution. If somebody could contact the relatives of the other dead bodies, one could arrange for a van and …'

He beckoned somebody with the ring of a bell, and asked, 'How many dead bodies were sent to the headquarters?'

Somebody replied, 'Five.'

'Are they from the same place?' asked the officer.

'One's from the village near the bridge, one is from Nimtola, another's from Simliguri …' the man stopped.

The room was filled with the cacophony of voices; voices that debated the number of bodies sent; where they have been brought from; what the injuries on the different bodies were; what were the cases they were involved in.

Pomeela Bengi was looking intently at a man who was selling something to the beats of his two-headed *dambaru*. She got up, startled, hearing the stomping of shoes nearby.

She suddenly rose and made her way outside. She looked at Manobai and said, 'He will have his meal.'

Mileshwar and Manobai, too, came out, following Pomeela.

The day was over by the time Pomeela Bengi and company reached their village, crossing the barriers of numerous army check-posts. The main road was also cordoned off; they had to take many detours to reach home. Bengi was another problem.

She would suddenly sit down somewhere, start moving her hands in a circular fashion, and keep repeating the same words—'My son is hungry and waiting. I have to cook.'

Darkness had almost entirely enveloped the village by the time they reached. Pomeela Bengi moved rapidly into her house. Manobai and her friends kept on observing her. She swept the house first thing after entering, broke a few firewood twigs on her knees and then went out to the public tube-well to get a potful of water. She proceeded to close the cages of the poultry after placing her pot.

Seeing her, Manobai said, 'I think we can leave. She would be busy with her chores now.'

Manobai came out of Bengi's house and saw a lit earthen lamp placed on the spot that had the blood stains. The lamp was in its last gasps, Manobai picked up the wick. The flame shot up once and died.

Pomeela Bengi's earthen stove roared up in flames. She put on the rice. There were a couple of eggs lying in the coop; she had picked them up too. She let the eggs boil in the pan that had a broken ear. She kept removing the egg shells and stirring the rice at the same time. The eggs were freshly laid, so the shells wouldn't come off easy; she had to pinch them off bit by bit.

When she was about to throw off the shells, she noticed two bundles wrapped separately in a *gamosa*. There were some lentils in the first bundle and the other contained a few potatoes. She washed the potatoes rigorously and the lentils, too. She put them on in a pan over the fire and added a little *khar* in it for effect. After pouring the banana *khar* in, she kept on closing and opening the bottle, again and again. She often looked outside while fiddling with the bottle cap.

She then got up and started moving around inside the house. The fire of the stove went out. Pomeela Bengi took the plate meant for her son, washed it and served rice in it. She placed the peeled potatoes and the eggs on one side of the plate. She went out and got a few chillies from the garden too, after placing a little salt on the plate.

The rice and the dal, the eggs and the potatoes, all turned cold. The stove filled with ashes. Bengi continued sitting with the plateful of rice in front of her. All her fellow women came to see her, but none could dare talk to her. The rooster crowed the hours of the night off, the lamp died, she kept sitting with her head in her knees. She started dozing off there itself.

The mongrel that used to sleep under Mohan's bed barked out loudly just when the pink of dawn was about to break. A tomcat had come to catch mice inside her house. Bengi woke up with a start hearing the dog bark. She looked at Mohan's bed immediately.

A swarm of black ants had covered the plate of rice, a couple of rats ran away hearing the approaching footsteps. She extended her hand towards the plate, and brought it back. She started moving around the plate now.

A blood-stained sack being carried by a group of people started floating in her hazy senses. She ran behind the door and sat down. A few pieces of burning ember flew before her eyes, she closed them instinctively. There was a deafening noise; that group of people wearing black masks ran past her, the bamboo platform was soaked with blood, only blood.

She ran out hearing voices at her door. All the women—from Manobai to Renumai—started coming in, one by one. Pomeela was mumbling to herself, standing in the corner behind the door, 'He will have his meal, he will have his meal.'

Her friends had tears in their eyes now. Bengi came out and smiled innocently, looking at them. She crossed them and returned after washing the plate of rice. She lit the fire again, filled the rice pot with water, placed the pot on the flames and kept staring at the sobbing Renumai. Her brawny young son was walking around in Bengi's muddled senses. She wove her hand around and said, 'He will have his meal. Oh, indeed, he will have his meal.'

Manobai and her friends were weeping loudly now, Renumai's sobs had turned into wails. Bengi stood up and started watching the girl intently. A blood-soaked sack carried around by a group of men floated up like a dead frog in a pond in her foggy senses; the sack went back into the water again. Her son floats up; her son goes down, the sack floats up.

All her friends were wailing loudly now. Pomeela kept looking at them, her head tilted at an angle. Her son was drowning in a whirlpool in her cloudy world. A blood-stained sack was lying in the middle, surrounded by grey darkness. Gun shots were ringing in her ears, flying embers were blinding her. Her son was drowning in huge puddles of blood; she could no longer see him.

Pomeela Bengi suddenly stood up and overturned the boiling water in the vessel into the cracking fire. Ashes spewed into the air with a hissing sound. She started crawling like a baby on the floor, watching the fire die. It was as if she was surrounded by deep craters, one wrong step and she could fall into one of them. She crawled into the corner behind the door. She started wriggling and rubbing her body; rubbing till she was all out of breath. Pools of blood began to fill up her increasingly darkening senses.

Pomeela Bengi broke into spasmodic, heartbreaking sobs.

Alekjaan Bano's Love

Sixteen-year-old Alekjaan sat kneeling on a sack, combing her hair. The mirror's stand had come off. She put a piece of brick behind it to keep it from falling. Taking out a bottle of oil from a blue polythene packet, she applied it to her thick, jet-black hair flowing down to her waist. A mild scent floated out.

Combing her hair, she tied it into a knot. She wiped off the extra oil stuck to her palms onto her face. Her dark face glistened at once like a ripe jamun—a juicy, over-ripe jamun—which has been touched by the slanting ray of the sun. She then stepped inside the small hut.

She was wearing the red blouse with the gold rolex work on it. She put on the yellow sari with the large pink flowers on it. Placing the bindi with the tiny colourful beads on her forehead, Alekjaan finished getting ready that winter afternoon. She took one last quick glance at herself in the mirror before putting it away.

The paint and beads on the earrings had come off. She had bought it at the last rasa mela at Haoli. The nose stud was also in the same state. As she tried to fix one earring, it broke and fell onto the sack. Dejected, she took off the other earring too, put them in the palm of her hand and started walking. She clipped the small lock onto the iron hoops of the door and tied the key to the end of her sari. Her stepmother, Hanifa, already had the other key.

Hanifa had gone out with Alekjaan's father, Miyad Miyan, taking their pair of children along. It was market day. The boat had been filled up with pumpkins alone. Alekjaan's brother had disappeared from home following an argument he had with his father over something. She remembered now that it was over money only. He wanted money to buy a pair of jeans and shoes.

Their mother had died when they were very young. Her father had gotten married within a month of his wife's passing away. That is, brought into his house Rahmat's wife Hanifa—Rahmat who had left Kasimmari, the high land formed by silt and sand on both sides of the river, to go work in Barpeta Road; or rather, Rahmat's wife had moved into their hut, which Alekjaan's mother had built with grass and reeds collected from here and there, like a bird collecting thatch for its nest.

Rahmat left the place for good with Lame Sofia, Alekjaan's father's sister. Rahmat, they had heard, had now set himself up at Falimari, far from Kasimmari. Sofia may have had a bad leg, but she had magic in her hands. She just had to poke the cabbage sapling once and it would start to grow luxuriantly. If she stuck in a couple of twigs next to the beans, the creeper would start climbing greedily.

Rahmat had apparently made so much money one monsoon from just growing beans that it was enough to fight a case. Aunt Sofia, limping, dragging her bad leg along as she threw the dung on the ground and as she toiled in the fields, came to Alekjaan's mind after a long time. Recalling her aunt's face, again and again, Alekjaan kept walking.

The winter's afternoon was slowly beginning to fade. She stood on the steep sand bank and looked towards the river. Exactly at this spot, the river bifurcated, with a Kasimmari-like island in the middle—a vast, high area of silt and sand. One branch of the Brahmaputra flowed away from Kasimmari, into the distance. The other branch flowed towards it, quite close by. On the side where the river flowed close towards it, you could bring a boat right up to the land in the winter. On this side, the river had washed away the soil, forming quite a steep bank.

The people found it difficult to come from the other side. The silt area had become considerably wide, so it had become strenuous to cross the stretch of sand, carrying all their goods, to get into the boat. On this side, the boat touched the land directly.

Other winters, the *bhotbhotis* stopped running. This time, however, they were still running. Actually, the people of Barpeta stopped running their *bhotbhotis* long back. The one still running belonged to Hasim Miyan of Bohri; he used to stay in Kasimmari earlier. Now, he plied the *bhotbhoti* and stayed in Bohri. The *bhotbhoti*'s owner stayed in Haoli, Hasim Miyan just plied it.

Hasim had run away from home when he was quite young and taken a job on the *bhotbhoti*. Just by looking at it, he could gauge the depth of the water, predict which way the *bhotbhoti* could go and where it would get stuck. Yet, even Hasim Miyan's *bhotbhoti* wouldn't run for long now. The water was getting shallow. Mounds of sand were rising up in all directions on the Brahmaputra's breast.

Alekjaan started going towards the north side. On this side, the people barely did any cultivation. They barely built any houses either. You could almost say they never built any houses here. During the last rains, this part of the sand area got submerged; during almost every flood, the sand piled up the most here. People didn't come over to this side much. Nothing grew here, except the tall reed-like grass that grows in flooded areas. Thatch-grass also grew in abundance. Except for the people who came to cut the reed and grass, few came in this direction.

Lately, a path had emerged in the middle of the grass and straw by people coming and going. On this side, the steep bank sloped down a little. Tying their boat to a peg, the people could easily climb up carrying their goods.

Alekjaan stepped onto the cattle path amid the grass and straw. A few minutes down that path, she entered the plot of tall grass towards the left, with narrow raised earthen boundaries. Right here, a path, just big enough for one person, had been cut through the grass—a path not used by many. The heads of the tall grass did not bend down to the ground, they still stood erect.

Alekjaan raised her sari and stepped carefully. Used to walking bare feet over the sand since her childhood, the soles of her feet had hardened. The heads of the grass, therefore, did not give her much trouble.

Now, she could clearly hear the sound of whistling; it was the tune of a song. She kept going, and reached the cleared area in the middle of the grass. Since three months now, this area had become familiar to Alekjaan. Towards its end, Kasimmari thinned out like the tail fin of a fish, before it merged into the river. But, here the sand was layered like a thick blanket. She could see from far, Samsoon sitting. He was wearing a blue lungi with black-and-yellow checks and a blue vest; the amulet around his neck. He was whistling as he looked at the river, absorbed. She kept watching him for a while.

Samsoon turned and looked at her. A smile broke out over his face. Getting up, he pulled Alekjaan by the hand, down onto the bed of cut grass. He was still whistling, a smile on his face.

He took out a small bundle from the knot of his lungi. Alekjaan watched him open the small bundle wrapped in the bright pink paper; her kajal-lined eyes wide open. There it was—a pair of earrings with red beads and a silver-coloured chain. He took out the things on his palm and sat there for some time. Alekjaan sat leaning against his back. He put the earrings on her. Then, he slipped the chain around her neck.

For some reason that she couldn't fathom, she felt saddened. No one had ever bought anything new for her like this. Only her mother had got her a dress once, and also some pairs of pants. She remembered only one thing clearly about her mother. At times, she used to bleed profusely, the blood soaking all her clothes. After that, she would not be able to get up from bed. So, Alekjaan would have to start fetching the water, cook and do all the work. Towards the end, it had grown worse. Whenever she tried to remember her mother, all she could see before her eyes were large clots of blood. Her mother, pale from losing so much blood continuously, was unable to get out of bed for some months.

Her father had then started openly going to Rahmat's wife, right in front of everyone's eyes. Fifteen days before her mother died, Alekjaan's father and Rahmat, who had just come from Barpeta Road, had had a *da*-fight, chasing each other all around the place with their long knives. The blood-soaked woman kept watching mutely. She was found dead soon after that incident.

No one was near Alekjaan's mother at the time of her death. Alekjaan's brother had meanwhile run away from home. Those days, their father had been fighting a case. She had been out in the field, picking peas from their strings. After collecting four baskets of peas, she had brought them all home, and was sitting, stretching out her arms and legs. Flies were buzzing all around her mother. But, they were always there. Alekjaan noticed her mother's hand, dry as a twig, had not come up in a while to shoo away the flies. She went to take a closer look and noticed that her mother's body had become stiff.

Remembering her mother, two teardrops flowed down Alekjaan's eyes and hung like beads over her dark cheeks, slippery with oil, for a few moments. Then a hard hand caused the beads to break. The hard hands moved over her young body, slowly letting loose all over her a small bundle of tinkling, black, glass beads. She rolled down and stretched out on top of the grass.

She gazed at the sky through Samsoon's embrace. The sun was about to set. The river, the sky, the grass, everything had been imbued with a red colour. The young maid named Alekjaan, too, had become imbued with a heady intoxication. The tiny flowers from the grass clung to her body, as did the glittering sand, as did the taste of a man's hand—intense and boiling hot. Like the flowers fluttering in the wind, she, too, was shaking uncontrollably; like the shiny sand particles flying in the wind, she, too, was soaring high.

Both of them got up startled at the sound of the *bhotbhoti*. Yes, it was Hasim Miyan's *bhotbhoti* approaching the river bank. They went off in different directions, tearing through the grass.

Her father and stepmother were already back by the time she reached home. She saw that her father had lit a fire outside and was sitting with several men around it. When she passed them, she overheard them talking about the erosion on the side where Hasim Miyan plied his *bhotbhoti*. It had never happened in such a scale in Kasimmari before.

A whirlpool had formed on that side of the river. There was a roaring sound, of water flowing fast, at the place—a sound never heard before. Piece by piece, Kasimmari was being eroded at that place. Every day, chunk by chunk, Miyad Miyan's pumpkin crop fell into the river. Rezaul chacha and Maimuna's grandfather, everyone, said this was not a good thing, the way the sand bank was getting eroded. Especially, the roaring sound and the whirlpool were not good signs. Chacha and the others suspected that the river was eroding away Kasimmari from the bottom. It was normal for land to get eroded every year. But seeing the way it was happening this time, the people were terrified.

That day, Alekjaan's father, Miyad Miyan, had gone and sold off the yet-to-ripen pumpkins at the Bohri market. He was sitting with his head sunk between his knees. He had worked hard on his pumpkin cultivation. He worked hard every year. His pumpkins were famous. They looked as good as they tasted. If one was as small as a sheared coconut, the other would be as big as a jackfruit; one was round as a football, another long like a bottle-gourd. But each of them was red and brittle. They made a smart swishing sound as they were cut into strips on the *bothi*. He always grew a breed of pumpkins that climbed over the ground; these didn't grow as profusely as the ones that grew to be the size of a pomelo. Every year, only 10 to 15 of them would grow. Each pumpkin grew to be the size of a big pan where the grains for the cows were cooked.

People stopped and stared at the fruit. He took one of these to the market every day, along with the other pumpkins. He would put it right in the middle, piling the others all around it. Soon, a crowd would gather around:

'What a huge pumpkin!'
'How much will you give it for?'
'It's big enough for a feast.'
'Is there any occasion or a wedding?'

Indeed, who would buy a pumpkin of that size unless there was an occasion, a wedding?

A big crowd would gather just to look at it, to touch it. In that crowd, all the other pumpkins—the ones that were like pomelos, the ones shaped like bottle-gourds, the ones as small as coconuts, the ones that looked like jackfruits—all of them would get sold. Tucking the money into the knot of his lungi, Miyad Miyan returned home, a smile on his face.

Miyad Miyan got the seeds of this crop from his father. When Alekjaan's grandfather had come to Kasimmari, he had with him just one pair of clothes and a handful of pumpkin seeds. Sand and earth from the banks of the Padma River still clung to those seeds. Kasimmari was not like a gradually thinning fish then; it looked like a big turtle. When he saw this tract of fertile land, sunning itself like a broad-backed turtle in the middle of the Brahmaputra, he immediately took out the seeds from their bundle. The big, broad leaves climbed all over the land, turning the whole place into a lush green colour; various kinds of sweet fruits started growing. The man stayed behind. It was from him that Miyad Miyan inherited his bundle of seeds.

This was the first time, Alekjaan's father was compelled to sell off the yet-to-ripen pumpkins at half the price. One side of the crops had been swallowed by the river. The leaves of the creepers were starting to turn black. The pumpkins had just started to grow, the green fruit with faint yellow stripes just beginning to peep through the broad leaves. All the people had been working. Miyad Miyan, too, had been clearing the weeds from the creepers.

This time, a weird thing was growing in the land; never before was such an evil thing seen in Kasimmari. It was the white-yellowish leafless parasitic vine called Ravana's Intestines, and it truly was like Ravana's Intestines. It refused to die. If it was uprooted from one place, it would come up in seven other places, coiling around the plants.

The yellow-coloured, thin, creeper didn't need land to grow, didn't need water, didn't even need to be planted. Wherever it fell, it latched on there. Like a leech, it stuck there. Whichever plant it coiled around, like a leech sucking blood, it would suck the juice out of the plant, turning it pale. The leaves would turn yellow and the twigs would start to rot. Slowly, the plant withered away.

God only knew how this Ravana's Intestines came to Kasimmari. Birds may have brought it. Didn't they bring all kinds of things while building nests? Or it could have come with someone's goods. Miyad Miyan was suspicious of Samsoon, too. Nobody knew when he became the owner of the land left behind by Rahmat. Last year, he made good money from growing a breed of chillies that were the size of round lemons. Apparently, this kind of heatless chilly was valued highly. They were taken on wholesale from Bohri, straight to Guwahati. They said this variety of chilly was needed in the big hotels of the city—hotels owned by the rich people.

Once, Alekjaan had fried some of these chillies for her father with new potatoes. He found them to be rather tasteless. How could they compete with the feisty dried-fish curry made with ground red chillies? He could now smell just one thing ... Pushing the plate of fried potatoes and chillies away, he brought the red-coloured dried-fish curry closer. He was amazed. The wholesale traders apparently sold these chillies for ₹ 30 per kilogram. In the city, they sold for as high as ₹ 78 per kilogram.

Samsoon was always eyeing his pumpkins, green with envy. Miyad Miyan kept cleaning those Ravana's Intestines, brooding about Samsoon, the boy who was obsessed with seeds all the time. Who knew, he only must have come and left one of those creepers there.

Suddenly, there was a commotion. A thin crack had emerged right in the middle of Miyad Miyan's pumpkin cultivation. Everyone understood the meaning of this narrow crack, as twisted as Ravana's Intestines. Pretty soon, the river would claim another bit of Kasimmari for itself. In fact, a tremor occurred right then. A block of land, along with Miyad Miyan's pumpkin cultivation, fell into the river with a loud thud.

Like a man who had lost his mind, Miyad Miyan started tearing off the remaining half-ripe pumpkins from the plants, and piling them all in one place. His hair, a golden brown from working in the sun, was flying about in a disorderly manner. His eyes had become big round orbs. He didn't look here or there, but just kept piling up the pumpkins. The slender man, his lungi tucked up, jumped around among his crops, like a grasshopper. The others around him tried to stop him:

> 'What are you doing? Hey, what are you doing?'
> 'Have you gone mad?'
> 'Leave it today, pick them tomorrow.'
> 'What, do you think you can pick the entire crop in one day?'
> 'The blood has congealed in his brains.'
> 'The man refuses to listen to anyone.'
> 'A man his age can't go on like this.'

'The man stood there, bent, his hands supporting his back. His face had become twisted with all the effort. He was trying to straighten himself up slowly. He felt as if someone was beating him with a cudgel on his back. With every movement of his body, this 42-year-old man's wrinkled and creased face twisted. In each hand, he carried one pumpkin, green with little yellow marks.

'I will die, yes, I will die.' The man shouted out, panting.

Alekjaan and her stepmother were standing nearby. He looked towards them. Alekjaan, her stepmother and the children started picking the pumpkins, too. Samsoon, who had been waiting nearby, also joined in. Hazera, Sayed, Saboor, Asmat, everyone started helping Alekjaan's father. The tender, half-ripe pumpkins were piled up in their hut made of reeds, straw and grass. Miyad Miyan was a creature of the soil. He just had to place his hands on the land to understand what was going on. He understood that day, too. That night, the river took away all the remaining land.

Miyad Miyan, was sitting with his head sunk between his knees. The wind was blowing strongly from the river. The fire made from thin and small branches, twigs and dry leaves gave neither warmth nor light. Again and again, the fire would be reduced to ashes. They were all quiet. Looking at his sombre face, everyone understood that this jovial man's heart was heavy; his dreams, too, were being turned to ashes.

Inside, Alekjaan's stepmother, Hanifa, was cooking rice on a fire built from dry cow dung. Suddenly, she noticed on her stepdaughter's ears, glittering in the light of the cow-dung fire, a pair of shiny new earrings. A sparkling silver chain hung from her neck. Hanifa peered at her, taking the earthen lamp. Just one glance was enough for her to know that her stepdaughter's maturing body had felt the touch of a man's hand. She flared up in an impossible rage of jealousy and hatred.

She grabbed Alekjaan by her hair and gave her a good shaking, 'The father sells seeds for a living, but the daughter wears gold rings. The father is on his death bed and the daughter is having an affair, secretly! Tell me! Who is your lover?'

Alekjaan kept quiet, even after her stepmother's slaps and blows. Seeing she was about to grab the chain from her neck, Alekjaan flared up, 'Don't you dare touch it! I am warning you, don't touch it! Yes, my man gave me this. What will you do, tell me! What will you do?'

Alekjaan had truly turned into a deadly black cobra, its hood raised. She was never able to accept this woman. Whenever she saw this woman, she remembered a pair of sunken eyes; a woman staring continuously with her sunken eyes, lying in the midst of blood-soaked clothes. Outside, two men were chasing each other with *da*s; the men going out at night, going out even in broad daylight. The woman just kept looking from upon her sack. The flies buzzing around her … Once in a while, a hand, dry as a twig, was raised and then went down again.

Hanifa dragged her out by her hair, screaming, 'Listen! Listen to this whore! She is talking about her man, showing off the earrings given by him!'

Miyad Miyan looked at his daughter, hand placed behind his hips. The man was dumbfounded. The little girl who used to roam around wiping her nose with one hand, and holding her torn pants with the other, had started talking about a man now?

'Which man has given you gold earrings? Is your stepmother telling the truth?'

her father's voice sounded weary, sad.

But she felt the love in his voice. Her heart swelled up. So many days had gone by without his saying a word to her.

'Samsoon,' she blurted out his name suddenly, her head bent.

The man bristled upon hearing his name—as if someone had piled a bunch of dry leaves and twigs on him, and then struck a match into it. Samsoon was close to that villain who had eloped with his sister, Lame Sofia. He worked on his land, he stayed in his house. And his daughter was in love with that fellow. He started slapping and hitting Alekjaan. These weren't her stepmother's slaps that she could fight back. Under assault from the hard-as-iron hands, she became helpless.

There was a fire raging within him.

He burnt with an all-consuming anger—anger against Rahmat for eloping with his sister, Lame Sofia; anger against Samsoon who had taken over his house and his land; anger against his daughter who wore the earrings given to her by Samsoon, the one man he despised; anger against the river which had swallowed up his land; anger against the wholesale trader who had taken away his crop of pumpkins at a nominal price.

The man took out all his anger on the 16-year-old girl. Everyone was stunned. Her stepmother became speechless too. It was true that in her heart of hearts, she didn't dislike it when her husband gave his daughter a slap or two, but to hit her like this? Nobody could tear this possessed man away from the girl. The small fire had died out a long time ago. Now, all that remained were the strong wind and the heart-rending cries of the girl.

No one knew when Samsoon reached there and who informed him. He came and tore off the girl from her father's hands. Everyone heard the strong voice of a young man, 'I will marry Alekjaan.'

Fixing her clothes and hair which had come open, she took his hand and walked away.

They kept going, the new hurricane lamp, shaking as they walked, tearing through the darkness. The people kept looking, as long as they could see in the light of the lamp, at the young couple.

Samsoon and Alekjaan kept walking towards the rotted, broken-down and half-repaired house that Rahmat had left behind.

Alekjaan and Samsoon entered the house Rahmat had left behind. The so-called house had no walls or anything; just a thatch roof on top with big holes in it.

After working the whole day, Samsoon would throw a sack on the floor and lie down there, curled up in a corner, till morning. Every day, he would wake up instantly. He had already decided on everything beforehand. He had already marked out a bunch of bamboo on the river bank that he would cut, as he went up and down to Bohri. He was going to bring Alekjaan, after the nikaah, to a house with new grass walls, bamboo posts and a new thatch roof. But it didn't work out that way; his plans got messed up.

Samsoon tore open the sack he slept on and spread it wide. Their bodies lay upon the mouldy earth littered with earthworm excreta, their heads on the sack which had got dragged to one side. As if exhausted from walking a long distance, the young children fell into a deep sleep, and lay there, holding onto each other.

Even before the sky reddened, they were up. She cast a glance around the deserted house. Everything would have to be started afresh. A broomstick would have to be made with straw and thatch-grass to sweep the house. A nice stove to cook in, a pot to store water in, a utensil for cooking rice, a *bothi*, two plates to have their meals in, and gradually, an iron pan to fry puffed rice in … Alekjaan kept sitting there. A house, children, crops, Samsoon … The pictures went round and round in her head.

She looked at Samsoon. He was all concentration, fixing the boat. The boat, made from sal wood, had been there from his father's time. The bottom was rotted. Samsoon was striking nails onto the planks on the bottom of the boat. Alekjaan felt a strong desire to go over and hand the man, working so hard, a cup of salted tea and a handful of puffed rice, like she always did to her father. She went inside the house.

There was a pot to cook rice in. There was rice, too, kept tied in a *gamosa*. There was salt and oil, and there was a clay stove, too, eroded in parts, and a sack of dried leaves and twigs. Alekjaan quickly put on her sari, then opened it the next moment. She had left behind her two saris, which Samsoon had given her, at home. If she wore this one to work, what would she wear after bathing? One sari, one blouse, one petticoat ... so many things to buy She felt gloomy.

She glanced towards the man drilling nails into the boat, focused on his work. He would forget everything else once he put his heart into doing something. She had heard Samsoon say that his father had been like this too. If he started doing something, he would forget everything else.

Samsoon's father once owned a lot of land. But the river took everything. Samsoon's father's land was on the side where Hasim Miyan brought his *bhotbhoti* close to the bank. When Samsoon's father grew a great variety of crops, in those days, Kasimmari looked like a big, round turtle, not like the curved ilish fish, thinning out at the bottom, like it looked now. The river took away Samsoon's father into its bosom too, you could say. A great flood had come. Samsoon's father thought nothing would happen to his big and sturdy boat.

In the middle of Kasimmari, there was a high piece of land, like the raised portion on the back of a turtle. He could easily get there. That time, too, they had been growing *bao dhan*. When one of that season's crops started rotting, he realised this was no ordinary water. It had come as Allah's curse. One day, he took his boat to see the *bao dhan* crop; the man never came back. Some said he was struck by a snake which had climbed into the boat from the water, the man had turned blue. Some said the boat got caught in a whirlpool, the river took him down. Others said some genie had possessed and taken him. Apparently, he had dreamt that night that he was wearing dirty and torn rags, and was eating some inedible food. It is in the *Khwabnama* that such dreams are a foreboding of some imminent danger. Anyway, the man disappeared into the water.

Alekjaan could not hear the sound of nails being struck any more. She looked up. The man wasn't there. She got up, too. Tying up her hair tightly into a knot, she wrapped her petticoat over her breasts. She scraped and smoothed up the clay floor with Samsoon's hand spade, and then swabbed it. She wiped the earthen stove too. She did it carefully, so as not to moisten the inside of the stove. It would be difficult to light a fire then. She decided they would have to get a proper stove soon. There were a lot of advantages of having a proper stove; during floods, you could lift it onto the roof. It wouldn't get wet at the bottom during rains. Where would she find a metal basin to wash things in or to keep things? A broom to sweep the house, one basin … Alekjaan became restless.

Samsoon was coming back, carrying some green vegetables in his hands. She stretched out her hands, took the vegetables from him and put them beside the stove. She kept staring for a while at the fresh vegetables kept on the clean floor.

A winter's afternoon. By the time Samsoon had his bath, the sun was already setting in the horizon. Samsoon had finished work on the boat. Somehow managing to stuff the rice in, he took the boat out into the water. Alekjaan went towards the steep bank of the river, the sickle in her hands. There, she cut a good amount of the tall grass bushes and piled them all in one place. Busy at work, she didn't notice her friends Farida and Maimuna cutting grass nearby. Spotting her, they all came towards her, surrounded her. Alekjaan poured out her heart and soul to them. There was no jharu, no stove, no *bothi*, no pot, no ladle. What was she to do?

Before Samsoon even got back with his boat, there were two straw brooms in the house, one pot for the stove and several bunches of grass. Samsoon took down the things from the boat, then headed straight for the Bohri Ghat with his boat. From the shops there he got sacks, one pot, a pair of ladles, a *bothi*.

On his way back after buying the things, he cut four long bamboo stems from a bunch that he had noticed earlier on a steep bank of the river; it was leaning out over the water. He cut a couple of leaves from a coconut tree on the river bank and placed them on top of the bamboo. He also got biscuits and tea from a shop in the ghat.

On the freshly cleaned stove, in the pot used for cooking rice, he made some salted tea, and opened the packet of biscuits. One by one, Maimuna and the others started to drink from Samsoon's leaky mug. Actually, if one closed the hole tightly with a finger, it would stop leaking.

After having the tea, they made a wall from the straw tied together with the thin bamboo strips that Samsoon had cut for them. Actually, it was Samsoon doing most of the work as Maimuna and the others watched him.

When he worked, his fingers moved so fast, they became a blur. As he tied the grass together, the muscles of his body, hard and strong like an oar, rippled. And when he smiled, flashing his even set of teeth, he looked like a small boy. As he worked, he would often look at Alekjaan and smile. His half-shy, boyish smile expressed a sense of complete happiness. Maimuna and the others felt a bit envious. Samsoon's smile fell on Alekjaan's face like a ray of sunshine. Her face glowed.

Just as Maimuna and the rest were about to leave, Alekjaan's father Miyad Miyan arrived along with some men, including Mansoor Miyan. Janab Mansoor Miyan was an important person here in Kasimmari town. From chasing fevers and to giving amulets for weddings and funerals, he was needed everywhere. He wasn't available all the time, as he roamed around here and there. Samsoon and Alekjaan were lucky to have him with them. He performed the nikaah for them. Samsoon and Alekjaan were pronounced man and wife.

The new moon of Muharram had risen in the sky. Mansoor Miyan raised his hand laden with gold rings, so that everyone could see. It was propitious to look first at the new moon and then at gold. It was also propitious to get married when the new moon rose. Everyone bowed their heads to the new moon. Mansoor Miyan announced in a loud and clear throaty voice that that Sunday, the new moon of Muharram had risen. He prophesied the occurrence of many hail storms that year. Lightning would strike, too. The paddy crop would be good. Domestic animals such as cows, sheep and goats would multiply. Milk and ghee would be cheaper.

Hanifa, Alekjaan's stepmother, gave her, in addition to the clothes she had left behind at home, a pair of clothes, not exactly new, but without a tear in them. Her father gave her a bundle of pumpkin seeds, which Samsoon had been eyeing greedily all these days. Mansoor Miyan had to leave. The grains were ripe; it was peak time in the fields, so no one had time to waste these days. Even if they had the time, why waste it on the motherless girl?

Everyone went their own way.

In Kasimmari, 8 pm was as good as midnight. The people here went to sleep with the birds and woke up with them. Samsoon got up to tie up his boat to a post. Alekjaan, too, went after him. After tying up the boat, as usual, he glanced towards one side of the river; his father's land was there once. Samsoon had heard from many people about his father's land which was swallowed up by the river. He had heard about the varieties of crops that grew there. Was it a long time back? He could recall in bits and pieces. It was from the time when he roamed around, without a stitch of clothing upon him, among his father's crops—bigha after bigha of watermelon, pumpkin, potato and bitter-gourd. He couldn't remember his father's face, but he could recall vividly the green colour of the watermelons. He could see them even now, in his mind's eye.

After his parents died, he grew up with Rahmat chacha. He had no recollection about when his mother died, and when and how his brothers and sisters died. The only memory from his past was that of a great swathe of water swallowing up the whole of Kasimmari. Whenever he looked back, he was aware of a severe and intense feeling of scarcity and want, an overpowering sense of lack—lack of love, lack of a mother, lack of a father, lack of a piece of clothing, lack of a handful of rice, lack of a piece of land to lie down on.

He had immersed himself in work from his childhood—in Rahmat's fields, in Miyad's fields, in Mansoor Miyan's fields. Samsoon started working on the land for a handful of rice, for a piece of cloth, for a piece of land to rest upon—sometimes with a hand spade, sometimes with a hoe, sometimes with a harrow. He worked for a while in a couple's house in Bohri. Rahmat took him there when he had gone to work in Barpeta Road. After Rahmat chacha took off with Lame Sofia to Falimari, Samsoon came away from Bohri.

If truth be told, Rahmat, a distant uncle, never felt any sense of responsibility towards Samsoon. Since then, Samsoon was on his own. He lived on somehow in this hut, devoid of a roof or walls.

How old could he have been then? Like the sand, which the river laid thick at times and sometimes swallowed up, his age, too, increased or decreased with necessity. When he went to work in Bohri, he was a small boy who was able to do household chores. When he started living with Rahmat chacha, he worked in the fields; he had become a responsible man who could survive without help from anyone.

Samsoon waited for a while, so did Alekjaan. Both looked up at the sky. Looking at the new moon, they cleansed themselves once with water before praying. The whole sky was like an overturned bowl covering the earth. Wherever the river flowed, the bowl—painted with flowers—broke into pieces. Wherever the soft light of the new moon fell upon the sand, it looked like a bunch of glittering kholi fish had been spread out. They stepped onto a bit of the kholi fish-like sand. The newly laid sand felt like fish eggs under their feet—fine, loose and soft. At this part, Kasimmari took on the shape of an ilish fish's tail bone, just like the beating tail of a curved fish.

Samsoon stepped down onto the place where the tail divided into two parts. He tied his boat there, every day. Alekjaan kept waiting where she was. She covered herself. She couldn't see Samsoon. His dark, brown body was indistinguishable in the grey light of the new moon. She looked around here and there, aimlessly. There was a noise coming from the side where Hasim Miyan plied his *bhotbhoti*. The whole river seemed to disappear onto that side. On this side, was just the weak current of shallow water here and there, and sand.

'Alekjaan, O, Alekjaan, come this side!'

Hearing Samsoon's excited cry, she rushed to him. She saw him standing on the boat, shouting loudly, 'Alekjaan, O, Alekjaan!'

She felt out of breath. She, too, went down the steep bank and got onto the boat.

'Look, Alekjaan, look!'

In his excitement, the man had forgotten everything else. He was pointing towards where the river turned, at something white, shining in the half light of the moon. Samsoon rowed the boat over to that side.

The river had taken a sharp turn here, and was curved like the new moon. The boat went a little ahead, then got stuck. It wouldn't go any further. It seemed to have got stuck on solid land. Samsoon struck anchor right there, tucked in his lungi, and stepped down. Truly, there was land under his feet. He pulled Alekjaan, too, onto the land.

Bubbling with excitement, they climbed up onto the white piece of land. Alekjaan was amazed; for as long as she had known, there was only the river here. She had crossed this part by boat countless times—on Hasim Miyan's *bhotbhoti* and on the boat that belonged to the merchant from Barpeta.

There, indeed, was land underneath. The river had kept it hidden all this time. Taking a new bend, the river now returned this piece of land. Alekjaan, too, became all excited like Samsoon. This piece of land, then, belonged to Samsoon's father. How many times had she heard from Samsoon's mouth about this piece of land as they lay together on the grass? What could he talk about, besides his seeds and land? What did she like to hear about, other than his land and seeds? What else did she know about, anyway?

Samsoon was now hugging her. He was crying. On his face—no longer that of a child but of a young man—tears of joy were flowing down like drops of black, damp mud. His tears got entangled in his new growth of moustache and beard.

Alekjaan kept staring at Samsoon's face; it looked like it had been carved from black, muddy, earth which had been tilled and made ready for planting seeds. His voice sounded like raindrops falling on ploughed land. The words were coming out drop by drop.

Very slowly, very softly, he said, 'Alekjaan, we will plant our seeds here …'

He wasn't able to speak. Neither could she. A pair of lips pressed down on hers; the taste of salt on her tongue …

The piece of fertile land, hidden for ages, had completely taken over the imagination of this young couple. The land on which watermelon, pumpkin, eggplant and chilly plants had grown so abundantly, formed a bed for them now.

The sky, embroidered with the new moon and the stars, engulfed the couple like a mosquito net woven with floral designs. Their young blood bubbled inside like a bunch of fish flapping about on being caught in a net. The smell of earth filled their noses. They were drunk on the smell and the touch of a piece of land that had been hidden under the river for ages. They kept saying in indistinct voices as if speaking to themselves, 'We will sow our seeds right here.'

Alekjaan's tender body was taken to bed for the first time.

Truly, the river returned Samsoon's land bit by bit. Day by day, the river took a new turn and a piece of land would emerge. Everywhere, not just in Kasimmari, the land was measured from over the water level. Samsoon's father's land was measured, even during the full spate. These days, there was an unusual flurry in Kasimmari. The surveyor had come. He came every year. He had come with helpers, and they had put up a tent. The surveyor was measuring the silt land. There were no rightful owners of the land. Whoever had been cultivating the land had the rights to it. Samsoon's father's land was also measured. Samsoon was now the owner of solid land. Neither the government nor any other power could now take over or transfer the land.

Samsoon and Alekjaan had a lot of visitors these days. One day, Alekjaan's father had come to visit them. The pain in his hip had completely taken over him. Whenever he moved, he cried out in pain. There was no saying how old he was. He had married Hanifa when he was 22; Alekjaan was born within a year of their marriage. She was turning 17 this year. The man's face was filled with lines and wrinkles.

Hanifa came, too. Twenty-one-year-old Hanifa had given birth to five children till date, three of them had died. When she gave birth to her third child, her teeth had started protruding. Her gums, which had turned black because of anemia, had become loose. By her fourth child, her teeth had become loose. Now, somehow, the front teeth remained stuck to the black gums. She looked strange when she smiled. At 21, Hanifa was an old woman.

Saboor Ali had also come; he grew his crops in two bighas of land. Twenty bighas were taken by the river. His four sons stayed in four different places. Two of them plied rickshaws in Guwahati, the other two worked as daily-wage labourers in Baihata and

Goreswar. The man suffered from a pain in the stomach. Just like Alekjaan's father, he, too, cried out in pain now and then, gripping his stomach. The 45-year-old man had shrivelled up, looking like a 70-year-old.

Rahmat had come, but not Lame Sofia. Her aunt had sent through Rahmat a bundle of potatoes, cabbages and mustard. Alekjaan listened to Rahmat's stories about Falimari. She laughed, hearing about her aunt giving a feast for him.

Everyone came to look at Samsoon's land, which was emerging gradually. Samsoon regained 20 bighas of land which had remained hidden under water for 12 years. It was no small matter. Different people gave different advice. Alekjaan and Samsoon listened attentively to everyone.

One night, they decided to go and meet Lame Sofia. After all, Alekjaan had grown up in her lame paternal aunt's lap. Her aunt, whose one limb was affected by polio, poured out all her love onto the land and this motherless girl. The whole of Kasimmari knew that Lame Sofia's hands were blessed by Allah. Whatever seed she planted, produced crop. Lame Sofia just had to touch the earth to know what manure, cow dung or urea, was needed; how the land had to be taken care of during the rains; and what was to be done during the winters. Some predicted that her power came from her lame leg. Wherever her lame leg left a footprint, seeds would spring to life. The plants bore fruit, the land became fertile.

Samsoon decided to take the boat out at the crack of dawn. Early morning, Alekjaan cooked a handful of rice, and served herself and Samsoon. They had packed their bundles of clothes and things the previous night itself. The vegetables for her aunt had also been all packed up. Samsoon woke up and looked outside—there was a blanket of thick fog. Both of them decided to set out only when the sun came out a little. As soon as the net of fog around them grew thinner, they pushed the boat out to the water.

When he stood on the boat, one leg erect and the other slightly bent at the knees, and his hands on the oars, he became a different person. He loved the slapping sound made by the boat as it tore through the water. On both sides, the small waves created by the boat gurgled to life like toka fish. The gurgling climbed up his body, made it tingle. The broken pieces of sky on the waves flowed upwards and caught at his throat. Gradually, the water, the sky, the gurgling of the waves—all came to stay there in his throat. Bending his knee a little more and leaning his body forward, he kept rowing. His throat would gradually become heavier. The river, the sky, the silverfish-coloured waves; he could never hold it inside him for too long. He couldn't hold it inside him that day, either. He burst out singing:

> Seeing the beauty of the silver river, you go mad,
> O, you fill up my eyes with your beauty.
> O, you will become mad if you see her beauty.

The beauty of the river as well as that of a dark-skinned woman intoxicated him. Alekjaan, peeping at him from under the veil of her sari, head tilted, smiling a little, too, has grabbed him by the throat, almost choking him. A tune in a young voice painted a picture of a house with banana trees in the backyard, banana trees with white flowers, and woman with long hair, on her parting a gold ornament …

> Brother, I have come to this house,
> Banana trees in its backyard,
> White flowers on the banana trees,

> Long hair on the woman.
> The woman ties her hair,
> Ties a jewel on her head.

As she laughed uncontrollably, Alekjaan's hair comes untied. She cannot hold her heart in any longer. Looking up to the sky, she, too, bursts into a song:

> I'll give you a pair of black dove
> Come to me in the form of black cloud
> Gopal of Harichand
> Slowly come to me in the form of black cloud.

Alekjaan calls out to the clouds, asks Harishchandra's son to come disguised as clouds.

By the time Samsoon reached Falimari and tied up his boat, the fog had disappeared and the sun was shining brightly all over. Alekjaan's eyes widened. She was not even aware of her head-cover falling away. It was the first time she had come out like this—no load on her head, no scolding and chidings from anyone.

Till then, if she ever came out of Kasimmari, it was only to go to the Bohri market. She would sit all squeezed up in the boat, among the goods that were being taken by her father to be sold in the market. He took everything to the market, and then spread it out there. Since he had been besieged by the pain in his back, every time he bent or picked up heavy things, he would cry out loudly in pain. Then he would become angry and restless, and would shout and scold her without a pause. Why did she place the basket of brinjals in a lopsided manner on her head? Why did she drop the brinjals? Why did she keep the sack of gourd that way? Why did she place the sack of gourd on top of the tomatoes?

Her hands would ache; she would not be able to move her head. On their way back, she would fall asleep, exhausted, on top of the empty sacks and baskets. She had come out of Kasimmari for the first time like this—not carrying a load on her head, not carrying heavy sacks in her hands, no one to scold or shout at her.

When they climbed up to Falimari, Alekjaan was amazed. For the young girl who had grown up seeing nothing else but the Bohri market, actually, everything was a source of amazement.

Falimari was nothing like Kasimmari, where she was born; it was very different. There were huge trees. She could see the trees lining the river banks as they were crossing by boat. She had never seen such huge trees from near; only the kind of grass that grew on sandy soil. But here there were many bamboo trees as well. A small rivulet ran through the middle of Falimari. Khalimari was situated right where this small river and the Brahmaputra merged. It was formed at that spot almost 150 years ago.

There were very few people in Alekjaan's Kasimmari. Falimari, on the other hand, was filled with people. There were so many things to see. She stood transfixed, almost forgetting to walk as she watched the crowds of *mekhela-chador*-wearing girls going to school. They had pharmacies here as well. Motorcycles, too, passed closed by her. Like in the movie she had seen at the Bohri market, those things passed right by her as they moved around.

Lame Sofia and Rahmat lived at one end of Falimari, where the sand had just been laid. Many of the people who had come here recently built their houses together; they all lived huddled in a bunch. During rains, it got flooded on this side. But these people, who were water insects, why would they fear the water? As always, they lived three months with the dry weather and nine months with water. Alekjaan and Samsoon broke into smiles looking at the crops grown by their aunt's hands.

Out of their aunt's five children, only two boys and a girl remained. The older boy sold *paan-tamul* on the *bhotbhoti*, the younger two stayed at home. The girl had inherited her mother's gift. She had been married off as a child, even before she gained puberty, but the husband had died from some ailment. No one could get her to marry again. Like her mother, she, too, gave her heart to the land. Her husband was a well-off man with land. Sofia's daughter, Parbeen, was only 10 years old when she was married off, her husband was 40. What did a man's age matter, anyway? What mattered was that he was a rich man who owned a lot of land. There was no question of any objection being raised.

After she attained puberty, Parbeen stayed with her husband for about six–seven months. Actually, the land that Sofia and Rahmat grew crops on was handed over to them by Parbeen's husband. Eventually, the land was settled permanently in Rahmat's name with his thumb print.

In the six–seven months that Parbeen stayed with her husband, she had run away from there several times. The first time she returned, she found a wide blood stain wherever she sat. Afterwards, if any boy came for Parbeen's hand in marriage, as did two or three, she would stop eating and drinking. Whenever talk of her marriage came up, she would wake up in the middle of the night, screaming. She would wail like an animal being put to halal, waking up not just her family, but even the neighbours.

Nobody talked to her about marriage any more. She talked only in the fields—while sowing the seeds, removing the weeds, digging at the roots—she spoke in a soft, low voice. She spoke with the seeds which were just starting to sprout, with the creepers crawling up, with the fruits filling up the trees—very softly. Just like Alekjaan talked to Samsoon as they lay together on their bed made of straw, and the way Samsoon talked to her, as they lay on the newly emerged, fish-egg like sand. Very softly, in a low voice, very slowly ... When she talked like that, people laughed at her, called her Crazy Parbeen. Gradually, like the thin, soft green covering that clings to the ear of a corn, the word "crazy" stuck to Parbeen's name.

Sticking her head into her knees, Parbeen cooked rice and a gravy of dried red chillies crushed with kholi fish, over firewood made from twigs and branches that had been covered with a layer of cow dung. Khalimari got its name from the kholi or khoil fish found there. Wouldn't Alekjaan and Samsoon have at least one meal with kholi fish during their visit here? Alekjaan laughed at Aunt Sofia's words.

Rahmat talked about the kholi fish of Khalimari. He pointed towards the darkness. In the part, where the Brahmaputra and the small river running through Falimari converged, there were a few river inlets without any current. Over there, if you cast your net, you could catch the shiny, silver-coloured kholi fish in bunches. Probably, that was the reason why the river that ran through the place was named Khoila. Some called it Khoila, others Kholi. Large schools of kholi fish would come in with the river water and cling to the nets like beads hanging from them. Now, they were no longer so easily available. Still, towards the part where Sofia and the others lived, you could still find a few fish in the inlets.

Waking up at the crack of dawn—Parbeen, Rahmat and Sofia—armed with hand spades, went to work in the field. Alekjaan and Samsoon also joined them. This time, they were growing brinjals. This variety bore fruit while the plant was still short. The tiny, light purple brinjals grew in abundance, covering the whole plant like bunches of flowers. There was a good demand for these in the market, too.

Between the rows of brinjals, the pumpkin creepers were shooting up. By the time the season of the brinjals got over, the pumpkins would be ready. Alekjaan recognised the pumpkin plants. How could she not recognise the rounded leaves with their black rings, which bore sweet pumpkins the size of small, sheared coconuts and which made a sharp, smart noise when they were sliced?

Parbeen was tending to the saplings which were just showing their heads, with great care. At this stage, the saplings were very soft and delicate. Parbeen handled the plants delicately, so as not to break the tender leaves. She cleaned the area around the saplings and patted the earth firmly around it. Rahmat and Sofia were telling them about the land. The land here remained submerged in water for nine months in a year. It was only during these three months that it remained dry. Last year, they could cultivate a variety of paddy that grew on low-lying land. This variety did not die even in chest-deep water. Actually, the year before that, it had rained for a much longer time. Even the hardy paddy plants rotted away.

All of Rahmat's neighbours were out working in the fields by then. Towards the place where Sofia and all lived, the land gradually became thinner and narrowed into a strip, before merging into the river. There were no trees of any kind on this side; only bushes of thatch-grass. Even in this dry winter, the bushes were green. The roots of the thatch-grass were long. Tearing through the sand, they kept travelling downwards. Even if the sand became absolutely dry, the green colour of the grass did not lose its lustre. The trunks of these leaves, though looked very delicate, were actually very strong. Walls made out of these, lasted for quite long, and used as logs, they also produced a good fire.

The people led a tough life. It was impossible for the crop from these few months to provide for the whole year. Also, it wasn't paddy they were growing, just green vegetables, which barely brought in a couple of rupees. That, too, was like pouring water on sand. Each household had many mouths to feed, at least eight–nine in a family. And every year, the number grew.

As soon as the crops were harvested, many of them would go off to other places looking for jobs. Some became bonded labourers somewhere, some plied rickshaws, some worked as daily-wage labourers, some started fishing. The people who wanted to hold onto their lands just clung on there, even during the rains; sometimes eking out one meal a day by growing paddy in the chest-deep water or by fishing, but they didn't care. They found it hard to leave behind their plots of land with the thatch-grass and paddy, and when they left, it was only because there was no other alternative.

Suddenly, Parbeen let out a loud cry. The people who were working nearby looked at her, but showed no signs of surprise. Obviously, they were used to her screams. Alekjaan ran towards Parbeen, who kept sitting, hands on the ground, in the same position without moving. There was clearly pain written on Parbeen's tender face. Alekjaan went and took her hand. The two women, who only understood the language of seeds and the earth, kept looking mutely at each other. A pumpkin plant lay between them. A pumpkin sapling with its new leaves, round and notched with black rings, thin white veins on green, was about to shoot up. The tender, new, leaves of the plant had withered away; the creeper, just about ready to climb, had become frail, weak and limp.

Both the women examined the plant, handling it gently. Pests had pierced the base of the plant; it was beginning to rot at those places. The sapling, which lay limp and lifeless, its face crushed down into the earth, would no longer bear fruit. No orange-coloured, sweet flowers would grow here any more, no honeybee or bumblebee would fly away from here—its legs completely yellow from the pollen. No brittle fruit, changing its colour as it grew, would hide amid the leaves. Alekjaan took the lifeless plant out of Parbeen's hands, Parbeen who still sat motionless, and flung it away. Parbeen kept sitting, looking towards where Alekjaan threw the plant away.

From that direction a tune floated down:

> Falimari is our home
> O dear brother!
> Settled in so many places have we,
> But no end to our miseries.
> Some grow crops and cultivate,
> Some become carpenters, brother.
> But all of us are poor, brother,
> Making a living on fish.

Parbeen's gaze was fixed in that direction. Looking at her mute face, Alekjaan tried to understand her. What was she looking at? Was she looking at the lifeless sapling they had thrown away? Was she listening to the song? The song in a male voice filled the whole area indistinctly, but had died away now. Parbeen started to take out the weeds by their roots under another pumpkin plant.

After returning from Falimari, Alekjaan and Samsoon spent all their time on the land. The more the river turned towards where

Hasim Miyan plied his *bhotbhoti*, more and more of Samsoon's land emerged. As soon as he was able to earn a little, he deposited the money with the government for the land that he inherited from his father.

Samsoon's grandfather had come to Kasimmari during the "gormor foot" (grow more food) scheme days. Samsoon's father had to keep paying the deposit for the land, although, the land was under water during his time. If he didn't, the government would immediately seize the plot of land. Out of the land in Kasimmari and Falimari, only 35 per cent was legally owned, 40 per cent was illegally occupied and the remaining 25 per cent was under the government. Because Rahmat's father continued giving the money, the land remained with Samsoon and was not taken over by the government.

Alekjaan and Samsoon spread out the bedclothes given to them by Lame Sofia, and lay down on it, immediately losing consciousness to the world. Samsoon had so many dreams. He would restore the land that had re-emerged and was gradually returning to its earlier glory. He was confident that he would be able to do it. He would not be able to bring back the river that once brought them unlimited supply of fish; he wouldn't be able to bring back the vast, round, turtle-shaped land of Kasimmari; he would not be able to bring back the storks, the kingfishers, the eagles and the other birds that lived on the wetlands of Kasimmari. But, he would be able to bring back to life the land which layers and layers of sand, deposited over the years, had made unfit for cultivation. Samsoon was ambitious.

The winter was slowly retreating. Now, the rains would come, and with it water and silt. In the area where thick layers of sand have been deposited, Samsoon was going to plant beans and other pulse-type variety of seeds that Lame Sofia sent him. The plants, which would grow to be taller than a person, would shoot up, covered with countless green leaves. The leaves would fall. They would rot in the water. He would lay water-hyacinths over them. He owned a boat made of sal wood that was 24-handspans long. There was a shop that sold manure in the Bohri market. He would breathe life into this lifeless piece of land.

In the land that had come back to life, he would grow—like in the days of his grandfather—green leaves, mustard, sesame, wheat, brinjal and pumpkin. Why couldn't he do it? He would.

They would fly kites, like they used to in his grandfather's time, while the crops were being weeded. The work would go on between the rows and rows of crops. There would be small lanes in between the crops. In these lanes, the fine strings of jute used to fly kites would lie buried under the earth. There would be many varieties of kites. They would mostly fly the snake kites with their long, flowing tails. At the heads of the kites would be the tiny bows made from thin, fine strips of bamboo. When the kites soared up, the bamboo bow would flutter noisily as it gets battered by the wind. The sound could be heard from far off. His father and brother would also hear them from heaven. They would know that the crop was being weeded on their land. Wouldn't they hear it? Of course, they would.

Alekjaan would grow koi leaves on this land. They would call in workers to reap the crop—red handkerchiefs tied around their hands and necks, anklets tied to their feet, drums around their necks, they would sing:

> O What happened in Janakpur,
> Lakshman's brother Ram came,
> He broke the bow in Janakpur,
> And married Sita Devi.

Everybody would join in with the workers' song. The hands of the workers would move faster and faster to the beat of the songs. Three days of work would be finished in one. Why wouldn't it? It would. Alekjaan's mother would hear the workers' song from heaven. Why wouldn't she? Of course, she would.

The winter was nearing its end. The late crop of cabbage Samsoon had grown on the two bighas of land left behind by Rahmat chacha, was infested with caterpillars. They weren't exactly caterpillars; they were a kind of green insect. Of course, most of them had been sold off already. This time, the cabbage crop did not turn out to be very profitable. He made a profit from the chillies though. He had grown these round chillies without heat while working as a help at the house that Rahmat chacha had fixed up for him. When he left the job, he brought the seeds with him. No one knew about it, he collected them, seed by seed, in the bamboo-and-mud house where he slept, in front of the granary.

He never laid hands on anything in that house. He only touched the varieties of seeds that were ordered and bought. The words Sutton Seeds from Calcutta had become familiar to him. He pronounced it Satan Sidis. They were very expensive. Samsoon's salary was ₹200 per month. Even if he saved the whole year, he would not be able to buy the seed packets from there.

His employer, Manib, was the owner of trucks, buses and land. He was a rich man. He owned a big nursery as well. Samsoon himself had sold many varieties of plant saplings and grafts of fruit trees to buyers who came there. On one bigha of land, Manib grew only the lemon-sized chillies, which were without heat. Samsoon opened the expensive packets of seeds, prepared them in cement pots as large as the utensils used for feeding cows and buffaloes, and kept them covered with plastic sheets. He mixed dry dung into the earth; then, sieved it till it became as fine as kuhi fish eggs. None of the seeds would go bad; from each seed came out saplings.

He prepared the land to plant the saplings himself. The land needed a slight slope; if it retained even a little water, the leaves of the chillies would turn yellow. The long, shallow pits to lay the seeds for germination also required a slope. If water collected in between these pits, it was also equally bad.

In the first burst of sunshine after some rain, the plants shooting up so luxuriantly would suddenly turn yellow, wither away and die. He spoke to his employer, got some sand and mixed it with the earth where he would plant the chillies.

He did one more thing to prevent the water from getting trapped under the chilly plants. In the nursery, there were two trees. When the wind blew, the two tall trees made a whistling sound. Samsoon was surprised whenever he looked at the leaves of these trees. The leaves, which looked like straw cut into thin, fine strips, never rotted. Even after the roaring rains of the monsoons, the leaves which had fallen down and collected in piles, remained the same. He asked his mistress the name of the tree; it sounded strange to his ears, "pine tree". The word became "fine tree" for him. He mixed these leaves with the earth.

As he prepared the land to grow the chilly plants in the nursery, he would often get lost in a dream while shuffling the bundles of seeds that he had siphoned off gradually and kept in a tin trunk. The trunk, with its colour almost peeling off, was a gift from his mistress, who had given it to him to keep his clothes and things. If he could put aside a little money, he would leave this place for good. He would settle in Kasimmari, where, he would grow chillies, papayas, tomatoes, brinjals and watermelons. He had collected quite a lot of seeds—a lot of good-quality English seeds.

Samsoon uprooted the pest-infected cabbage and cleared a piece of land. It was a small piece of land. In the blink of an eye, the plot was prepared to grow pumpkins, then, mustard. At one point, it was filled with sesame plants, and at another, with green, juicy, watermelons. Then, followed the sweet-scented snap melons; the flowers of the ribbed-gourd made the land shine, even in the dark. There were papaya trees, so heavy with fruit that they had to be propped up with supports.

Samsoon grew restless, looking at the papaya seeds. Where would he plant the papaya trees in this small plot of land? The land would get tied down for several years. The seeds of the English tomatoes were still lying in the tin trunk in a loft of his thatch house. He had put the papaya seeds for germination in a wide cement pot, in the same way he had prepared the chillies as well. He had sieved the loose earth, then, mixed in rotted leaves from the mango tree and dried cow dung to prepare the pot. He dug holes, put compost manure and made the land ready to plant the saplings.

Samsoon was amazed at the quality of the seeds. Not one of the plants turned out barren; each of them bore fruit. He had named the breed honey papaya. His employer had read up a book before ordering the papaya seeds. He sat on a chair, Samsoon at his feet. In that book, there were pictures of the fruits alongside the names of the seeds. The name of that papaya breed was honeydew. Not understanding anything, he laughed, 'English papayas and their English names!' His employer had explained to him the meaning of "honey" and "dew". He didn't understand! But he knew what dew was. In the winter, the mist would fall and make their Kasimmari all wet. It meant that honey would fall on the papayas like dewdrops and make them all sweet. So, Samsoon named them honey papaya.

Truly, his heart calmed down when he grew the honey papaya. Each papaya would grow to be the size of a medium water-gourd. When they ripened, they really filled up with honey. When he sliced them, they looked like the beautiful, round, sliced pieces of pumpkin which were sold at the market in the evening.

Once, some guests had come to his employer's house. They were served the honey papayas sliced lengthwise, on a big plate. The guests mistook them for pumpkins, and were surprised at being served the vegetable. They had come to take saplings from the nursery. Samsoon loaded them into the car as they sat in the chairs placed outside. The guests, the host, everyone laughed out loud, even Samsoon.

Samsoon had the honey papaya seeds with him; he would plant them on his land. His children would eat the honey papaya that looked like big red pumpkin pieces when sliced. Whenever Alekjaan liked something, she would make a sound with her tongue—the same kind of sound she made when eating something sour. Samsoon imagined his wife carrying a slice of honey papaya towards her mouth with both her hands, her eyes half-closed, her forehead creased a little, her lips slightly twisted to the right, and she was making the slurping sound with her tongue. Samsoon's mouth watered. He imagined a soft and sweet taste, like that of milk that had been cooked with sugar. Suddenly, like Alekjaan, he half-closed his eyes, twisted his lips slightly to the right and made a slurping sound with his tongue on the roof of his mouth.

The rains came early that time. That day Bordoisila was on way to her mother's for Bihu. Her uncontrollable hair was all spread out. Darkening the sky with her flaming hair, she flew over Kasimmari's sky. The waves crashed in the river. The sand flew about wildly like the small red birds that flew here and there in the paddy field. The wind was full of sand. You couldn't see the other side of the river. It looked as if it was covered in a winter's mist.

Bordoisila flew, howling and roaring over Alekjaan's land that was returned by the river. Samsoon and Alekjaan looked at Bordoisila's streaming, dark, locks that covered the entire sky, their hearts filling up.

Two days later, the dark sky descended in a torrent upon the earth. That was the beginning of rain, and more rain. As a matter of fact, it rained a lot in Kasimmari. The clouds banged against the hills that lay to the east of Kasimmari. The rains had already filled up the river; Bohag, had barely ended and Jeth begun.

These people who belonged to the water, were not afraid of it—they were like fish in water. Samsoon had already steeled himself, he steered the 24-handspan-long boat around for the last time. He bought a stove from the market, and had already stacked up on kerosine. He also bought rice, dal, potatoes and cooking oil. Alekjaan kept the packets of matches bundled up in cloth as well a lamp and an earthen lamp. The river swallowed up the land in the south, where it looked like a fish tail. Meanwhile, the people who stayed on that side went off to Guwahati to ply rickshaws. They would go off every time. It's just that they had to go a little early that year.

Samsoon's piece of land was still not covered by water. There was knee-deep water in some places, and even less in other. After 10 days of incessant downpour, the rain receded. Now there was just black silt all over the land. Samsoon and Alekjaan planted thatch-grass there.

The rain, which had stopped for a while, resumed. The thatch-grass shot up abundantly. It did not take long for the thatch-grass to grow on this kind of loamy land. The seeds of these plants which fertilised the land and which grew to be the size of a person, blossomed abundantly and were passed down from generation to generation. They always kept these lentil-sized seeds with them. The thatch-grass grew on almost any kind of land. On fertile land, they flourished with branches and leaves, and grew to be as tall as a man. Even in harsh and barren land, they would grow into the size of a bush. The leaves fell off soon after the tree matured. On the ground, they would start to rot. Thus, the land was fertilised.

Early morning, Samsoon and Alekjaan had a cup of salted tea and some green chillies mixed with flattened dried rice. The sun was shining strongly after many days of rain. As they stepped on the earth, it felt like they were plunging their feet into a warm blanket. Alekjaan smiled, just like that. In just these few days, the straw-grass plants had grown to be a foot long. The plants had spread out their branches and become bushy. Very small, tender leaves were sprouting. The two of them walked around, treading again and again on that warm blanket. Even after the land was cleared, there still remained some twigs, branches and garbage. Samsoon started pulling away at them, removing them. Alekjaan, too, gave him a hand.

On hearing Alekjaan exclaiming, 'Aah, aah, aah!' as she worked, Samsoon broke out in laughter. The silly girl thought these straw plants were as tender as the ends of the pea plants. She thought them to be like cauliflower and pumpkin plants. She started pulling out the weeds and garbage from under these straw plants very slowly and carefully. This time, a whole lot of weeds had come in with the silt, God knew from where, and had taken root at several places. As she pulled out a weed, a branch of the straw plant snapped. 'Tsk-tsk!' she exclaimed again.

Samsoon snapped the branch into two, 'Silly woman, see, the plant will grow again. These are not your cabbage plants. They are strong.'

Looking at the straw plants that had come up, pushing through all the weeds, she realised he was right. The plants that had come to life and survived in such a lifeless land, indeed, had to be strong. She went back to cleaning up the weeds again.

As the sun started climbing the sky, the land started getting warmer. She looked at Samsoon's face and paused. The sweat from his face was pouring down onto his chest. His whole body was wet and sticky with sweat.

'Aah!' he suddenly let out a cry.

The skin had torn open near his knee and was bleeding. Tearing through the mud, she reached him. He smeared some mud over the wound. A few drops of blood flowed down to the earth, and mixed with the black mud.

Seeing Alekjaan look with concern at the wound, he smiled, 'Your man is strong like this straw-grass.' She smiled too.

Early that year itself, Samsoon had scattered the seeds of a breed of paddy on the land that the river had returned. This was his first batch of seedlings that he was preparing on this plot of land. Fertile with the silt, the paddy seedlings were shooting up wildly. They had grown up to be more than a foot now. Meanwhile, on the side where he grew straw-grass, the land got cleared quite a bit. He decided earlier that he would grow the paddy on the north side—not too much, just a little. There was no need to plough and prepare the land; it was moist from the silt. They just had to stick the paddy saplings in. The remaining three-fourths of the land were already filling up with straw-grass.

Samsoon had not been able to hire any workers. In fact, he could not even get a few men from his own place to help him out in exchange for some tea and flattened rice. His pockets were almost empty now. The monsoons loomed ahead.

The paddy saplings had to be lifted very carefully. It needed more care than the cauliflower saplings. He had to pull out the saplings, which were about a foot to a foot-and-a-half long, one by one, along with their roots. You couldn't just grasp and pull them out. Alekjaan was the one to do this job—not even a single string of peas broke under her careful hands. She had inherited Aunt Sofia's skilled hands.

Samsoon kept watching. Alekjaan was on her knees, holding the paddy plants one by one between two fingers, pulling them up with one upward jerk, then, piling them nearby. Not one root broke. Samsoon kept cutting off the ends and planting them in the loamy earth. They had to be planted with some space between them, as each would become a paddy stalk that could be grabbed by one man alone.

Samsoon's land filled up. Soon after that the torrential rains started. You could ply a boat on that piece of land. The higher the water rose, the more the paddy and straw plants grew. The water current was not on Samsoon's side; it was on the opposite side. The more land emerged on Samsoon's side, the more the water submerged on the other. There was so much erosion on that side that Kasimmari looked like a fish that had been bitten off in the middle by a cat.

All the people living on that side fled, leaving behind their houses and their belongings. Rezaul chacha had started living on his boat. Chacha suffered from knee pain, so there was no question of him working elsewhere. Therefore, he somehow carried on in Kasimmari. His four sons took up odd jobs here and there, and sent him whatever they could. With that, Chacha survived, sometimes on one meal a day. Chacha had land. He filled up his land with varieties of crops. That part of Kasimmari that looked like a fish that had been bitten off was Chacha's land. He would go back there when the water dried up. It was all the same to him, whether he had a house or not. He just needed a place to lie down.

Most of Kasimmari's residents kept working, even when the water entered their paddy fields. But, of course, all of them weren't as lucky as Samsoon. They would raise paddy in two–three bighas of land, and keep the land locked till Magh. During the remaining three months, the land had to be made ready for the Rabi crops. No one had time to waste.

Then, a stomach flu visited Kasimmari. Caught between the steaming water from the ground and the strong sun, the people carried on with their work. Every year, at this time, some ailment would occur. The previous time, it was the fever—and, what a deadly fever it was! It wasn't malaria or typhoid. It came without any warning. They didn't even have enough time to go to the Bohri market to fetch a fever-reducing pill. The people died in huge numbers, there was no one left to perform the last rites even. They just threw the bodies of the small children into the river.

The stomach flu was similar. It came without warning, no rumblings or anything—just a little loss of appetite, followed by diarrhea. It didn't last long. After three days, the diarrhea would stop on its own. But the person became weak. The body would be dehydrated, the eyes grew weak and the knees would start trembling. When the diarrhea stopped, the people would be relieved. Before the body could replenish the lost fluids, the people would return to work with their plough and spade, in the scorching heat. As they worked, they would start sweating and collapse right there. They died on the spot.

The number of people suffering from diarrhea was increasing daily. Everyone was perplexed and terrified, seeing the people die.

Mansoor Miyan was not able to keep up with the demand for amulets. There was talk all around that all this was the doing of a genie. It grabbed the person by the throat, squeezing the breath out of him. The man died, sweating profusely, arms and legs all twisted up. The genies and spirits, and ghosts and demons took many lives.

This time, the genie possessed Alekjaan's father. After recovering from four days of diarrhea, the man had taken the boat out and gone to see the paddy. After many days of rain, the sun was shining with its full might that day. The water was drying up; the whole place was like a geyser. He had just entered the fields, when the genie caught him. Shivering violently, his arms and legs got all twisted up. The man started shouting loudly. The people found Mansoor Miyan's amulet gleaming in his hands. The genie was there in spite of the amulet! The crowd felt weak and helpless. Right before their eyes, Miyad Miyan dropped dead.

Alekjaan cried for two days, and on the third day, went to work in the field. The paddy seemed to be competing with the water. If the water rose one inch, the paddy stalks, too, would shoot an inch above it. The dhoomsar plants were also rising along with the water. The paddy stalks were now just a little shorter than a person.

For a few days now, a small red insect had started flying in between the paddy stalks. Samsoon had become a man possessed. Plying his boat around, he kept smoking out the pests. All Alekjaan did was look up at the sky, and pray. Let the genie spare Samsoon. Let nobody's evil eye fall on his land and crops.

It was raining in leaps and bounds. The river grew in volume. Hasim Miyan's *bhotbhoti* had stopped plying. Day by day, the river kept swallowing the land on that side. Each passing day, Kasimmari became smaller and smaller.

The water entered Alekjaan and Samsoon's house. But, they were already prepared for this. They left the house and got onto the boat. Samsoon had already fixed a roof made of bamboo strips and blue plastic. They took the kerosine, stove, rice and flattened rice, and anchored their boat. Many people had tied up their boats right at that spot.

It was raining that day as well. Lightning flashed in the sky. Alekjaan and Samsoon were looking at the sky after dinner. The line of lightning shone twice as bright in the reflection on the river. Thunder followed the lightning immediately. The roaring sound was all over the overflowing river.

A great golden creeper glittered from one end of the sky to the other. The creeper spread out on the river even more brightly. On the river, it looked like a golden necklace broken into many pieces.

Samsoon kept watching the black silhouettes of the paddy and grass that had raised their heads above the water, and which he glimpsed momentarily again and again, in the lightning. He placed his sore hands on Alekjaan's back.

'Look Alekjaan, what good rainfall. Just one more month; after that, the paddy will be down on the ground.'

'They will rise again.'

Alekjaan was looking at the paddy clusters.

'The crop will be good.'

'After the grain is reaped, we will plough the land.'

'The dhoomsar leaves will bring the land back to life again.'

'There will be good crop in this fertile land.'

Suddenly, Alekjaan vomited noisily.

'What happened, oh, my Alekjaan?'

Samsoon ran so swiftly up to her, the boat shuddered. Who knew, the genie may have got to her too! What would he do without Alekjaan? Who was this land and crop for?

'O Alekjaan?' Samsoon enquired in a raised voice.

Several replies came from many different boats:

'Samsoon, what?'

'What happened, Samsoon?'

'Alekjaan, are you unwell?'

'Keep quiet!' Alekjaan scolded Samsoon.

'What happened, Alekjaan?' Samsoon saw before his eyes a slippery demon, the lower part of his body missing. He had Alekjaan by the throat. A couple of men were throwing her stiff body over the boat into the water.

'Oh, Alekjaan!' watching Alekjaan vomit once again, Samsoon felt helpless.

From the boat next to theirs, Jakir's mother stepped onto their boat. Alekjaan asked, 'Pisi, for a few days now my head has been swimming and I throw up, am I ...' Alekjaan covered her face.

'Oh, Samsoon! You will be a father soon.'

Hearing her words, Samsoon broke into a smile. At that exact moment, he saw in the flash of lightning that the land was returned to him by the river.

'Alekjaan, you will see this time, what a crop we will have. What a crop we will have on my land,' said Samsoon, his eyes filled with hope.

'Of course, we will, why not? You have worked so hard,' said Alekjaan as her face reflected the glow of the light from the earthen lamp lit by Jakir's mother.

The month of Saun passed, Bhado started. The people who had left Kasimmari, returned. This time, the land to the north where the thatch-grass grew, and was uninhabited till now, also filled up with people. The river had severely eroded the land in the middle. Rezaul chacha came and put up a thatch roof right next to Samsoon's. He cooked and ate by himself. Anyway, it wasn't much. He cooked rice in one saucepan for three meals. A pile of salt and a couple of green chillies was all he needed.

Chacha couldn't stop smiling when he saw the paddy clusters on Samsoon's land. Nobody told him, but he had taken up the responsibility for Samsoon's land himself. Chacha sat on Samsoon's land, his legs spread out wide. He propelled himself forward on his behind. Seeing Chacha's hands work, one would think they belonged to a young man's. Samsoon got a lot of help and relief. So did Alekjaan. Her body was beginning to grow heavy gradually.

The paddy stalks were beginning to bend down, and were almost flat on the ground. Chacha said that it was very good indication. They would rise back up shortly. When the water dried up just a little, the thatch-grass leaves would start falling. The ground would be covered by feet-deep leaves. Those leaves rotted, turning the earth black. Chacha said they would start ploughing in 15 days.

Alekjaan was feeling restless. But this was not enough to shake her mind or her body. She was unhappy these days. There was no reason to feel otherwise. Her only brother had returned just after their father's demise. She had heard all kind of things about him. People noticed that he didn't do anything for a living. He just flaunted a watch and a cycle, and spent extravagantly on fraudulent lottery tickets. The way he spoke, the way he walked, the clothes he wore, Alekjaan felt sick just looking at him. He gave her a sari, a shirt to Samsoon. Neither she nor Samsoon had ever worn such expensive clothes.

Alekjaan was not at all mollified by all the gifts brought by her brother. He was no longer the boy who roamed around clinging to her clothes. He would disappear from Kasimmari, on and off. When he returned, there would be a pile of stuff in his house—TVs, tapes and utensils. After a few days, he would disappear again, and so would the things. It was a week since he was arrested. This time they didn't find things, but found a gun instead.

For a couple of days Kasimmari was abuzz with Alekjaan's brother, the police and the gun. Then everything went quiet.

Samsoon was getting ready to plough over the dhoomsar leaves. The dried plants were taken out; they were very good to make walls with. If they didn't get wet, they would last a long time. Samsoon had built a hut for Chacha, tying their stalks together with thin bamboo strips. You could hardly call it a hut actually, it was just a roof put up right next to theirs. Chacha would mostly have his meals in their house. After having a handful of rice, limping and dragging himself, he left for Samsoon's field, where he worked the whole day.

The paddy stalks had all tumbled down, but the ends had raised their heads, like a cobra that had raised its hood, and were pointing upwards again. The clusters of paddy, reaching up to the sky, were becoming heavier day by day.

Chacha roamed around, pushing himself, between the paddy stalks, 'Aah, aah, what a crop! See, the more the water has rises, the taller the paddy grows. The water disappears, the plants tumble down. Not a single plant has broken; they have just gone to sleep. Aha, what crop! Look, they have raised their heads again. What a crop! Look, Samsoon, look!'

Samsoon also looked at the crop. The ends of the stalks that had fallen down raised their heads again. The plants looking upwards were filled to the brim with clusters of grain.

Samsoon ploughed the loamy earth which was covered with a foot of grass. These days, he would just sit looking at his bundle of seeds that lay open before him. His land filled up again and again—once with honey papaya; once with white and green cauliflower; then pumpkin; then perfectly round cabbage; and with paddy, mustard, sesame and black cumin. If he could, he would pour all the crops of the world onto the land that was returned to him by the river.

Lame Sofia and Parbeen once paid them a visit. Alekjaan did not let Parbeen leave. She did not like being all by herself. As she cooked for Samsoon and Chacha, she often wished there was someone to lend her a hand. So, Parbeen stayed back.

Samsoon had just finished ploughing. Without anyone telling her what she needed to do, Parbeen helped Alekjaan with her household work and was getting ready to go to the fields. No one had to say anything to her. Without a word, she started working alongside Chacha and Samsoon.

Truly, Samsoon's land was filled; just how he dreamt it would.

Alekjaan, too, was growing. She calculated that they would bring in the grain by Magh. Her lap would be filled, too, by then. She also joined in the work on the field, along with Parbeen, Chacha and Samsoon. So much work was left! Four pairs of hands were hard at work, yet, every day there would be something new to be done.

The honey papaya saplings had to be taken care of. The water hyacinth had to be placed on the base of the pumpkin plants. A low, temporary bamboo platform had to be erected over the peas. The earth had to be brought close, and small outlets for water had to be dug around the cabbage plants. The land had to be made ready to plant the heatless chillies.

That day, too, they were all at work. Chacha was singing, like he did every day:

> We came along the Padma River, to Assam's land,
> But the Brahmaputra broke down our beautiful,
> golden homes.
> Where will we go leaving that house, pray tell,
> Whole life has gone in sorrow, can't bear more.

Suddenly, Chacha jerked himself up. His face had turned dark. Never had Samsoon or the others seen Chacha's face like this. Samsoon, Parbeen, Alekjaan, they all got up. Chacha was kneeling down and praying, looking up at the sky. They all waited a moment. Chacha always read the namaz like this, twice in day, but not at this time of the day. Tears were rolling down from his eyes. The man was visibly scared. Chacha dragged himself from the fields and reached the middle of Kasimmari.

Chacha had been right; the land was heating up. Everyone felt a strange heat coming up from the land. Almost 10 days passed by like this. Anyway, these people did not pay much heed to things. At this peak season, there was even less time to think about it.

There were about 20–25 days left for the rice to be reaped, and also for Alekjaan to go into labour.

It was exactly 12 noon. All the young boys, old men and women of Kasimmari were working in the fields. At this time, Kasimmari looked like heaven. Apart from the small hutments built from the stalks of thatch-grass, straw, dried branches, etc, the entire land was green.

Kasimmari looked like a new bride dressed in a patchwork design of various shades of green. Work was being carried out in Maimuna's land. The people were working, their backs turned to the sun, and they were singing.

> I am gone, my friend, to graze my buffaloes
> I have no umbrella, have no japiFriend, with a wet
> gamosa tied around your head
> Come to my house, friend,
> Buy me an umbrella …

At that time, these people, without umbrellas or *japi*s, were out grazing their buffaloes and calling out to some unknown friend to come visit them in a wet *gamosa*. The out-of-tune, discordant notes from their throats rose and fell, keeping rhythm with their hands at work.

The people could feel the heat emanating from the ground. But no one paid any attention. When it was bright, the wet earth naturally heated up. It was nothing out of the ordinary. No one knew who noticed it first, probably Maimuna's father. There was a bubbling sound rising from the earth. At first, even he paid no attention to it. It was coming from a crab's hole or a snake pit. Water had probably gotten in, hence, the gurgling noise. But, gradually, the bubbling started getting louder and louder. Slowly, the potato-sized hole became the size of a cabbage.

All the people drew closer. Samsoon, Chacha—all of them came and peered into the rumbling hole. The area was gradually widening.

Someone shouted out, 'It is an earthquake.'

Indeed, they felt the earth was vibrating slightly. The tremors increased. Now there was panic among the people. Rezaul chacha ordered everybody to leave the land and get into the boats. The trembling grew. The waves around Kasimmari were also getting bigger and bigger.

Some of the people scrambled into the few boats tied there. The young ones jumped into the water. The muddy water was rising up fast at the place where Maimuna's father first noticed the bubbling. The bubbles looked like gemstones coming out of the earth, except that they had no colour or light. The people were struck with terror. These fearless people who went after snakes and tigers with sticks and knives, who braved the floods, and who soaked the land with their blood and tears for a handful of rice, did not know how to fight this strange new danger. Kasimmari had suddenly become a live turtle that was now starting to shake itself. The people scrambled to get away as far away as possible from the heaving land.

Samsoon got into the boat along with Alekjaan. He was not aware of who all had got into his boat made of sal wood. He caught a glimpse of Chahca in the midst of the people.

Then, all of a sudden, Alekjaan gave a shout, 'Where's Parbeen? Parbeen, Parbeen!' Her voice broke and tumbled into the rising river.

The bubbling gems of mud were rising even higher. The higher they rose, the more Kasimmari shook. There was no reply from Parbeen.

It was like as if someone had cleaved through Kasimmari with a sword. The cloth with its green designs was torn into two, from north to south. There was muddy water coming out through the crack also. But it didn't burst upwards; it flowed outwards now. Samsoon's blood, Alekjaan's blood, Chacha's, Maimuna's, Rahmat's, Mansur's, with lumps, bits and pieces of their broken hearts—all were flowing together.

Alekjaan shouted out, pointing with her finger, 'Parbeen, our crazy Parbeen!' Everyone on Samsoon's boat looked that side. Crazy Parbeen was sitting on Samsoon's land.

Only Samsoon could dare to take the boat that side.

'Come, Parbeen, come here.'

'Hey, Parbeen!'

'Crazy Parbeen!'

'Parbeen, can you hear us!'

'Parbeen! Parbeen come!'

Many people were shouting out to Parbeen from the boat. Crazy Parbeen was sitting towards where the cabbage plants were. She did not look here or there. She sat like she always did when she worked, with her legs wide apart. She kept working with her hand spade, her head facing down.

Kasimmari was shaking. The river was getting ready to take back again into its womb the land it had given birth to. Yes, this happened all the time—Rezaul chacha had seen, so had Maimuna's grandmother. They had witnessed rivers swallowing up huge land masses, taking away people, houses, fields and crops. Most of the people had heard about it.

Only thatch-grass and straw grew in this region. There were no big trees to hold the soil together. The people knew that the land on which they poured out their blood had only sand beneath it. There were no rocks under the land, only sand. The river could wash away those layers of loose sand any moment. The land under their feet could disappear anytime.

This time the crack appeared on the piece of land that the river had given back to Samsoon, the land to which he and Alekjaan had given their lives. From the safety of distance, they saw the muddy water flow over the heavy clusters of paddy which would have been ready to cut in 10–15 days. The muddy water was rolling over the land set with green stones.

Alekjaan burst out crying, sobbing loudly. So did Maimuna and her mother, Hanifa and Latifa's mother.

Rezaul chacha spoke up, scolding them.

'Why are you crying, huh? Didn't you know before you came here that there are no trees on this land, no shrubs on this land, no rocks-stones under this land! Didn't you know?' Chacha sounded helpless.

With a sound, Kasimmari—without rocks-stones under it, without the roots of trees clasping it, without any shrubs—started collapsing.

Alekjaan was still shouting, 'Hey, Parbeen! Parbeen!'

As more and more parts of Kasimmari fell into the river, the shouts and noises from the boats increased. No one knew who got left behind. Even though they stayed on land without rocks, the people's hearts were not made of sand, after all. The swiftest river in the world couldn't take away the people's hearts and their feelings, the way it washed away Kasimmari.

Crazy Parbeen did not here anyone's voice. She sat there, staring abjectly at the cabbage plants, which had been growing luxuriantly, but was now covered by the muddy water. Crazy Parbeen was wielding her hand spade like one possessed. She thought that by just doing that she would be able to salvage the cabbage plants.

When the mud had buried her and carried her away into the bosom of the river, she was still carrying the shovel in her hand.

Alekjaan was still screaming, 'Parbeen, crazy Parbeen! What will I tell Aunt Sofia? Where will I tell Aunt Sofia you have gone?'

Kasimmari disappeared completely, without a trace. The people who remained, went away towards another piece of silt land at midnight—a piece of land that had just emerged. There were no rock-stones under it to make it stable; no big trees with roots to clasp the soil together; no firm land where bamboo shrubs could grow. There was only sandy soil, where nothing but thatch-grass and hay grew. But it would do, at least it was a piece of land—land on which they could stand. It was a piece of lifeless land, but it would do; they would bring life to this land with their tears and sweat.

Alekjaan continued shouting, 'Parbeen, crazy Parbeen! What will I tell Aunt Sofia?' In between Alekjaan's shouts, there was now a moaning. Gradually, the moaning increased, the shouts waned away.

There were still 15–20 days left for reaping the paddy. Alekjaan's time, too, advanced by 15–20 days …

Life, An Overflowing River

The lock on the big gate had rusted and taken on an earth-red colour; it was hardly ever opened. Bani and the others always came in and went out through the small gate. Besides, no one ever came to visit them in a car. The owner himself visited only once in a year, and even then, he never brought the car in. His hands behind his back, the man would make a round of his whole compound once, peek in at the well, then, as always, ask Bani's mother, 'Does the tea water look black?' Like always, Bani's father would reply, 'No sir, you can drink straight out of the well.' After that, he would get into the car parked by the gate and take off.

This time, too, the owner came and made a round of his compound. He didn't take a look at the well, but came and sat down in the verandah of their thatch hut. Just a few days back, they had bought a wooden sofa set. Bani's father made him sit down there. Drinking a cup of black tea with a coconut laddu, the landlord informed them of his plans to build a house on that plot of land that year. They were alarmed on hearing the news. Would they have to leave this place?

The owner stood up to leave. Stuffing the *paan-tamul* into his mouth, he said, 'Right after the house is built, I will be going abroad for a few years. Right now you are looking after only this piece of land, later you will have to look after the house, too. And listen, I will make your house concrete too, with a proper bathroom and latrine.'

Indeed, one day, the big lock was hammered open. Trucks came, pushcarts came. Bricks, sand, cement, iron and wood were unloaded. Then, arrived a truck-full of woven bamboo walls. Right next to Bani's house, there came up a temporary building for the workers, makeshift toilets, new pumps—everything. A crowd of workers and helpers arrived, stoves were lit. Work went on day and night. Huge lights flooded the area and transformed the nights into days.

The desolate, lifeless piece of land was now humming with activity: the thud of bricks, the sound of sand and stones, the noise of wood being sawed, the outbursts of laughter and noisy quarrels of the workers. The mornings, the afternoons, the evenings, and even the nights came alive, humming with activity.

The 21-year-old, average-looking, young girl's life, so long uneventful, came alive, trying to keep with the rhythm of what was happening around her. Bani was just two years old when Dr Atanu Barua brought her father, who often worked as a daily labourer at his house, and his whole family over to Guwahati to look after his acre of land. The doctor had even got a house built for them. Her hard-working father filled the pot-holed land, and under his watchful eye, the coconut and banana trees started bearing fruit. The shop financed by the land owner started to prosper.

Bani grew up to be 21; she was quite well looked after. She had even attended a school nearby and taken the matric exams twice. But she couldn't pass the test, so left it and started helping out her mother with household work instead.

All around Barua's land, the area swiftly filled up with shops, cars, vehicles and people. Bani, too, flowered into a young adult. There were a couple of marriage proposals from the village, but the mother protested vehemently. The girl had grown up in a city, how would she adjust to village life?

Bani's mother herself found it difficult nowadays to visit both their extended families in the village. Bani's brother was better in his studies than she; he was learning to play table tennis at the club just opposite their house. He played quite well, too. He, too, couldn't stand the village at all. How could she send her daughter back to the mud and dirt of the village? So, in this way, Bani entered her 21st year.

Until the lock was hammered open, there hardly was any work for Bani: she swept the courtyard after waking up in the morning, washed a couple of clothes and cut the green vegetables for her mother. After that, she was free. She would at times go and stand by the gate, but what was there to look at? Just the same road, the same cars and vehicles … At other times, she would play the cassettes brought by her brother, but what was there to listen? The same old *dhik-dhik dhak-dhak* sounds. But after the temporary building with woven bamboo walls came up, Bani was never free.

The workers were young; they were always laughing and joking. Bani had to fry pakoras for them, make tea, and sometimes, even cook chicken or fish. After all, they were building a huge house, there was so much work. How could they do everything on their own?

And her ears! Her ears were abuzz with the rhythm of different sounds. For a few days now, Bani's ears had become as sharp as a rabbit's, picking up the slightest of sounds. Her ears filled up with sounds in the middle of the night, too; through the fence came floating the sound of a flute being played, sometimes snatches of Bihu songs even. How could she sleep?

In the day time, a soft and pleasing whistling rang in her ears, sometimes a few words: 'Banilata! Where are you headed to, all dressed up? Bani Kumari! When you wear a churidar, you look absolutely … Banimati! Why are there no bangles adorning your hands? Wait, I'll go to Fancy Bazaar and …'

She couldn't even shut her eyes for a minute; a smiling face, a hard, tanned body constantly floated before them, disturbing her peace. There arose a humming inside Bani's body, too.

The blinding flashlights came on; the workers worked constantly, day and night, on the concrete roof. Bani's days and nights, too, merged into one inside that three-storeyed building, where only the plaster work and door-window fittings were left to be done.

When that boy with the hard, tanned body placed his hands on her, Bani drowned in the floodlights which lit up inside her; when he spoke, a huge cement mixer whirred noisily inside her; her eyes glittered; she became deaf—oblivious to any other sound on earth. Whenever he explained to her the rooms in their new house that was being built, he always talked about a paddy field leaning against a hill and about a small house with a courtyard. He also told stories about a plump boy playing there and he spoke about the deep love between the boy's mother and father. He left victorious over Bani.

Barua's house-warming ceremony was over. Gradually, their eyes got used to the glitter of their new half-walled house; in place of the temporary workers' building, a creeper of green was growing luxuriantly.

One day, the boy with the tanned body came forward and informed Bani's parents directly about their affection for each other. Bani's mother and father would not think of sending their daughter off to that dump of a paddy field next to a hill. They wouldn't. On top of that, they had a marriage proposal from a peon working in an office in Guwahati. He had already come to see Bani and given his approval. True, the peon was not that good looking, but so what? Did one look at a man's looks or his qualities? Bani went mad crying, and stopped eating and drinking; she would not marry that mole with the protruding teeth.

Finally, with no option left, Bani's parents gave Mineswar Mistri the condition that he would have to stay in Guwahati. Barua had built three rooms for them; he could stay in one of them. There would be no dearth of work in this growing city for someone who could work with his hands.

Mineswar put his foot down; he would not be a man who lived with his in-laws, a ghar-jowain. He had played for far too long with hard sand and cement; now he wanted to play with soft earth and be amidst greenery.

Meanwhile, he had already bought a piece of land and even started building a house when he went last Puja. He pressed them saying that he had built a bathroom-latrine as well for Bani. Bani's parents warned her angrily saying that she wouldn't be able to survive in a village in some remote corner; she should marry the peon who had land and a house in Guwahati, and who had a job, earned money. But Bani was lost in the story of the amorous couple, sitting in that wide courtyard under a moonlit night; that story beckoned her wildly. Bani followed the strains played by the tanned and hard-bodied boy on his flute, and followed him to that wide verandah, in reality, too.

As expected, there was uproar in that village by the hill over Mineswar bringing home a girl from Guwahati. The average-looking girl, who had only lived within the four walls of Barua's piece of land, became a fairytale princess in that village by the hill.

The people in the village couldn't stop talking, completely in awe of this girl from the city: 'One can go on looking at her face forever,' 'She speaks so sweetly,' 'She can't walk without sandals, even inside her home,' 'Mineswar built a bath and toilet for her, even before he got married,' 'Her parents had fixed a well-off guy with a government job,' 'How many boys do we have like our Mineswar?' 'He works in Guwahati, hasn't he done well for himself?' Mineswar's looks, his smile, his words …' The clusters of paddy in Mineswar's newly cleared fields' … Caught in the whiff of the fairytale princess's glory, Mineswar, too, became a prince.

While going to light an earthen lamp in Mineswar's paddy field for Kati Bihu, the royal princess stood still. The field leaned against the hill, the paddy stalks swayed with their heads bent—heavy with the milky-white liquid which hardened into grains of rice when mature. Everything had taken on a golden hue in the setting rays of the sun.

All of a sudden, darkness descended on the field, as if the hill had hastily grabbed the sun and hidden it in its lap. In the darkening sky, a flock of herons were flying towards the hills. Were they going looking for the sun? This was the prince's magical kingdom. The prince was looking at the sindur bindi on her forehead, and saying, 'It looks like the sun has stayed back on your forehead.' The princess was almost falling on him with laughter. Bundling up the sun in its arms, the hill very tenderly spread darkness like a sheet over them.

The field was aglow with a golden light; a light of its own, not from the rays of the sun. How happy the man was. Hadn't he taken great care to protect the paddy field from the tiny pests which would have destroyed the crops? The man would stay in the fields itself, if he could. Those days, without being aware of it, she, too, became totally immersed in his face; lighting a lamp under the tulsi plant, she would pray daily, 'Lord, the man has been working so hard …' She could never complete her sentence; her eyes would fill with tears. Only when the paddy stalks swelled out with grain was the man able to breathe easily. Smoke, pesticides … so much care he had taken. The man worked at night too; there was still a bit of work left on the granary, when that was completed he would harvest the crop.

Then, suddenly, like the all-enveloping darkness over the field when the sun dropped into the midst of the hill, terror spread a film of panic over the village by the hills. Herds of elephants started coming down from the forest-depleted hills to eat the ripe grain. There was a furious hunger inside the huge bodies of these huge animals; they couldn't find enough in the bald hills to fill even one-fourth of their bellies.

Elephants had come down to the village earlier as well; they got into the sugarcane fields to feed. Sometimes, they would drink the rice liquor from Ratiya's house and get tipsy. The villagers had never seen this ferocious side of the animal before.

The village folk started to severely rebuke the young men who were involved in the timber trade. 'You have sold Ganesh Baba's home out of sheer greed, for a few silver coins. Now, suffer. What else is there to do?'

What was their timber business, anyway—cycling the whole night to town with two heavy planks tied to their cycles, so that they could sell it to traders in the morning? And what about the men who had appeared from nowhere—the men with their stamped and sealed papers with the permission from the powers that be? They left as quickly as they had arrived, disappearing without a trace.

Within six months, the hills had been robbed and stripped bare. The timber was taken away, truckload by truckload, to God alone knew where. The squirrels, who stole food, climbed into the trees and disappeared. The innocent were being punished for no fault of theirs. Could anyone catch the squirrels that darted in and out of the branches?

The people were confused and helpless. As soon as dusk set in, the elephants descended, herd after herd, and destroyed everything in their wake—the paddy in the fields, the sacks of salt in their shops, the grains spread out in circles in their courtyards meant to be threshed by cattle and the banana trees from their compounds.

The herds did not seem to be afraid of anything. Earlier, they would eat whatever they found at the edges of the hills and go away. Sometimes, just a few fires and sounds of broken tin being struck were enough to chase them back to the hills. They never dared to come towards the human settlements. Every village that bordered the hills, not just this one, was struck by the same terror. The people were all panicking. How could tiny humans fight with these huge animals?

The herds of elephants had come down and reached Botabari village; the crowds chased them by lighting fires and making a huge clamour. But they refused to go back to the hills. After being chased from Botabari, they travelled along the river and reached Lichubari, from there to Sunjuli, and then to Hugrajuli.

The herds moved from village to village, there was no way to send them back to the hills. The people were naturally terrified and panicking. As soon as evening set in, the villagers collected branches and bamboo strips, and sat in their courtyards warming themselves by the fire. Night meant hundreds of elephants blended in with the darkness. No one knew whose house would be demolished, who would be trampled upon, whose field would be razed, whose shop would be destroyed, whose destiny would go up in flames. In the evening itself, you could hear the cries and shouts of people in terror, of tin being struck loudly, the sound of fire-crackers, and in between, the shrill, heart-rending trumpeting of the elephants. Every dawn, crying and wailing.

The princess from the city could not see the road, as her eyes were filled with tears. In the dark night, she sat on the wide courtyard, staring at the sky filled with stars and the bright moon. Lost in thought, she forgot to put the rice on to the stove. With nightfall, there was only hue and cry—fear. She stopped going to the kitchen to cook, out of fear, and remained seated on the cold bed, sobbing.

Every evening, the men in the village, including her husband, would head for the fields with torches in their hands. Half of the grain in the fields was yet to be cut. The rest had been cut and just piled in the courtyard. There was no time for anything else; they were all just running after the elephants.

All day, she moved around sleepily; all night, weeping on her bed without sleeping a wink. All she could think of was the city with its dazzling lights, the safety and the comfort of their three-bedroom, half-walled house, which lay right behind Barua's shiny new three-storeyed building.

Rubbing her eyes, she made up her mind—she would leave the next day itself. She couldn't take it anymore. Her parents wouldn't send her back, would they? No, they wouldn't. Didn't her mother send her a pair of clothes with someone who once worked with Mineswar? Yes, she did. He told her that her parents had both burst into tears after inquiring about her. She started sobbing loudly. She would go; after all, it wasn't for good. They said the elephants went away as soon as the grain was reaped. When the elephants retreated, she would come back to the village once again. Wasn't it normal for girls who were married off to visit their parents' house? Of course, it was. She would also go. What was the big deal about it then? It was nothing.

Early in the morning, Mineswar returned from the fields. He washed his face and hands as soon he returned. Asking her to make a cup of tea, he pulled a *murha* and sat down, 'You know, the elephants have not yet come to our fields. They are still on the other side of the river.'

Bani carefully handed over a bowl of tea and sat down nearby, 'What will happen if they cross the river? Our house isn't that far from the fields, is it? What if they come till here.'

'What can you do, you will have to chase the elephants with the others,' Mineswar was smiling a little.

A burst of anger flared up inside Bani. She did not look at his face, but sat with her face turned away.

He continued, 'You know, our village is going to arrange for electric current, just like in the tea gardens. After collecting money, Ratan will go to the city to get the batteries. If we can surround the fields on all sides with electric wires, the elephants will not be able to come this side.'

He asked for another bowl of tea. It wasn't a matter of joke staying up all night in that watch-post on top of a tree in winters. Bani got up. She was waiting for the right moment to say what she wanted to.

Taking a sip from the cup, he dragged the *murha* closer to the fireplace, 'It seems, the elephants have also become very clever. If a fence is put up, the big-tusked one pushes the pillars down with its legs, and after the pillars are down, they slowly cross over the wires.'

A shudder ran down Bani's body. She didn't look at his face. If she looked at him, she wouldn't be able to tell him.

'You know …' she started.

He was drinking his bowl of tea very slowly. Adding a few more logs to the fire, he said, 'Did you hear what happened to Jagat, who lives on the other side of the river, last night?' Mineswar was laughing loudly, his head thrown back, 'It seems he woke up at night to take a leak. In that sleepy state, he thought he saw eight jujube berry trees in his compound. Jagat was stumped, they had only one berry tree in their garden. How did it become eight? Then, the trees started shaking. From the light of the torch his son brought him, he saw that it was a herd of elephants. They were feasting on the banana trees. He put the fire out and lay down. One of the elephants came forward towards him as he lay among the potato plants, but Baba didn't do anything. It just shoved earth on him with his legs, buried him, and went away.'

Bani was barely able to breathe. She felt as if she had been buried by the elephant too; as if the earth had formed a blind over her eyes. She couldn't see Mineswar's drawn, sleep-deprived face.

Warming his hands over the fire, he was laughing again, 'They've dug deep pits all around the tea gardens. When the elephants come, the labourers hide in them, and are thus, saved. This time, it seems, the elephants have learned to throw branches or stones at the labourers, killing them.'

Bani suddenly said it, 'I am going home.'

Mineswar was startled, he roared back, 'More than half the grain is still left in the field, we have to bring them in within two days, and she wants to go home!'

Bani replied harshly and abruptly, in equal measure, 'I can't live in this hell, I have said I will go, and I will.'

Mineswar planted one tight slap on her cheek. Crying inconsolably, she went and fell down on the bed. At night, she dreamt of that rat-like man with his protruding teeth. He came and was speaking to her in his thin, squeaky voice, 'Let's go, Bani,

I have come to take you.' A huge herd of elephants was chasing her; she was running towards the man. He was still calling her, 'Come Bani, come, hold my hand.' He was holding out his thin hand, his skin was withered like an old man's. She looked behind her. The herd of elephants was almost upon her. She now grabbed that thin hand. What powerful hands! One tanned hand grabbed her now. Whose hand was it? Was it the peon's or that man's?

She woke up with a loud scream. She saw the hard, tanned hands in the fold of the cloth upon her. Those hands had very tenderly placed over her the soft blanket that he had bought for her from the city. She jumped out of bed. She got down from the bed carefully. A nail had been sticking out from it and her clothes had got caught on it a couple of times. But she saw that the nail was no longer there, it had been smoothened down on the wood. What hands that man possessed! Always looking for something to do … Was it any wonder, then, that she teased him saying those hands belonged to Viswakarma's son? Whichever way he turned, his hands always found some work to do.

Outside, the sun was shining bright. She went to the bathing house. The buckets had been filled up with water. Even with so many things to worry about, the man did not forget that she found it difficult to fetch water from the river. She took the new piece of pink soap in her hands. The earlier one had thinned down and broken into three pieces. The man had brought six bars of soap from the city. Even now, she picked up the small white, broken piece, and started scrubbing her heels against a rough corner of the bathroom. Viswakarma's son had made this rough corner for her to clean her heels. He did it by placing a lot of small stones in the floor when he was constructing the bathroom. Pouring a mug of water over herself, she picked up the thinned-down piece of soap to wash her face, then seemed to hear a rough, yet soft voice,

'Bani, why don't you take the new piece?' Smiling a little, she said softly, 'As if he would get me the moon from the sky if he could!'

By the time she put the bindi on her forehead and had come out, she had forgotten all about the elephants. Humming a song, she entered the vegetable garden with a basket in her hands. The yellow-and-maroon speckled marigold under the tulsi plant, moist with dew drops, glittered as the sun's rays tumbled upon it. Sticking tiny pearls in between the specks, the sun moved on to the vegetable patch.

The bamboo gate made by Viswakarma's son took a long time to open. She had laughed looking at the beautifully crafted, perforated bamboo fence, 'My, my! I've never seen anyone take so much effort to make a beautiful design over a fence, just for a vegetable patch corner.' Smoothening down a piece of long split bamboo over and over, the man had smiled, 'This fence is the first thing you behold when you wake up, isn't it?' His smile spreading over his eyes and the whole face, he had said, 'I'm weaving it for your eyes only, so there.'

She gazed around, savouring the sight of the beautiful garden. The eggplants looked like round, plump balloons. The ends of a couple of plants looked like they have been squeezed by someone. With great care, she pinched and broke off the ends which were eaten by insects or had withered away. She has been forgetting to add ash-manure to the soil for quite a few days; she would have to while the dew was still there—it would stick well, then. She placed two eggplants into her basket.

The papaya trees looked like they were about to snap with the weight of the fruit, if she didn't put up a support. She tore off a papaya from the branch that lay broken; the whole tree wasn't uprooted, it was possible to save it by supporting it with earth. The man worked so hard, right from preparing the seeds to planting the trees. The whole garden was filled with tender green vegetables and leaves; she couldn't resist picking them up. The spinach, the coriander, the sorrel, everything was growing luxuriantly.

He had bought the seeds from a shop in Guwahati the very day he had brought her here. She was so angry that day. She felt that the whole world was looking at this woman, without her wedding bangles and sindur as she stood like a shadow by the man. And, what was the man doing? He was totally immersed in buying tomato and pumpkin seeds, oblivious to everything. She bit her lower lip and smiled; that memory still fresh in her mind.

The peas were also growing inside their pods; some of them were maturing, too. She broke off a few, tore open one, took out the tender green seeds and placed them in her mouth—sweet. Seeing him plant a whole row of peas, she wondered who would eat them all. What did he say? What was his reply as his eyes twinkled and a smile lit up his face?

A plump little boy got in among the peas and started breaking them off. She ran and quickly took him into her arms, 'Naughty boy! Your father has worked so hard planting them …' The man was smiling once again, 'Let him break. Who have I planted them for, anyway?'

She bit her lower lip and smiled again.

One of the plants was full of white flowers; the flowers were all strewn on the ground as well. How could she not pick them up? The small tomato plant looked like a piece of cloth with red and green prints, strewn on the ground. Poor things! These plants had taken seed and grown by themselves, and were now bearing so much fruit. She lovingly picked up a handful of the bright-red, juicy tomatoes and put them in her basket.

From the vegetable garden, she went on to the enclosure were the ducks were kept. There were quite a few eggs lying around.

These eggs were laid by ducks which ate new rice; the whole lot was good. She collected all of them and entered the kitchen. She poured all the things from the basket onto the big sieve. White, green, red, purple—all the colours spread out onto the sieve.

Bani opened the small kitchen cabinet door and took out the fried kurhi fish pieces that she had kept covered. There was really no need to cover them up. Viswakarma's son had made the water-tight doors of the shelf to keep the cockroaches and ants from getting in. She had teased the man, 'Looks like you are building the merchant of folklore, Sandu's round and impenetrable fortress of a house, which no one could enter or come out from.'

Actually, she was filled with pride when she saw this man take up his hammer and tools at home, even after a hard day's work. Looking at him holding and fondling those pieces of wood, she thought of them as her rival. Why were his hands on those wood pieces, when they should be on her?

She placed her hands on the beautifully crafted rim of the sieve; a tingle ran through her whole body. Two hard hands were beginning to weave an intricate pattern all over her freshly washed body, arousing beautiful feelings; they were lifting her body tenderly, as tenderly as they lifted the young gourd creepers onto the hanging platform made of split bamboo; enclosing her lovingly, as lovingly as they put up the long bamboo supports around the papaya trees, without even one tender fruit falling; bringing warmth to her body, touch by touch, as they brought the earth close around the flowering peas which had fallen onto the ground, without even one of the cane strings around it breaking. She blossomed, she matured. Bani placed her hands on the sieve, 'white green, red, purple'. She kept standing like that for a while.

She hurriedly put the rice to cook. The man had risen even before sunrise. Very soon, he would arrive, gobble his food somehow, and run back out again. The brown-skinned man, whom even the strong sun and wind couldn't weaken, had turned quite dark in just these last few days. She put the kurhi fish heads into the papaya *khar*, dropped the fish pieces into the tomato and greens gravy, and fried the smoked brinjal that had melted as soon as she placed it on top of the flame, along with the duck eggs. She also fried a few greens dipped in rice flour, took out the poker stick from the clay stove, scattered water over it to put out the flame, scattered the ashes, and put the iron pan with the fries back on top of the unlit stove. 'Let it stay there. They will remain crisp,' she said to herself.

A huge crowd was coming towards the village from the fields, with cries and shouts, making a loud clamour. All the people—old men, women and children—came and crowded together on the road. All the young men were out in the fields, fighting off the elephants. There was a loud hue and cry. Who could the victim be this time? Who had been taken by Ganesh Baba today? Some of the women started sobbing. Bani, too, started crying.

A couple of old men scolded them, 'Patience! Don't bring in bad luck!'

The crowd came closer. On a bamboo stretcher was a man who had been trampled by the elephants, all his intestines out, a couple of them hanging down from the stretcher.

Someone cried out in a loud voice, 'We told you so many times, don't go chasing them because they were eating grain from your field. Can humans win against Baba?'

The people lowered the stretcher in the open area outside Bani's hut. Jogeswar's wife flung herself onto the body with its intestines all hanging out. She, too, was painted red in patches of blood. Who did the elephants kill—Jogeswar or his wife?

Bani fainted on the spot. When she came to her senses, there were people all around her.

Mineswar placed his hands on her forehead and asked, 'Have you eaten?'

She shook her head.

Someone said, 'Go on, everyone, go and eat your lunch!'

The people started dispersing.

'Only one has gone, but the others have to go on living,' someone remarked on his way out.

Mineswar was just toying with his food, instead of eating it. Placing his hand on the plate, he spoke very slowly, 'I will drop you in Guwahati and come. Just let Ratan come back from town with the batteries. If we can put up the electric wires, we needn't be so afraid.'

He took a bite out of the fried greens reluctantly, 'It will take at least a week to bring in the grain,' he said as he poured water over his rice and stood up.

Bani followed him. He did not look at the *bota* in her hands, but stood looking outside, holding onto a door post.

His voice was very low, 'I had thought as soon as the grain was brought in, I would add one more room to the house. I would go and bring your parents here for a couple of days.' He stood there waiting, head bent, 'If you want to go, I will drop you and come ...' His voice was getting muffled; he stomped out, without glancing back.

Mineswar had stopped eating, sleeping. Ratan returned from town with the batteries. The electric wires were put up on the field on the side of the river. Most of the grain had been brought in. It was the custom of the people to collectively harvest the grain; many men were invited to work, and they did it without wages. That way, the work got done faster. In the day time, toiling in the fields and spending the nights at the watch-post, the young men had no time for anything else. The ones who stayed back at home were also in the same state. Sometimes, the cows remained tied to their stakes the whole day. The day Bani heard from Rupahi and the others that several herds of elephants had gathered on the other side of the river, her ducks remained in their enclosures the whole day. On this side of the river were the fields—in the fields in their watch-post were Mineswar and the others ... She couldn't sleep a wink. She couldn't swallow a handful of rice.

A huge herd of elephants, after being chased away from the tea garden, had come through the forest reserve and had now gathered on the other side of the river. Bani woke up hastily at night. There were loud shouts and cries coming from all around; the deafening sounds of cymbals, drums, gongs, firecrackers, clanging of broken tin pieces ...

She woke up and saw that Jethai had already lit the torch. Jethai was staying over with her those days. Mineswar had been staying over at the watch-post at night, with all the other young men. The light from torches lit up everyone's houses nearby. Holding onto the door frame, Bani started sobbing and crying. She thought about the peon, not in her dreams now, but as she stood there. She should have listened to her parents. Jethai returned from Nongolamukh. The elephants had crossed the river; the shock from the electric wires had sent them away, shrieking wildly.

The very next day itself, Mineswar called the workers to harvest the grain. After bringing in the grain, he would drop off Bani in Guwahati. He couldn't bear to see her this way, deprived of food and sleep. Bani also got engaged in making arrangements for the harvest. The rhythmic swish-swish sound of the sheaves of paddy being bound together remained with her wherever she went; it got tied to her like anklets to her feet. Bani felt like she was dancing all the time, not walking. Grain filled up the whole house—the verandah, the sleeping room, the main room, and even the kitchen.

The next day, Ratan and his family would be calling in the workers. Almost everyone in the village had finished bringing in the grain. The young men spent every night at the watch-post in the fields. They were all gone that night, too. Jethai didn't come that day; she had gone to her daughter's house. Bani was all alone in the house. She was dead tired after the harvest, falling asleep on her feet, too tired to even feel afraid. Even in her dreams, she heard the sound of the anklets tied to her feet.

In the middle of the night, she was awakened by loud cries and shouts. The elephants had brought down the electric poles, crossed the empty fields, and were entering the village; they were unstoppable. She got up and opened the door; every courtyard had fires burning, except theirs. She rubbed her eyes and looked again. Just a little away from the bonfire stack which waited to be lit, a bunch of berry trees was swaying slightly in the wind. Bani froze. There was just a haystack between her and the herd of elephants. Bani started shivering violently, uncontrollably. Her throat dried up. That night Rupahi jethai hadn't come either. Her man was on the watch-post, on the other side of the field.

On the other side of the haystack, the trees were shaking. Trembling, she picked up the torch; as always, he had dipped it in kerosine before leaving. She lit the torch from the earthen lamp kept lit just by the head of the bed. The golden-coloured sheaves of grain kept stacked all over, almost touching the roof, took on the orange glow of the flame from the torch. She swiveled her head and looked all around her. The orange-coloured light had spread between the paddy sheaves, crawling like a child in between them.

She felt the roof of her mouth with her tongue that had dried up and become as stiff as wood. She took a deep, long breath. She stood there for a moment, immersed in inhaling the smell of ripe grain. Then she stepped outside.

She was surrounded by tumultuous noise and deadly cries. In the light of the fires that had been lit all around, the vegetable garden glittered—its gently swaying greens, the front ends of the broad banana leaves, the beautifully crafted bamboo strips on top of the newly woven thatch roof, the fence made by Viswakarma's son through which not even a hen could slip, the ducks cackling wildly in their wired enclosure … the lily bush … the speckled marigold … Bani went wild. With the flaming torch in her hand, she rushed to the courtyard and thrust it into the middle of the haystack. The stack of hay caught fire with a roar. As she watched, the flame reached up to the top of the betel trees.

Bani stood standing there, watching. The elephant herd was slowly turning and heading away.

Mrigananabhi

The Musk

My Childhood

Immediately after crossing the pitched road was a small wooden bridge over a trickle of water. A flock of pigeons could be seen on the banks of the barricaded pond. They reside on the ceiling of the *naamghar*; nobody harmed them. The pigeons fed on prasad taken from the palms of the devotees. Beyond that were two huge coconut trees, with leaves and branches drooping on all sides. A silver-coloured iron gate in between the two trees opened on to the T-patterned house with a huge compound.

I would go on looking at the calendar, yearning for a long vacation; waiting eagerly for the day when school, teachers, discipline, homework and Guwahati city, with its traffic, can be all left behind to board that Jorhat-bound bus.

During the journey, I peep through the windows of the bus and feast my eyes on the sights on both sides of the road, enjoy the greenery, look at towns and villages, pass through the thick quietness of the green jungles of Kaziranga, and eat peddas and laddus at Bokakhat.

After that Ma and I would go in a rickshaw across that wooden bridge; then silently bow in obeisance at the *naamghar*. Soon, throwing open the silver-coloured gate, I run between the coconut trees to the house—the house with the long corridor—and hide under a chair in the living room. Putting aside the *gurguri*, Koka would accuse Ma, 'You have left behind my Goddess!' Coming out of the kitchen, Aita would be saying, 'What sort of a person are you? I have prepared so many *pitha*s in vain.' Runu aunty will look under the chair and say, 'How did the frock that I stitched for Sontara during the last Bihu get under the chair?' I will then jump onto Aunt's lap, and everyone would get occupied with me. Packets of peddas and laddus that Ma bought from Bokakhat, cake that Deuta sent from Guwahati would be opened. My mother, while opening the suitcase to change my dress, will take out the sari brought for Aunt, the cardigan for Uncle and the dhoti for Koka. Purnima's sister-in law will be coming over to meet Ma. Aunt will serve tea to everyone in the backyard. Ma and Aita will be busy catching up on the news. Taking advantage of the situation, I shall run away, clutching a few sweets wrapped in a paper.

Six of Ma's uncles lived side by side in the area. On crossing their compounds, I find myself under the litchi tree. I take a good look around. When I am certain that no one is around, I step on the stairs which are decorated on both sides with splendid architectural design of elephant tusk. Alert, I try to listen to the sound of betel nut being ground in the mortar. I push open the closed door. In the darkness, covered with cobwebs, lies a huge hand-carved bed. Somewhere amidst the dark house with walls made blackish by the smoke of the hearth, is Ramen aita in a tattered dress, grinding betel nut. I sit near her. Aita touches me with her rough fingers.

'Who is this?' she asks. She keeps forgetting my name. 'Kiran's daughter, Sontara?'

I feel uncomfortable saying Ma's name out loud. Revealing my identity, I sit a little away from her. The untidy dress, the untrimmed nails and the knotted hair—it was not to my liking. I open the wrapped packet. Ramen aita sees the sweets in my hand. Her eyeballs are white; in the corner of her eyes are two drops of tears. Sometimes they drip down, and at others, they linger on.

Ramen aita takes the packet of sweets from my hands and starts relishing them in her toothless mouth, deriving extreme pleasure. Even after she has eaten the sweets, she goes on licking her fingers. She tries to find me and when she does, she plants a kiss on my cheek with her stained mouth, which smells of betel nut. I flee from the house before that happens.

No one approved my visiting Ramen aita. If it was found out that I went over to her place, I was sure to be reprimanded. Once I was bitten by caterpillars; my whole body had swollen into patches and turned red. My grandmother rubbed the cool mud dug out by the earthworms. Aunt applied some ointment on the rashes. Uncle suggested taking me to a pharmacy, as my eyeballs were swollen.

Aita applied a little limestone powder on my ears. She scolded Kanau kaiti, 'How many times have I told you to clean the shrubs. My granddaughter is coming and she will run about everywhere. No one pays any heed around here.'

My mother went on checking for caterpillar stings amidst the earthworm mud and reprimanded me, 'Where did you go? Speak the truth, or else you shall get a beating? Today itself I will ask your uncle to send a telegram to your father. He will come and take you back.'

There was still a whole month left for school to reopen. Koka wanted to go fishing in the pond. The following Sunday, a religious festival was being organised in the *naamghar*. Aita was soaking rice to prepare *pithas*. I was planning to pay Nanda aunty a visit, and…

I replied casting my head down, 'Ramen aita's place.'

Aita and Aunt uttered in unison, 'Why did you go to that dirty place? The old lady can see her plate of rice even from a distance, but can't keep her place clean.'

I dare not utter another word. The itching recedes, and so does the swelling. But my inquisitiveness about Ramen aita grows by the day.

My grandmother prepared rice for Ramen aita on Sundays.

'Grandmother! Why does Ramen aita not prepare her food? Why does she not have a kitchen?'

'Aita cannot see with her eyes.'

'Does she have children?'

'No.'

'Why do you call her Ramen's mother?'

'Oh! Why so many questions? Aita had a son named Ramen who died.'

My grandmother goes to her with the plate of rice. 'Ramen's ghost will come. You'll get a good scare.'

'Ramen's ghost?' I stare at my uncle, shock written all over my face.

After the birth of my brother, we did not visit our grandmother for two years. I had to stay in Guwahati, even during my vacations. During those two years, I found out a lot about Ramen aita from my mother.

Ramen aita was my mother's aunt; she being the sister of my grandfather. My grandfather had six brothers and only one sister. Ramen aita was given away in marriage at the tender age of 13 to the Barua family of Tarajan in Jorhat. At the age of 15, she had to come back to her birth place, clutching a baby in her arms.

In the big joint family of seven brothers, Ramen aita had to serve till dusk in exchange of mere food and shelter. Ramen started his studies. With the death of my great-grandfather, the joint family broke up. The brothers started to live independently, although they lived right next to each other. Ramen aita started staying in her parents' room.

The seven brothers shared amongst themselves the expenses. Squabbles among the brothers involving these expenses once led Ramen aita to comment, 'Let Ramen grow up, he will repay all the debt, along with interest.'

But Ramen did not grow up.

He turned into a ghost.

At night, amidst the darkness, a shrieking cry spins in the wind, in the very place where Ramen was crushed to death by a military vehicle. The shrieking sound comes to a halt at Ramen aita's doorsteps. She goes towards the bridge at night pounding her chest, shouting, 'Have you heard it or not? He is coming.' Afraid, the children would clutch their parents. The parents complain angrily, 'Why does this inauspicious woman shout?'

Gradually, the darkness of my great-grandfather's house merges into the white eyeballs of Ramen aita. She, who could effortlessly bear the heavy load of grains in the big vessel, now had trouble moving the small mortar from one place to another.

The seven brothers stopped quarrelling over the money that had to be given to Ramen aita. Their wives, too, tried to shrug off the responsibility of serving the plate of rice to Ramen aita. Tara's mother would frequently become indisposed when it was her turn to serve rice to Aita; Ranju's mother's excuse, as always, was that she got late while shopping; Maina's mother was unable to do so, as she had guests over. Amidst all these, Ramen aita still somehow managed to get two square meals a day.

We went to Jorhat again after my brother completed two years. That year, Ramen aita held a function at the *naamghar*. The women-folk were served rasogolla and kheer with the money that Aita got by depositing her earrings as loan. Aita was taken to the *naamghar*. She was made to sit leaning on a post, with some help from Tara's grandmother. Ramen aita was dressed in a faded *mekhela-chador*, the colour of the champa flower. Her earlobes hung low with the holes prominent, being devoid of her earrings.

At the end of prayer, the women blessed Aita. They said in unison, 'Oh God! Please release her from the trouble of hell and take her to heaven.'

I was shocked. The old women were asking God to bless Aita with death. On that day, I could not bring myself to join in their prayers and say 'Amen' at the end of it. A cry choked my voice. Ramen aita went on sitting with folded hands, even after the prayer service was over. Two teardrops sparkled in her colourless eyes, waiting to trickle down, any moment.

The coming years brought with it many changes: my grandmother passed away; my only aunt was married off; my uncle's wife joined the family; the fireplace was replaced by a gas stove; instead of squatting on the floor during meal times, food was being served on the dining table; the meat-safe was replaced by a fridge; and the stairs adorned with elephant tusks gave way to a porch. The house that beckoned me during my vacations was lost somehow, and with it, my memories of Ramen aita.

But in the college art exhibition, the painting that I exhibited was drawn from those memories of my childhood. It was inspired by my recollection of Ramen aita's dark house. Against the green background was the portrait of an old woman with colourless eyes, gazing at the sky with folded hands. Two teardrops hung in the corner of her eyes, ready to trickle down any moment. The picture fetched me the first prize.

The judge asked me, 'Why have you applied green colour to the background?'

I replied, 'The woman's sorrow is not yet over, it is still unripe.'

The judge laughed, probably not expecting such serious words from a college girl.

Why did my bright and happy childhood choose to keep this gloomy picture alive in my memory? Why did I make Ramen aita's dull eyes the subject matter of my painting? There were many other vivid memories of my growing-up years: the bright nights of Guwahati; my brother's charming smile; my mother's loving face; my friends' bright eyes; the green paddy fields by the side of Koka's house; the ponds full of fish; the altar covered with hand-woven, bright-flowered *gamosa*; the bonfire of the *naamghar*. There were many more memories from my happy childhood.

The only thing that tinted my otherwise happy childhood with sorrow was the memory of the folded hands of Ramen aita. The happy smiles scattered like sand particles; only one cry stood out in my memory like the coloured snail shell sparkling in the lap of sand.

My Adolescence

The annual examination of my eighth standard was on. It was the day I had my science and maths paper. I came out of the bathroom, screaming like a deranged person, 'Ma, Ma!' My mother came and held my shivering hand. She made me lie down on the bed which was reserved for guests. I spent the next seven days on that bed, eating only fruits and milk. No male member was allowed to come near me, not even my father and brother.

On the seventh day, a small prayer ceremony was organised at our house, to which a couple of ladies were invited. Ma cleared the drawing room, removed all the pieces of furniture and arranged the *namghosa* on a *xorai*. She arranged the soaked chickpeas and some fruits beautifully on a dish. I was made to wear a pair of new *mekhela-chador* and kneel down in obeisance. Lowering my head, I felt shy and hesitated to look at the familiar faces of Run's mother and Lata's grandmother, and even my own family members.

On my way home from school, I came across a group of boys in Ramu's paan-shop, and the same shyness I felt at home, during that ceremony, took over me. My ears and head turned hot. One of them uttered in a suppressed nasal voice, 'Age will make her very beautiful.' It was followed by a loud roar of laughter from the whole gang of boys.

I wanted to hide from the whole world the changes that my body was going through. So, I hid behind a cardigan—I wore it long before winter set in and did not give it up, even long after the cold months passed.

Sister Louisa once told me, taking off my cardigan, 'Take it naturally, take it easy.'

After completing school, I got into college. The person who was always hiding behind the cardigan, was now filled with the colours of a thousands of petals of the krishnachura flower.

Juliet, sitting by the window, made Romeo fall head over heels in love with her.

My heart, filled with the colours of the petals of krishnachura, fluttered.

John Donne rebuked the sun: 'Busy old fool, unruly sun', for disturbing him while he lay in the arms of his beloved. I heard the fluttering sound of the flowers' soft petals in my heart.

Antony mocked the world, calling it inferior, while he was entrenched in his love for Cleopatra, the Queen of Egypt:

> Let Rome in tiber melt, and the wide arch
> Of the rang'd empire fall! Here is my space,
> Kingdoms are clay.

My heart was completely filled with the red of the petals.

Like the golden-coloured ridge-gourd flowers blooming in the soft light of the dusk, a delicate dream made my heart its abode ...

A man will come into my life—a tall and polite young man with eyes as grave as the deep pond; with long, delicate fingers; and with a fondness for poetry, art and flowers. We will sit in the verandah that is covered with ivy creepers from summer to winter. At night, he will run his fingers through my tresses and speak like Romeo, 'I never saw true beauty till this night.' This deep love will immerse me. Paintings of bunches of red flowers against the background of the azure sky were imprinted in my canvas. There were sewali flowers lying in the midst of dew-drops, too. There were landscapes of the ivy creeper-covered verandah in the starry night. The beauty of the golden-hued ridge-gourd flowers in full bloom was imprisoned in that canvas.

I loved looking at myself in the mirror, almost like Narcissus. I was growing into a beautiful and slim young girl with a rose complexion, black eyes and cheeks with dimple. My thick, black, wavy hair hid my face when I left it open. I was myself surprised at how fine and soft my tresses felt when I touched it. I felt like somebody was eulogising my beauty to that person with deep-set eyes. I felt like a Goddess. Thousands of petals fluttered like butterflies in my heart.

Immediately after I took my Part I exams, a white car arrived at our doorstep, filled with a number of handsome and dignified men. After relishing the special dishes prepared by my mother, they left our house in a in a spirit of friendliness.

I found out later that some tea planter's family from Sibsagar had come to see me. The son was expected to arrive in the next couple of days.

I was shocked.

Lying down on my bed, I started howling. Ma came and gently touching me, said, 'If you are a girl, you must marry at some point in your life. Such a good boy has come in marriage because you have a wonderful destiny. He is currently looking after his tea garden. He is a graduate. Theirs is such a prosperous family. You will live like a queen in their house.'

'Queen? I never longed to be a queen.' I simply went on crying, biting the pillow, 'I don't want to get married. I want to study further. My teachers keep telling me that if I try, I will be able to achieve the first position in my honours paper.'

Two days later, two men came to our house in that same white car. Deuta welcomed them from the gate. I peeped through the window curtains. One of them was dark and lean with specs, the other was fair, fat and short. My mother forced me to go to the drawing room, carrying the tray with tea. I never had the heart to disobey my mother. But I refused to dress myself in a good pair of *mekhela-chador*, and wore a crumpled sari, instead. I wiped off the bindi from my forehead and applied kohl to my eyes.

With a sullen face, I walked down with the tray and sat in a corner, my hair in disarray. Ma looked at my dirty sari in disapproval. The men asked me some questions; I do not remember what they were. The only thing I remember was biting my lips and saying as loudly as I could, 'I shall study.'

The short, fair, fat man wanted to slip a ring into my finger. I closed my palms tightly. The man handed the small red box to my mother. I wanted to take out the ring and throw it at his face, and run out of the room. But I could do nothing. Like a doll, I went on pulling the threads from the cushion.

Everybody at home said that I shall be married only after my BA examinations. Ma forced me to put on the ring—blue, red, white and green stones crafted into a peacock design. The ring seemed to turn me into a puppet; someone was pulling the strings. I was a lifeless doll and someone went on winding the key to make me move.

After about 15 days, the short, fair man came to stay in our house, alone. After lunch, he took me out in the afternoon. Like a doll moving to the winding of keys, I wore the sari my mother asked me to and sat in his car.

I felt very uneasy sitting alone in the car with the man as he smoked. His body odour mixed with the smell of the cigarette got on my nerves.

Smiling at me, he asked, 'Sontara! Why are you feeling shy?'

He took my hand. I freed my hand from his grasp.

He stopped the car near a sari shop at Fancy Bazaar. He took me along with him. I followed him around like a doll. He purchased six saris in the shop. Seeing the man pay quite a few thousand rupees for the saris shocked me. My father also purchased a number of saris for me. I had two suitcases of clothes. But never did I buy saris worth so much at one time. I kept the saris on the car seat.

Lighting another cigarette, he pecked at my cheek, 'Nice girl, all girls love saris.'

Whenever I get a new sari, I try it at home. But these expensive saris did not stir any feelings in me. Actually, I did not even think that the saris were purchased for me.

His car came to a halt near a river-side hotel. The sharp scent of the handkerchief that he took out from his coat pocket made my head spin. I felt awkward entering the semi-dark room. One of the things that my mother forbade me from doing was to go to hotels with friends.

I followed him into the dazzling bright hotel. He selected a quiet corner table for us. The sofa could barely accommodate two people. From somewhere, a musical note came floating. Otherwise it was quiet. The whole place was dark, except for the colourful lights that fell on the round plates of food on that silent table. My heart pounded slowly. While he was eating, I went on holding the spoon and the fork. In the darkness, his small eyes, buried in fat under the thick eyebrows, sparkled like that of a cat's.

After finishing off his food, he smiled at me. He put his hands around my waist. Lips smelling of cigarette and mutton came towards me. My whole body, from head to toe, turned cold. Suddenly, I felt a sharp bite on my lips and the sticky feel of a tongue. I stopped myself from shouting—only tears flowed down my eyes.

I am used to being teased as a cry-baby. Whenever I am upset, I clutch the pillow under my stomach and weep. Whenever I cry, someone in my family pampers me. The more affection they show, the more I cry. On that day, in my life of 18 years, I wept alone, with no one to wipe off my tears.

It was past 10 pm by the time we reached home. My feet trembled as I got down from the car. What would my parents think? Ma might be waiting outside. Whenever I go out alone and it gets dark by the time I get home, Ma usually waits for me at the gate. I take long strides towards home as I look up at the streetlights. Guilty, I scold myself—Why did I go on chatting at Maitreyee's place for so long? Why did I have to stay back for tea when Junuka's mother insisted? I was scared; scared of Ma scolding me and of the darkness around me.

No, my mother was not waiting outside for me that day. She was working in the kitchen. My father was reading the newspaper inside. My parents did not ask me anything. Everybody got busy with the man.

In the bathroom mirror, I saw a black patch just at the centre of my lips. I tried to get rid of the mark by scrubbing it with soap, but couldn't. Trying to hide the patch with red lipstick made me realise that the red petals of krishnachura in my heart were shrouded by the artificial colour of my lipstick. I stared at my pink lips that had turned black—like the colour of coagulated blood.

The next day, my mother asked me about my black lips. I did not cry. I simply looked at her without so much as blinking, 'Ma, I do not want to marry him.'

'Why?' Ma asked, surprised.

I felt devoid of any shame or hesitation. Wiping off my lipstick, I showed her the stained lips. I almost shouted when I said, 'How can I accept the man who could treat me like this on our first encounter?'

I was hoping that Ma would understand. But, she was not shocked. She remained calm.

'Your marriage has already been fixed. This is nothing serious,' said my mother as she caressed my back.

She continued, 'Sweetheart, as you are a girl, you have to learn to tolerate many things. The female body is meant for a male. Things will be like this at the beginning, but later on, it will become easy. My own …' Ma probably wanted to say something about herself, but stopped short of it.

I cried loudly, 'I won't marry, I won't marry, I won't …'

Ma made me lie down, as I was hysterical.

'Sweetheart, do you have any preference somewhere else?' Her question made me sit up. She continued, 'Anyone among your friends—Ratan, Bidyut, Utpal, Hamid?'

'No, Ma. How can I love them?'

'Then, Sharma sir, Jinu's uncle, Junuka's brother, Maitreyee's uncle …' she insisted.

No, it was Romeo who could immerse my life in exciting love. There was none other who could fill my heart with the colourful petals of krishnachura.

'No, No …'

That night, I heard Ma telling Deuta, 'After the marriage has been fixed, it is not proper to keep the girl at home. Please, write to them. Let the wedding take place soon. She can pursue her studies later also.'

I did not hear what my father replied. I only realised that the flower petals blooming in my heart were being blown away by the wind. In the empty heart, crawled an ugly black patch.

My Marriage

On the day of *juroon*, my Part I exam's mark sheet and the people who had come to attend the ceremony arrived together. I grabbed the mark sheet from my uncle. I managed to secure even better marks than I had expected in my Honours Papers. I missed first-class marks by a hair's breadth. I jumped with joy, dressed in all my bridal finery.

I was over the moon.

His family members started taking out the articles for *juroon*. I was probably staring at the gorgeous jewellery sets and the beautiful *mekhela-chador*s kept in front of me.

Aunt whispered in my ears, 'Don't stare like that! What will people say?'

The house was filled with people. I always found my aunt's words—'what will people say'—resounding in my ears. What will people say if I wake up late? What will people say if I take my bath late in the day? What will people say if my *uroni* slips while eating or while serving tea to the guests who come to see the bride? The same words kept ringing in my ears—'what will people say? What will people say?'

After a certain point, things got a little less complicated. All the people who had come to attend the wedding went to their respective places. In the huge house, besides me, were my ailing father-in-law, the servants and the occasional visitors from the tea garden. His uncles, aunts and other family members, and sometimes, even his friends visited us.

I had very little work around the house, yet I did not have a single moment to sit all by myself. Kancha's work was to cook, Lakshmi's was to wash the utensils and my duty was to serve guests with a smile forever plastered on my face. Tired of serving guests, I wanted to venture out of that house with its high walls and pine trees on all sides. I longed to take off my expensive sari and put on a simple, soft dress with a scrubbed face. I wanted to silently sit in that verandah covered with ivy creeper.

A sharp pang of loneliness crept into my life. His father was bed-ridden, almost dumb with paralysis. He was only able to utter some indistinct sounds.

I had very little interaction with Santanu Chaliha. During the first few months of our marriage, I was actually afraid of him. The more he kept himself busy with the tea garden and business, the more relieved I was.

After we had been married for three months, he took me to Darjeeling, Kashmir and Bombay.

Leaving the familiar faces behind, we embarked on our journey to new places. Travelling with him alone and staying in hotels, I somehow found myself drawn closer to the man that I avoided out of fear. I had come to terms with the fact that if I wanted to live, I had to keep my man satisfied.

It was drizzling the day this realisation dawned on me—the realisation that I had no choice but to live with this man. I was sitting in the verandah of an expensive hotel in Darjeeling; he had gone out after having his breakfast. The sun was hesitatingly peeping through the clouds over the Himalayas. The azure sky was tinged with the pale light of the rising sun. The sunrise brought to my mind a picture I had drawn in the sixth standard. The sky looked similar that day. There were only mountain peaks, no string of pine trees.

On a blank paper, I started sketching the monsoon clouds with black and blue pencil, and rubbed it in long strokes with an eraser to show the sun's pale light. The gift packet of canvas and paint from my friends on my wedding was tucked under the costly dresses that filled my suitcase—the suitcase with the overpowering smell of naphthalene balls. The sky of Darjeeling reminded me that I still had that packet stashed away.

By that time he was back, the Darjeeling sky was half imprisoned in my painting.

He started shouting, 'Get ready soon. I've got two tickets for a very good film.'

There was a smile on his sullen face. I understood that he was in a good mood. It is only when he is pleased that traces of a smile appears on his face. The sunrays playing hide-and-seek through the clouds in the Darjeeling sky continued to keep me enchanted.

I told him with excitement, 'Let us not watch a movie today. I am tired of shopping and watching movies. Take a look at the picture that I have drawn.'

The sparkle brought out by the sunlight over the snow-covered Himalayas, made my eyes glisten. I did not see his angry face. He went downstairs and did not return till midnight.

Putting away my painting, I sat alone in the room but not a single drop of tear trickled down my eyes. When he returned after midnight, his walk was unsteady. I was aware that he drank socially, but I had never seen him in this state. When he lay down on the bed with his shoes, I went to remove them.

He pushed me and muttered, 'Pride! What are you so proud of? Are you proud of your beauty or of the fact that you can read and draw? Santanu Chaliha never begs a woman.'

He fell asleep.

I went on looking at the man I had known for the last three months—brown eyes, overweight and rosy complexion. That night in the soft blue light of the Darjeeling hotel, I saw him in a different perspective.

A while back, sitting in that empty room, I heard many sounds—footsteps on the other side of the wall, many knocks at my door. There were also shadows on the window panes. But now only silence everywhere. It was the same hotel room, the same twin-bed, the same carpet, the same wall-hanging, the same plant with red and yellow leaves in a tub. Just a few moments back, the room reeked of trouble and conspiracy. But now, somehow, I knew that I was safe in that room with him.

He was fast asleep. He was drooling and the smell of wine emanated through the gap in his lips. I heard the sound of somebody treading with heavy shoes outside. I clutched his unconscious body, and after sometime fell asleep, my head on his arms.

In the morning, when he was getting ready without uttering a single word to me, I cried holding his feet. That evening, he took me out to watch a movie. I don't remember the name, some English film. To me, the movie felt like a broad canvas filled with white, lifeless pieces of flesh. The lumps of flesh were running about in the canvas. In my eyes floated a healthy face.

The boy in charge of our hotel room was Mon Bahadur. Flashing his fine white teeth, he used to chat with me while I was alone. His mother was dead; his father worked in another hotel. He invited me over to his house, as he and his father had a day off. I felt inquisitive. I wanted to see how Mon Bahadur lived after seeing such richness, such luxury in the hotel. I tried to imagine him on the canvas ... Mon Bahadur wore an ironed uniform over his torn vest, his hair in disarray. Did his small, round eyes hold two drops of tears like Ramen aita? No, his eyes would be better if painted with a sparkle of laughter.

The movie was coming to an end. On our way back, he gave me a costly white nightie with white lace.

That night, seeing me in the lace nightie, he said, 'Sweetie! Mini Liz Taylor.' When I saw myself in the mirror in that transparent nightie, I felt like a lump of flesh—a lifeless lump of flesh. Lighting up a cigarette, he smiled at me. The lifeless lump of flesh, too, smiled back—like a mechanised doll.

The next 15 months of my married life was nothing but the story of my relentless effort to bring a smile on his sullen face.

He never read. At times, even if he did, they were either business-related books or English pornography. I never read near him. I used to hide and read at times, but not as much as I used to before.

He thought painting was for people who had nothing better to do. I stopped painting.

One day I told him, 'All my books are here. So, I would like to take my BA exams. In my Part I, I was very close to securing first class.'

He smiled crookedly and said, 'If that is what you wish, then do it, but I do not think that degrees are of any importance. Take yourself as an example, you secured first division in matric, a position in pre-university and very close to securing first class in your Part I exams. But, do you know more than me?'

I never raised that topic in front of him again.

He always wanted me to dress up nicely. My wardrobe was filled with clothes and ornaments gifted by him. I decked myself up in different dresses. I flipped through the pages of the various magazines that he brought me and tried the different hairstyles in it. I changed my dress, my ornaments, my lip colour; changing from the day look to the night look. He wanted me to keep smiling. So I went on smiling, without any reason. He teased me, 'Colgate toothpaste's advertisement.' He started smiling more frequently; I felt relieved.

Once he asked me to paint. We had just got our house painted around that time. An old picture that he got during his visit to Gangtok hung in the drawing room. The faded picture was a sharp contrast against the newly painted wall—the black satin cloth was shredded, tongue turned almost pink.

He asked Lakshmi to take down the picture, and looking at me, said, 'Sontara, why don't you make a nice painting? The wall looks so bare. Manager Saikia is going to Kolkata. Ask him to bring you whatever you need to paint.'

He was right. The wall in the living room did look bare, without any picture.

I reopened the packet of canvas and paint gifted by my friends and started to paint. Bunches of white flowers were the focus of my painting. The heart of the flowers depicted through small red drops of colour. Like a mad person, I went on filling the white flowers with red drops of colours as if they were drops of blood.

After taking a good look at my painting, he said, 'Good! Even the ones in the market look like this. But the white flowers do not go well with the light yellow-coloured wall. Do one thing. Change the colour of the white flowers to bright yellow—the effect of bright yellow and red flowers will be marvellous.'

I changed the colour of the flowers from white to bright yellow. He got the painting framed in red. The drawing room had a red carpet, red and yellow curtains, and a pale yellow sofa-set; and right in the middle of the pale yellow wall, imprisoned in a red frame, were the bunches of red and yellow flowers.

A few days later, I vomited. This continued for many more days at a stretch.

My Distress

Death! John Donne mocked death: 'Death, Be not proud'. Shakespeare made death seem mysterious: 'The stroke of death is as a lover's pinch, which hurts and is desir'd'. Thomas Mann regarded death as a symbol of beauty: 'Don't you like the sight of a coffin? I really do. I find it a handsome piece of furniture, even empty; when someone is lying in it, then in my eyes, it is positively sublime'. Eliot's conception of death was philosophical: 'I can show you fear in a handful of dust'. Death, as depicted in books, is always mysterious, weak, wonderful and romantic.

In my 20 years, I had encountered death from close quarters; once, being that of my grandfather's demise. The newly framed photo of Koka; the fragrance of a bunch of incense sticks stuck on a piece of banana; prasad being distributed; lit earthen lamps placed on banana leaves and obeisance being paid to God: 'Madhava

Madhusudan, Jadava Jadunandan, O, you Nitya Niranjane ... Narayan, Narayan'. My aunts, dressed in *mekhela-chador*, walked around the house silently, tending to the rituals and guests who had come to offer condolences. My uncles were in tears.

Everyone consoled my grandmother. They said, 'The dead has left for heavenly abode after completing all earthly duties. So his soul should not be disturbed by crying.' Someone said, 'How many people have the fortune of dying so peacefully?'

I could never forget that picture of death—such a calm and peaceful end.

After that, I saw another death; death treated in the simplest manner, as if it was as natural as eating and breathing.

We found out about the existence of shopkeeper Ramcharan's father only after his death. The old man had been suffering for a long time. On hearing a noise, I opened my window and saw a group of people gathered in front of Ramcharan's paan-shop. I saw clearly a dead body covered in a white cloth, lying in front of the shop. A man stepped on the dead man's shrinking knee and it straightened with a crackling sound. I screamed.

My parents scolded me, 'Close the window. What is there to see?'

The sound of broken bones kept ringing in my ears. I remember going to Ma's bedroom that night, carrying my pillow.

But I never knew that death could be so fearful, so terrible, so cruel. I never knew that such death could bury a man, even in life.

Santanu Chaliha used to come to Sibsagar from the tea garden every Sunday. It was the second day of September. I was walking in the lawns of our house which was covered by hedges on all sides. The gardener was watering the plants. My father-in-law was brought out to the garden by the nurse. He was in his wheelchair, staring with blank eyes.

The doctor had advised me to go for walks during those nine months. My heavy body was draped in a bright yellow sari. He loved it when I wore big bindis with sindur on my parting.

While walking, I could feel my child in the womb. I was expected to deliver in three months. I had so many dreams: I would tell him stories, he would laugh and he would clutch me when afraid ... I stopped for a few seconds. He will be very naughty—he moves around so much in my womb. I smiled to myself.

His car arrived, but along with a few other jeeps. He did not come out of the car, fiddling with his car keys, as he always did. A lifeless body was brought down, instead. On seeing the bloody body covered with a white cloth, I froze. There was confusion and a lot of noise around me. Someone lifted the white cloth. For a split second, I caught the glimpse of an arm hanging loose. Dry blood covered the body. I had no recollection of what followed after that.

Waking up, I tried to sit, but could not. I was on saline. A sharp smell affected my nose. A nurse in white uniform came near me with a bundle of cotton, 'Your baby is healthy despite being premature.'

I tried to sit up with a jump, 'But he?' I had a vision of a body with a loose arm and blood clots.

I saw many people through the open door, heard them weeping.

His aunt came in rubbing her eyes, 'Let her see the face of her husband for one last time.'

Somebody took me outside.

The priest sitting near the body covered in a white cloth said, 'The wife is still wearing the dress of a married woman.'

The yellow sari I was wearing—the sari that was the colour of the evening autumn sky, and the ornaments adorning my hands, ears and neck were all taken off, one by one. Aunt made me wear a white pair of *mekhela-chador* and made me sit at his feet. Someone held his big toe and rubbed off the sindur from my forehead and parting with it. How cold his body was. That ice cool touch spread through my body, both inside and outside, gradually.

He was taken in a truck. Somebody helped me lean on a verandah post.

I also felt like dying. The sound of people weeping was all around me. Then, there was silence. The familiar faces, the sky, the trees, the sunrays—everything disappeared from my mind.

I could not bear to look at the truck. My eyes stopped at a particular spot. Three house pigeons were making a fluttering sound amidst the red and green leaves in the hanging tub that I myself planted. For an instant, my consciousness was surrounded in the chirping of the birds.

I felt my hand, infused with saline, itching. My body from the waist down was in severe pain. My shrill shout was mingled with the noise made by the birds, 'Where is my boy? My baby? Why is he not in my arms? Why don't you say what has happened to him?'

Someone carried me to the bed. I asked my mother who was caressing my forehead, 'Ma, was my brother also not a premature baby? My son? Have you seen him?' I wanted to tell her many more things. 'Oh, my son! What happened to him? Is he alive?' The vision of my brother's muscular body floated in front of my eyes. 'Ma, you also slipped once and fell down before my brother's birth, is it not?'

My mother left my side.

A few moments later, the nurse came in with a baby covered in cotton. Ma was there too. He opened his blue eyes. I was engulfed slowly in a deep drowsy feeling.

A lit earthen lamp and incense sticks were placed in front of his newly framed photo. Prasad was distributed among the guests who had come to pay their condolences. Prayers from the holy scriptures were read. The priests blessed me, 'Let her live like a Sati Savitri, thinking only about him. May God bless the baby!'

My body was in pain. The stitches on my body made me suffer. I could not kneel down. When I tried to kneel before the holy priest to take his blessings, my body could not bear the pain.

Soon after, the house was empty. In the huge house, the only ones remaining were my paralysed father-in-law, the nurse who looked after my baby, the servants, my baby, my mother and me.

After about a month, my two brothers-in-law, the one who lived in Digboi and the other who lived in Shillong, arrived. My father and brother had also come from Guwahati. My father and brothers-in-law had discussions regarding the property. My brother-in-law, the one from Digboi, asked me to sign a paper stating that I was entitled to a part of the Sibsagar residence, part of the tea garden and properties in Guwahati. Santanu Chaliha's elder and younger brothers' properties were to be made into a guest-house by some company. My portion of the property was the northern side.

The day Lakshmi and Ramu shifted my things to the room in the northern side of the property from the room that I had stayed in since my wedding, I knew that my time in this house was coming to its end. I sat the whole night in the new room filled with my things. Ma was in the bed next to mine. A little further away, in the long room, were my brothers-in-law's servants. My brothers-in-law were in their respective rooms.

Beyond the house that was covered with pine trees and hedges was a world with so many people. Still, I felt alone in this world. In the strange loneliness, I trembled. The whole world seemed silent, without a sound. I could hear my own breathing. I felt everything drying up inside me. The baby sleeping in the cotton bundle cried, invading my helplessness into pieces. I murmured to myself, 'Be near me when the light is low …' I placed my lips on his cheeks; his warm, soft and smooth cheeks.

My elder brother-in-law suggested taking me to his Digboi home. My younger brother-in-law wanted to take me to Shillong.

After two months, Ma and I came to Guwahati with my baby. My brothers-in-law also accompanied me home. Ramu, Lakshmi and my father-in-law continued to live in our Sibsagar house.

And me … When I was getting ready to come to Guwahati, I glanced at my dress—it was unkempt and stained. I could not find even one clean pair of white dress in the closet full of new clothes.

My Reality

After my marriage, I used to visit my parents quite frequently. I also visited my friends and relatives. Everybody used to ask, 'How long will you stay?' Once again, I found myself at home … only this time, I had a baby in my arms and tears in my eyes.

This time, nobody asked when I would be going back. Mrs Bora came visiting. Presenting my newborn baby with a metre of cloth, she asked, 'How will the mother live looking at this burning fire?' Pari's grandmother came over as well. She brought a five rupee note for the baby. The old lady touched my forehead with her rough fingers, 'Ma! It is all God's will! What can you do? Remember your husband and take care of your son.' Two drops of tears trickled down her wrinkled cheeks.

My friends came to see me, but this time, they did not tease me asking about my married life as they would on other occasions. Neither did they eye my expensive clothes and ornaments with envy. They looked at me from a distance with dumb horror.

I felt like a falling star. I tried to remember the words of Pari's grandmother—'Husband's memory ...' The sight of a bloody body floated in front of my eyes; the feel of his cold feet when it was rubbed against my sindur bindi.

The premature baby wrapped in cotton, soon blossomed into our Sonmoni. He learnt to sit up, and then to crawl. He could fetch the red ball, even. One day, he took a few steps holding onto the bed. Books and newspapers got him all excited, and he would make strange sounds, as if trying to read. He was particularly fond of colourful comic books. After planting a kiss on my cheeks, he would go off to school.

Soon after completing his studies, my brother landed a job in Guwahati. He renovated the house built by Deuta: he got it repainted, changed the curtains and furniture, and planted new flowers. He even insisted that I bring more colour into my dress. One day, he brought me a blue-and-white-flowered sari and said, 'You should take your finals. I have already spoken to the Head of your department. And, why do you always drape yourself in white? Wear this.' Another day, he brought for me paint and a canvas.

One day, my brother took me for a ride in his new scooter. He stopped near a special restaurant in Panbazar and almost forced me to have a cup of tea there. Placing the order for tea, he looked at me and smiled, 'While in college, you all frequently came to this restaurant. Isn't it? OK Tara ba! How long have you not set foot outside? Sonmoni will complete six years on the second of September. That means for the last six years you kept yourself confined to one room. Ma is pursuing a normal life, enjoying movies and buying new clothes.'

I yelled at him, 'Don't talk about Ma like that. I have lost everything, she hasn't.'

He retorted, 'Tara ba. I am 23. You are only one year senior to me. What have you lost?'

I got up slowly, 'Let's go! Sonmoni will trouble Ma otherwise.'

What could I tell my brother? He was shining with such youthful purity. How could I explain to him our society's hard and fast, cruel rules; that the repetition of customs were meaningless?

Dressed in a borderless silk dress and a neat bun, I went to Runa's house at noon. She had asked me to help her in wearing the bridal finery. I made a garland of red and white roses for her bun. Combing her hair and tying it into a bun, I was about to put the sindur bindi on her forehead, when her great-aunt snatched it from my hands. She put the bindi on Runa's forehead with her thumb, instead. I had carefully drawn the placement of the bindi, but her great-aunt rubbed it in the hurry. I turned static. Spitting out some betel nut juice, she said, 'Woman without sindur should not put sindur on others.'

I rushed out of their house. While walking home, a big red sindur bindi burnt in front of my eyes—shapeless, rough and ugly.

On the day my brother was about to go for an interview, I came out with a rose bud to wish him.

My mother, in a rough tone, told me, 'Sonmoni is crying. Go to him.' But to my utter surprise, I found Sonmoni sleeping in the other room.

In the living room, I overheard Deuta saying, 'She just wanted to wish her brother good luck!'

Ma, in a suppressed voice, replied, 'He is going for a good purpose. So, why should he look at her bare forehead?'

In our next-door-neighbour Pari's house, there was a ceremony held during her younger sister's attaining puberty. I remember sitting in a corner. Someone told me that they were about to offer the prasad. Just as I was about to carry the tumbler of prasad, someone expressed dissatisfaction, saying, 'A woman without sindur and bangles should not prepare offerings for the deity.'

I realised that it was better to be stay confined in a room. Through the window of my room, I could see a portion of the fig tree, where birds came to devour the ripe fruits, and also the clear, blue sky through the gaps in the leaves.

From my childhood days, I suffered from chronic headache. If I studied too late or knitted a little too much, that simple headache would gradually turn into migraine. After that I could neither see the changing colours of the blue sky through the gap in the leaves nor the little fingers of Sonmoni pressing my forehead. My blood pressure, too, would shoot up. I had to rest frequently, either due to my blood pressure or migraine.

I appeared in my exams, just as my brother wanted. Handing me the mark sheet, he said, 'We will look after Sonmoni. You go to some university outside of Assam. I will bear the expense as well.'

Discussions regarding my brother's marriage were going on. Suddenly, his marriage was fixed with retired Magistrate Pranab Barua's daughter. The girl had an MSc in Zoology with first class distinction. She was fair and belonged to a respectable family. Everybody was pleased.

Our otherwise-quiet house was suddenly buzzing with activities and people as my brother's wedding drew near. I was trying to get some sleep. Sonmoni, afraid of all the commotion outside, sat by me in our room.

Suddenly, my brother slammed the table and shouted, 'I will not marry that girl.'

Ma asked, 'If you did not want to marry, then why did you give her the engagement ring?'

My brother retorted, 'At that time, they did not give these conditions.'

My father's voice was sober, 'I do not like this type of attitude on the part of the bride's house. She will stay here. The daughter-in-law will come, but that does not mean I shall send my daughter away.'

Ma started crying, 'How many proposals have gone back for this reason? I shall look after her till the time I am here. If she wishes to, she is free to make herself a cup of tea or cook a meal. She is free to read, even. But then will a girl from another family understand the situation and accept it?' Ma's voice was immersed in sobs.

Deuta said in his soft voice, 'You do not have to worry about her and Sonmoni's expense till I'am alive. But, once I close my eyes ...'

My brother shouted frantically, 'Is she not my sister? I understand her more than you do. I love her more than you do.'

'But if your wife does not wish, you can do nothing about it. There will only be trouble in your marriage,' Deuta said in his choked voice.

I turned static and felt a severe hatred for myself. The others in the house were earning, the others were working and putting things on the table, and all I did was to live off their money. I was nothing but a parasite, dependent on others. I slapped myself. Arranging the mosquito net and putting Sonmoni to sleep, I went to sit in the living room. Ma, Deuta and my brother were also there.

I said, 'What you all are saying is true. You are affectionately providing for me and giving shelter to my son, but a girl from another family should have no reason to do this. Brother! What Rima is saying is right. Why should she compromise her feelings and other necessities with an unknown woman?'

They wanted to say something to me, but I did not listen. I told them about my decision.

I did not listen to anybody. I had made up my mind. I took the job of a school teacher.

My brother eventually got married to Rima Barua.

Sonmoni and my small world started, a new life. The rented house was small. Water had to be fetched from far. We had to share the bathroom-latrine with the owner of the house.

There were five rented houses, including ours, in the owner's compound. When my brothers-in-law found out that I no longer lived with my parents, they proposed to build a house for me in Beltola. My brother wanted to find a comfortable house for us and he insisted on paying the rent. Ma started to cry when she saw me fetch water from the roadside tap. Deuta scolded me when he saw my Janata Stove, and the cheap bed and chair-table that I purchased from the street near Dighalipukhuri. I firmly refused my father's offer of wanting to buy me a new gas stove and some essential pieces of furniture.

With my school job, house work and taking care of Sonmoni, I hardly had the time to breathe.

We kept two pots of rose plants on the steps of our house. Sonmoni would scream in delight every time he found a new leaf on the plant. Two buds appeared in the plants—one red and the other white.

Sonmoni drew the flowers in his copy with a sketch pen. Gradually, my blood pressure and migraine grew less frequent. My son learnt to sing and play the guitar. I, too, was thinking of taking my MA exams.

At night, I would recite passages from *Paradise Lost* to Sonmoni:

'Fallen Cherub! to be weak is miserable Doing or suffering …' 'All is not lost, the unconquerable will …'

Not understanding a word of it, he would simply stare at my face awestruck.

My Sin

I passed my MA exams with good marks. I took over the responsibility of running Hostel Super. Sonmoni was in class V. The students respected me. The other teachers of the school liked me. My parents, brother and brothers-in-law frequently enquired after my welfare. If I was quiet, even for a short period, Sonmoni would create pandemonium. I purchased as many books as I wanted every month.

In the two-roomed quarter, I had created my own world. Still my fear seemed never ending. That day I feared for my body ...

At around 9 pm, Dharani Sharma came over—MLA Dharani Sharma. Two days before, I had gone to meet him, along with my colleagues, for some work related to the hostel. He came in connection with that meeting. I offered him a seat, but kept standing myself.

Sharma took a piece of betel nut and stuffing it in his mouth, said, 'Grants will be sanctioned for the hostel and your quarter will also be extended.'

He kept on staring at me.

Sharma was slightly inebriated, 'Sontara, when your new quarter is built, I will come over occasionally.'

I pulled my chador to cover my back. Conversing on various topics, Sharma left an hour later.

That whole night, I sat with a book open and couldn't switch off the light. The way Sharma stared at me made my skin crawl. It was as if a hairy caterpillar was crawling all over my body. I could only go to sleep very late at night. I had a dream—I was running in an empty street and was being followed by Dharani Sharma with a limp. I was wearing only that transparent nightie given to me by Santanu Chaliha. At one point, I simply shouted out. I was unable to run any further. I must have shouted very loudly in reality too, as the boarders came out of their rooms and knocked at my door. Sonmoni was shaking me. After that I could not sleep for many nights. The hairy caterpillar went on crawling through the curves of my body. I simply went on imagining about the time when my body would be devoid of any curves—no curves for the hairy caterpillar to crawl.

I waited eagerly for the day when my forehead would be adorned with a white bindi, like that of my grandmother. The bindi would match my white dress and my grey hair. Sonmoni will look at a shy girl and say, 'I am selfish in my love.' The purity of the sandalwood bindi will engulf me.

I saw a grey hair near my forehead. I kept staring at it for a long time.

I moved towards the safety of the sandal paste bindi.

I thought that my calculations would be correct. But in spite of my desperate wish, there were no more grey hair.

The day Aditya first visited us, Sonmoni was not at home. The hostel was almost empty, as the exams were over. I was basking in the soft sunlight of the wintry morning and leafing through the pages of a new book. I was not reading anything specific, but pondering over a question in the foreword: 'What does woman want? No doubt what man wants, the unattainable and the unattainable is precisely what women were not allowed to seek'.

The question created turmoil in my mind.

He came inside. Offering him a seat and putting the book on the table, I sat a little away from him.

Taking the book, he went on turning the pages. I went inside to prepare some tea for him.

Taking a sip of the tea, he went on looking at the painting on the wall. The portrait of Ramen aita was hung on the wall by Sonmoni.

'Who painted it?' he asked.

I smiled; the smile that was a disease at one time.

Sadness, despair or anger? Is it not sad that women were not allowed to seek the unattainable?

I laughed loudly—a hearty laughter.

He drank another cup of tea.

We talked a lot.

At the time of departure, he said, 'While talking to you, I've forgotten to tell you the actual matter.'

He told me about a vacant post in their college. The principal had asked him to inform me. I had written an application regarding the opening a long time back.

I handed him the application. His tall body gradually disappeared in the moonlit night. Closing the gate, I looked at the sky. Many stars clustered round the moon.

Shutting the door, I came to lie down on my bed. Can one feel so relaxed after talking to another person? Did anyone ever experience the feeling of fearful loneliness shatter to pieces after talking to a stranger for two hours?

I left school to teach in college. The pay increased, while the work load lessened. I had more time to spare.

During my free time, he frequently visited our newly rented house.

Sonmoni used to roam around in his motorcycle. He used to play with Sonmoni. He also played the guitar, sang and read the new poems written by Sonmoni. During the time when he and Sonmoni were busy in the drawing room, I would quietly observe them. At times I would prepare tea, at times I read, or sometimes just lay on my bed.

He loved Sonmoni. But, did he come to our house for Sonmoni alone? The question threw me off. While leaving, he would always look into my eyes. I could not look at his serious face for long. I kept myself away from him. I tried to escape from him, but was unable to.

A good movie was playing in a theatre. Sonmoni insisted that we go to see the movie. We made Sonmoni sit between us. I went on sitting quietly. But while returning, I could not help talking excitedly about the film.

He arranged a small picnic on the occasion of Sonmoni's birthday. Sonmoni made me bake a cake. When I was reluctant about going out for the picnic, Sonmoni threw a tantrum. When we reached the spot, he and Sonmoni moved about holding the camera. I went on looking at the dry autumn river. I was cold.

He was standing near me. He opened his half-sweater and kept it by my side, 'Why did you not bring any warm clothes? Put this on.'

Keeping the sweater near me, he disappeared with Sonmoni, walking along the banks of the river.

I did not touch the sweater. I was irritated—angry at him, at myself, and even at Sonmoni. What need had he? I was moving towards the purity of the sandal paste bindi. My calculations have not gone even slightly wrong.

It was raining; I was walking home after class. Why did he have to say: 'It is raining, no need to get yourself wet. I shall send a rickshaw from the square'?

It was getting late while I was sending off the answer scripts of final exam. Why did he have to say: 'Mrs Chaliha, I will enter the marks for you. You look tired these days. I hope you are not keeping yourself awake'?

Once when Sonmoni had a fall while playing football, why did he have to take him to the hospital?

When I was suffering from a mild cold, why did he have to bring me the medicine? I am capable and independent. I can walk two furlongs in the rain. I can take care of my child. I can exert the required effort for my job. All my calculations have been done. I was only waiting for the purity of the sandal paste bindi.

The sweater kept lying right where he put it. We were about to come back before sunset. It was slightly dark inside the car; outside, was the golden light of the evening. The orange hue of the outside world was new to young Sonmoni. A light breeze blew through the car window. I covered my body with the chador. He quietly put the sweater over my body; Sonmoni must have brought it along with the rest of the things. A part of his palm touched my cheek. He rested his hand on the back of the seat. My eyelids turned heavy. I fell asleep.

Was my sleep real? Shall I wipe out the purity of the sandal paste bindi? Should I allow my calculations to go wrong?

One day, he came with two books. I had forgotten that it was my birthday. Sonmoni must have told him about it. He kept the books on the table.

In quite a firm tone, I said, 'It is not my age to read love poems. The day of my coming to this world had stopped being special with a particular man's death.'

With trembling hands, he picked up the books and went away.

He did not come back for two weeks at a stretch after that.

When Sonmoni informed me about his fever, I replied bitterly, 'What should I do?'

That day I had a severe headache; four analgins also did not help. At one time, I was totally washed out with the frequent vomiting.

I went to his house the next day instead of going to college. Sonmoni had left for school. Sonmoni often visited him, but I had never gone to his house before. I hesitated at the doorsteps.

The door was open. The whole house was filled with books and paper—haphazard and messy. He was lying down in the inside room. On the table, lay a half-opened packet of bread and a few tablets. He did not realise my presence. I stood near his bedside.

'Barua! Sonmoni told me that you are not well.'

He sat up. His deep eyes were red, hair unkempt.

'Did you eat anything?' I asked, putting a packet of amla and lime on the table. He kept on looking at me with his red eyes.

'If you do not eat something …' I asked him if I could cook him something.

Suddenly, he jumped from the bed and embraced me, 'Sontara! I want you. I love you. I love you!'

I was stunned. 'But …' I looked at my clear white attire.

'Sontara! I do not want to comprehend anything. I won't listen to anything. I want you.'

He grew anxious. His feverish lips touched mine. I pushed him away and dashed out of the house.

His passion secretly made me lose myself. If I did not see him for one day, I grew anxious. I definitely tried to fight this anxiety, not with emotion, but with reason. I tried to sort out my feelings.

Was this attraction sexual? Was this the age-old carnal relation between a man and a woman? I did make love—the nights spent with Santanu Chaliha, those savage nights which meant waking up at 8 or 9 in the morning with the strong sunlight piercing the eyes, a burning body and pain. Santanu Chaliha craved to be with a woman; he was a womaniser. I understood that in that burning fire, I was only a straw. He had been with our servant,

Lakshmi, the labour girls of the tea garden and many others. I never acknowledged it. I wanted to go on living, pretending that I knew nothing. Those savage nights did not excite me, but only brought hatred.

But with him, it was different. For him, I felt this anxiety; the touch of his warm lips made my blood burn with desire.

But I knew that this was not just physical attraction, not just pleasure of the flesh, not just savage passion. What was it then? Was it safety that I was looking for in his embrace; safety in all forms—financial, social, emotional?

I had a job. I had a plot of land. I should be getting a loan very soon. Sonmoni had planned the design of our house. My maternal instinct was satisfied with Sonmoni's kindness. I was respected in the society. Then, was I mad? What was happening to me?

I tried to remember the blessings of the people, 'Keep yourself alive like a pure Savitri, thinking about your husband's feet.' I felt the rough fingers of Pari's grandmother on my bare forehead, 'Think about your husband's feet and bring up your son.'

Husband's memory? Can a person remain alive on someone's memory alone?

Possible! June aunty is alive—such peace in her eyes.

June aunty married Air Force Pilot Rustom Mehra while she was studying in Delhi University, in spite of opposition from her family members. Aunty wore the white dress only after two years of marriage. She did not even have a son, like I had Sonmoni. I had seen her many times sitting with the bundle of letters from Mehra; she kept her husband's uniform in her wardrobe. She would always bow down in front of Mehra's photo, offering fresh flowers and lighting incense sticks. Mehra died saving the lives of a whole plane of passengers. He made his wife proud.

I was afraid to talk about Santanu Chaliha's death and the circumstances that led to it. The more I tried to convince others that it was a car accident, the more they talked. The truth was that he had deceived a labour girl in the tea garden and the labourers had hunted him down. Sonmoni didn't know about it. But one day, he would find out everything.

Santanu Chaliha's love? In the memory of that love there lay stacks of expensive clothes in the suitcase and expensive ornaments in the bank locker.

Can one enjoy the moonlit night with these memories alone? Can one face the silence? Can one listen to music?

I plucked the grey hair. Neruda, Keats, Hikmat and Ghalib came out of the suitcase onto my table. I listened to music in the silence ...

Secretly, I fell madly in love. It was a stormy night. In the silence of the night, my blood was infused with the warm touch of his lips. His passionate touch excited me. I could not control myself and gave in.

Drying my wet hair, I tried to sketch a picture of that night—orange landscape, the colour of the red sun melting into the river bed.

He asked me to show him that portrait.

My Disease

The orange colour of the sunset loses itself in fearful darkness. The enchanting beauty of the setting sun turns into something eerie. How many people remember the fearful darkness that follows the beautiful orange light of the setting sun? I, too, did not remember. But even if we do not remember, the darkness still follows.

I, too, was engulfed in that darkness.

Many wrong things were said about us. There were obscene words written on the posters of the college wall, on the trees and walls near my house. My family stopped coming over to my house and so did my brothers-in-law.

I was nervous. But he was quiet and unmoved by everything happening around us. Nothing changed for him. He would come over frequently. He would be busy with Sonmoni. If I sat with them, he talked about the paintings of Ganesh Payne, Bikash Bhattacharjee and Picasso. He conversed on various topics—books, poems, cinema, school, college, China, Lenin. The fear in my heart evaporated in his presence.

Whenever he went away, the uncertainty of what lay ahead weigh on me like stones. Nobody said anything about the incident. I understood that my relatives had stopped thinking of themselves for a change and had started thinking about me.

Both of my brothers-in-law had come over and were staying with my parents. I called them over for lunch, but they did not come. They came the day before leaving. Sonmoni was leafing through the pages of a magazine. While I brought out the tea to serve them, I saw him coming towards our house with long strides. I thought that seeing the car parked outside, he would turn back, but he did not.

Handing me a packet of fish wrapped in leaves, he said, 'I found it on my way, so brought it.'

Some of the fish fell onto the floor. My brothers-in-law said goodbye to Sonmoni and took off, food still on their plates.

He stretched out on the sofa. His friendship with Sonmoni kept me amazed at times. He was telling Sonmoni, 'Shall we not eat fish fry?' While picking up the fish from the floor, I realised that my fear had become as light as the leaf.

There was joint protest after that incident, just as I expected. I was called to my parents' place.

The picture of gulinahur flowers that I painted hung on the wall of the drawing room. I sat staring at the picture.

'I have prepared all the papers needed to transfer Santanu's property in Sonmoni's name once he grows up,' said my elder brother-in law.

My elder sister-in-law added, 'A portion of mother's ornaments are for Sonmoni; a seven-stringed necklace …'

I grew impatient.

'No need. I too have a lot,' I retorted.

My other brother-in-law said in a severe tone, 'Even if you do not want, our family's tradition is such that Sonmoni's bride will have to wear that.'

My elder brother-in-law's tone was serious, 'Even if Santanu died, and though you are earning, you are the daughter-in-law of the Chaliha family of Sibsagar. You cannot do anything that will bring a bad reputation to this family. The things that we have heard related to you …'

My other brother-in-law interrupted, 'We saw that day with our own eyes.'

My younger sister-in-law shook her short hair, and grimaced, 'My family also knows, I was ashamed when they asked me.'

My parents, and my brother and his wife sat quietly, in support of what they were saying.

I clarified, 'Aditya is Sonmoni's friend. Sonmoni prefers his company. I do not have any special relation. He is simply my colleague.' My tears followed.

'Santanu has gone. I will be relieved if I see you all happy,' said my elder brother-in-law.

'We always talk about taking Sonmoni to Digboi. But we did not take him thinking you will not be able to part his company,' said my elder sister-in-law.

Both my sisters-in-law said in unison, 'Biju will come from Delhi next week. Ranju will come from Darjeeling.'

My elder brother-in-law rose from the sofa, 'Both of you come, I have a big bungalow now, after my promotion.'

I said resentfully, 'I have to check answer scripts.'

'Then let us take Sonmoni with us,' said my younger brother-in-law, lighting a cigarette. He continued, 'You tell me when you finish your work, I will take you.'

'No need of you to come. One of us will take her,' Ma assured them as she came in with the tea.

While having her tea, my younger sister-in-law took one good look at me, and said, 'Sontara, you've maintained your figure very well. Do you exercise? I have a lot of fat.' She removed her red chiffon sari from her waist—layers of white flesh. I turned away my eyes.

My elder sister-in-law whispered, 'He loves some fat.'

The younger one said, 'Same as the elder brother, after all they are siblings.'

Then she leaned towards me and asked, 'What did Santanu have to say? He was also not a simple one.'

I felt as if my breathing had stopped. I was filled with severe hatred. I rose to leave.

My elder sister-in-law said, 'Don't talk about Santanu. She will feel sad.'

Even without looking back, I knew that my younger sister-in-law was grimacing as she said, 'These are all a show.'

I dashed out of the house. It was only when I was on the street that could take a deep breath.

Sonmoni had gone to Digboi with my brother-in-law. I felt lonely without Sonmoni who used to be constantly by my side. He always kept me on my toes—he would want to eat this or that; want to go here or there. Without my impatient young boy around, my time turned to stone.

One evening, I was sitting in the verandah. A familiar long stride came into my view. It was him. Taking out a paper packet, he placed it on the table and looked around.

'I brought cake. Where is Sonmoni?'

'He is not here. My brother-in-law took him to Digboi.'

'You did not go with Sonmoni?'

I went inside.

While preparing tea, I saw him standing at the kitchen door. I hurriedly carried the tray to the drawing room. After having the tea, he kept looking at me—that intolerable stare. I gazed down and sipped my tea.

His voice was shaking, 'We want each other. We should marry soon. You, I and Sonmoni, we will make a happy family.'

I did not say anything. After some time, he left.

I went to stay in my parents' house during Sonmoni's absence.

After about 15 days, Sonmoni came back from his uncle's place. We also came back to our house.

I was tidying the house; Sonmoni was getting ready to go somewhere. He had put on a pair of blue corduroys, tennis shoes and a shirt with LOVE ME written on it. It was given to him by his elder uncle. The red bicycle was also a gift from his younger uncle.

He had come over that day.

Sonmoni looked at him in a slightly different manner. He was not excited like on other days.

'What Sonmoni? How was your holiday?'

'Fan-tas-tic.'

Hearing the word, I realised that Sonmoni had recently picked up this English accent.

But how?

'I learnt to drive with Ranju dada, went to hunt with Biju dada. I even watched a lot of movies at night.'

'What movies did you see, Sonmoni?'

'This and that.'

Sonmoni's young face revealed some sense of guilt, an attempt to hide something.

Sonmoni changed the topic, 'Ranju dada taught me how to drive. Ranju dada drives very fast. My uncle told me that my father never drove below 100 km per hour. He also told me that the money in my father's name will be transferred to mine when I am 22. Then I shall buy a car. OK Ma?'

For the first time, I heard Sonmoni utter the word "father". I did not like those words—money, car, etc.

'Sonmoni! Will you not show us what Biju dada and your uncles gave you?'

Sonmoni opened the huge suitcase. There were some paperback editions of English fiction. Most of the books had covers of nude females.

He slowly, but firmly said, 'These books are not for you, Sonmoni. You cannot go to Digboi any more.'

Sonmoni was looking at him. His eyes bore some unknown savage anger when he said,

'I have heard about you from my uncles and aunts. I have seen all the posters. That day, Bidyut and all were asking me, "What, today your father did not come to school? Why do you allow him to come? Don't you feel ashamed?"'

'Sonmoni!' I slapped him.

Sonmoni's chest with the words LOVE ME written on it was heaving when he said, 'You marry him and go. I shall go to stay with my uncles and cousins.'

Sonmoni went away riding his new red bicycle. He went out with his head down. I was surrounded by the dark sky which was orange some time back. The beautiful orange of the setting sun was followed by a spell of darkness.

Sonmoni came back at nine in the night. He did not take his dinner. I, too, did not eat.

That night, suddenly I woke up and saw him. It was a moonlit night. The white flowers looked like small pieces of light that had fallen from the moon. Who is that near the flower tree? I saw clearly that it was him. A young girl was standing near him. Who is she? Who is that girl who is as bright as an angel in the moonlit night? Is she the girl named Rupjyoti whom his family had selected for him? Or is she the newly appointed lecturer Bandana who liked to talk with him? Or is she his childhood friend, the lady doctor? Or is she the beautiful student who gave him flowers during Bohag Bihu? Who is she?

In every curve of her body were bunches of flower. Like the bright red hibiscus flowers, her whole body was bright and beautiful in a floral-print sari. He was looking at her raptly. He embraced her slim waist. She surrendered like a shy creeper. Who is she? I was envious. I jumped from the bed and went to the window. Why should he stare at her so raptly? Why should she touch him? His touch is only for me. Who is that by his side? Is she as tall as me? Her face—is it long or round? How does she talk? Is she shrill or gentle? What is the colour of her hair?

Cleopatra understood that Octavia could never snatch away her lover. Did Cleopatra know any magic? What base was there for Cleopatra's pride? Was Cleopatra very beautiful? Do I not possess such beauty? Everybody thinks I am beautiful. False! I was ugly, draped in white clothes. My plain clothes were like the cover over a dead body. So many colours and flowers fill the world, yet my dress is so plain. Her sari had bright red flower printed on it.

I pulled open my plain white dress; it felt as heavy as leather. I took out a red dress, red as a ripe tomato, from my suitcase and wore it. I was covered in red: red sindur on my forehead and parting, the bright red dress, red-stoned ornaments. The red and golden colours made me shine. I gazed at myself in the mirror. With great care, I arranged my hair into a bun and put on a pair of long earrings, earrings which were like pomegranate seeds.

The moonlight fell on me through the open windows. Am I less beautiful than Cleopatra? I wished I had a garland in my bun like the white pieces of the moon. Sonmoni can bring it for me. How many times have I received flowers from Sonmoni?

Sonmoni was not in his bed.

Who was talking to Sonmoni? 'I am selfish in my love. I cannot breathe without you …' To whom was Sonmoni reciting the eternal love-infused lines of Keats. Who was Sonmoni embracing? Who is that bride in the arms of Sonmoni? When did Sonmoni grow up into a man? Is that shy girl with her head lowered, my daughter-in-law? Covering her head, the girl was coming towards me with Sonmoni. They were trying to kneel in front of me. I must escape; otherwise they will read my mind. Have they seen me? Is the new bride shocked to see my red dress and ornaments? Where is my white dress?

The red dress was clinging to my body. The ornaments were like ropes tied to me. I should take them off before Sonmoni and the new bride sees me. The whole place was filled with torn clothes and broken ornaments. Where shall I hide these? The new bride is coming towards me.

I must go to college before Sonmoni and the bride sees me. What if I reveal myself to the new bride? What if Sonmoni realises that I tried to compete with the beauty of the girl beside him; that I tried to be lovesick Cleopatra! I should go soon. What shall I teach? What shall I teach in class today? Shall I teach that wonderful poem of Browning? That healthy, that ugly girl!

Her heart burned in the fire of jealousy, her heart was snatched away by her lover's healthy beloved. She became mad. She wanted to murder the beautiful girl, death will eat her beauty. She was wearing the glass mask of the chemist; the light white smoke in the chemist's laboratory was moving up in curls, like that in a devil's workshop. She was looking on. She was getting excited. Where is the poison that she is going to give? Where is that poison? Is it this soft blue chemical? It would surely be sweet. Can poison be so attractive?

'Which is the poison to poison her, prithee?'

Are the students listening attentively? A few of them were telling her that the poem was not prescribed in their syllabus. It was there. It was in the BA syllabus. What! This is not the BA class? This is the Higher Secondary class. This was not my class? Bandana madam was waiting outside.

'You all forget everything and concentrate on this poem! Such a beautiful poem! Listen to what she told the chemist—"Give her the sufferings of death. Let her die a slow death. Sufferings of death will make her beautiful face … "'

The bell was ringing.

'Let it ring, you listen to this poem by Robert Browning. Syllabus, exam, question, forget all those and listen to the poem:

> Not that I bid you spare her the pain!
> Let death be felt and the proof remain;
> Brand, burn up, bite into its grace—
> He is sure to remember her dying face!'

A few boys went out of the class.

'What happened? You all like my class. Even if it is the last period, you wait up for me. Why are you not willing to listen to the poem today? Listen, what the girl who lost her lover said … "Nor that".'

'Aditya?'

Suddenly, Aditya dragged me out of the class. He took me towards the canteen and started scolding me,

'What is happening to you today? For the last two hours, you have been taking the same class. A few students told us in the common room.

What is happening to you? What are you doing? Why are you wearing so many ornaments? One earring! Every day your hair is tied tightly. What is happening to you, Sontara? Why are you not wearing any shoes or sandals?'

I felt like laughing, seeing the shocked expression on his face. How will he know? He had not kept tabs on how time is changing. Sonmoni! My Sonmoni has grown up. My daughter-in-law … I went on laughing.

'Aditya! You cannot hold me any more. I am going away … very far away …'

'Sontara! Keep quiet, Sontara! Come here, get in the rickshaw. Arrange your chador.'

Aditya sounded desperate. His deep and serious eyes were wet.

I said, laughing hysterically, 'You cannot come near me. On both my two sides are my son and daughter-in-law. You cannot touch me!' I had not laughed in a long time.

Why are there so many people in my house? My parents, my brother, my sister-in-law. . . What were the passers-by looking at? Why were there so many people looking at me? Who was this sweet looking boy running towards me? This is my Sonmoni! The young healthy man of last night! My daughter-in-law! Sonmoni was embracing me. My brothers-in-law, my sisters-in-law and their children were coming in a group to take my Sonmoni away. Biju was showing Sonmoni the paperback editions with the nude females on the cover pages. Why was his uncle trying to give him the money? Wearing the red sporting with LOVE ME written on it, Sonmoni was going towards Biju on his new bicycle. No, Sonmoni cannot go towards them! I will tear up Sonmoni's red sporting. I will drive them away from my house! They have always underestimated me. I will not be afraid any more. He has rightly said, 'Man has created society.' I shall face the whole society. I shall live according to my wish. Love has come into my life. I want to accept it. Am I dead because you have wiped away colour from my body? 'If you prick us, do we not bleed? If you tickle us, do we not laugh? If you poison us, do we not die?'

Being a woman, does it mean I shall not bleed if you prick me? Won't I laugh on being tickled? Will I not die if poisoned? I do not want to harm anybody. I shouted, 'If you …' I embraced him.

Someone gave me an injection. After that it was silence, only darkness.

When I woke up, I found that my limbs were tied to the bed. Sonmoni was moving around me. Once, I saw Sonmoni's arm bludgeoned and stained with blood, almost about to fall. Sonmoni, my son and labour girl … My head was burning. Once I saw Sonmoni in hunting shoes, just like that of Santanu Chaliha, and kicking Mon Bahadur. Mon Bahadur's flower, like the young girl, was being … by Sonmoni. Everybody said Sonmoni looked like his mother, but in reality, he had become like Santanu Chaliha.

I could not recognise Sonmoni standing next to his uncle. Just as I frantically searched for my premature baby after Santanu Chaliha's body was taken away, I tried to find Sonmoni.

The fire inside my head was burning. Many people came to assault me—my parents, brother, brothers-in-law, sisters-in-law, MLA Dharani Sharma. Someone gave me a glass of water; the water smelt of poison. All around me was the sound of knives being sharpened. I tried to chase away the mob.

Again another injection, then silence ... Gradually, I was immersed in darkness.

My Mind

The pale yellow sunlight flickered for a moment on top of the row of devdaru trees, and then disappeared suddenly. The remnants of the sunrays seemed to crawl indecisively over the flowers, like a child who did not want to stop playing with water.

'Madame! Namaste!' The gardener tending the dahlias smiled at me. The aged man cared for the flowers with such devotion. His rough and dark hands helped me plant many flowers. Mrs Pooja Malhotra was coming to see the work of the gardener. Seeing the beautiful woman, the gardener abruptly left the dahlias to tend the chrysanthemums. Sister Mariam kept an eye on the woman. The ward boy Ram Ratan came and took Mrs Malhotra away. Sister Mariam was talking to the boy named Kaushik.

One by one, Maya who always carried a bundle of clothes in the crook of her arm, Mrs Sethna and Mrs Kapoor, were taken inside. I could feel the nip in the air; the last rays of the sun crawling on the flowers had vanished. The gardener was about to leave. Ram Ratan went too, maybe his shift was over.

Sister Mariam approached me, 'Won't you go inside? It is not a moonlit night.'

'No, I won't sit any more,' I said and looked at the flowers being tended by the gardener.

'You love moonlight and flowers, isn't it?' asked the nurse.

How did she know what I am fond of? How much time do you need to spend with someone to know what one likes and dislikes? How long have I been in this mental institution? What happened to me?

'Let us go inside, the dew drops are starting to fall. It will be cold,' said the nurse.

The nurse, the doctor, the gardener, everybody behaved normally with me. Nobody forced me on any issue. I passed my time as I wished. I was not given any injections. I had not taken any medicine for a long time. Then why do I have to stay here?

Sister Mariam was about to leave, maybe someone else would be coming in for the night shift.

'Goodnight, Sontara!'

'Sister! How long have I been here?' I asked.

'It will be one year. You came here last winter,' she replied.

'One year! I have been here for a whole year? Who brought me here? What did I do?' I was shocked.

'Your family members brought you here.'

'What did I do then, Sister?'

'You assaulted an aged man on his head.'

'An aged man?'

'He was a fair, fat, short man with specs. You did not do anything. You simply chased the man away. He was on duty at that time. You were calm again once the man was taken away.'

Sister Mariam rose. Taking out a peacock-blue sari from her bag, she said, 'See, I will wear this sari, John gave it to me. I shall go directly to the movie hall. John will be waiting.' Humming a song as she walked down the long corridor, the girl named

Mariam disappeared. Her song's tune seemed familiar. That old song … Sunday morning … The tune reminded me of sunrays falling on the sea waves.

I had heard the song somewhere. It was cold, like it is now, and I did not have warm clothes on me. That tune was accompanied by so many other melodies: the sound of a hilly river flowing; birds singing and chirping; a soft whistle and a deep male voice. The tune of that song, playing from the small tape-recorder kept on a rock, jumped over the waves of a hilly rivulet and crashed into pieces. The pieces merged with the bird's voice, the soft whistle and the deep male voice. The tape stopped playing a long time ago, but the tune sprung all over—'Sunday morning …'

He went on singing. Sonmoni was playing the guitar. And I? Unknowingly, I too started humming … I was lost in the song.

I have not seen Sonmoni for so long! Where does he stay now? With whom does he live? Why has he not come to see me? With whom will he come? Where is he?

Sonmoni scolded him after coming from Digboi. I slapped my son; his soft cheeks bore the mark of my fingers. The books he tore, the savage anger in his eyes—I remembered everything. But who brought me here? Sister Mariam told me that I was agitated seeing a short, fat, bespectacled man. Who was he? Was it my brother-in-law? Yes, he did look like Santanu Chaliha. Maybe I mistook him for Santanu Chaliha. It meant that my mental equilibrium was unbalanced—my past, my present, everything was a blur in my head.

Dr Joseph would come as usual—grey-haired, old Dr Joseph would take a look at me once in a day, just as he looked at the others. I will ask him everything about me. I don't feel like putting on the white hospital gown. Don't I have any clothes in my suitcase? Yes, this is a new sari, still crisp. Who purchased this sari? Where is my favourite white sari with small white flowers? In my suitcase, there lies a canvas, paint and design that I never used. Who gave me those? These new books still smell so good! Who has got so much time to read them?

I looked clean in my crisp white sari, the corner of my eyes were slightly dark, my forehead seemed larger and the new growth of hair made it difficult for me to comb neatly. Maybe my hair did start falling, but it was growing back again. When people suffer from some serious disease, the hair starts to fall. I must ask Dr Joseph if I have to stay here like this forever. If I am suffering from some disease, why am I not treated with medicine and injections?

Dr Joseph brought a white rose for me. With blue eyes and creased skin, he looked like Somerset Maugham.

'How are you, Sontara?'

'Fine.'

Dr Joseph checked my pulse. Today, I must ask.

I began, 'Doctor! Will you spare some time for me?'

'Certainly!' Dr Joseph guided me outside.

In the soft rays of the winter sunlight, the flowers looked radiant.

The gardener greeted me and the doctor—the familiar address.

The doctor started talking to me, 'See, Sontara! The gardener's duty is from 10 am to 3 pm, but he stays from 6 am till the evening. Nowhere will you find such beautiful flowers. There lies the love of the gardener in these flowers.'

A sister was coming towards us. She was probably looking for Dr Joseph. I must ask soon.

'What is wrong with me, Doctor? My hair, my dark eyes? Why am I not given any medicine? Why am I kept here?'

Dr Joseph smiled, 'So many questions! Ask one by one. Nothing is wrong with you. A simple disease has affected your mind. Now you are on the path of recovery.'

But I insisted, 'What is wrong with me?'

Asking Ram Ratan to bring him something, he continued,

'A simple disease has affected you. It is a disease of the mind where thoughts, feelings and actions lose their balance.'

Taking a seat near me, he picked up a stone. 'Sontara! Can you break this?'

How could I break a stone? Why was Dr Joseph joking and not answering my questions?

Ram Ratan gave an ash-coloured stone to the doctor.

'What is this, Sontara?'

'A piece of stone. But Doctor ...'

'Can you break this piece of stone?'

The doctor gave me the piece of stone. It was cracked. A chip came off at my touch.

'I have never seen such stone.'

'This piece of stone is schist; it comes off in bits and pieces. Your mind has become like this stone,' said the doctor.

'My mind cracked?'

'It is not possible to join the broken pieces of the stone.'

But the doctor tried to give me hope, 'Man's mind can be patched!'

'I do not want to stay here,' my tears fell in gushes.

'I know what you want. You told me everything,' Dr Joseph smiled.

'What did I tell you, Doctor?'

'If I cannot find out what is in your heart, then what is the use of my life-long studies?' he smiled.

What did Dr Joseph find out about my heart?

I was afraid to look at the doctor's blue eyes.

'Doctor, you look like Somerset Maugham,' I said, trying to change the subject.

Dr Joseph smiled like a little boy. Maugham's mother had come to me. She recovered and had just gone back. Surely now she must have made Rosalind her daughter-in-law.

The doctor rose, 'You too will go from here—you, Aditya and Sonmoni. Your family will be very happy. Happy families are very rare in this perverted society.'

'Aditya!' I must have shouted.

'Why are you shouting? Don't get excited,' Dr Joseph's face hardened.

'But I love Sonmoni very much, doctor,' I said, trying to stay calm.

'Sonmoni too loves you. You must recover to love him. Does any child want his mother to be mad?' asked the doctor.

Then I really have become a mad mother? Suddenly, my head was spinning. The nurse called Dr Joseph. He went away, without even looking back at me once. For him, I was just a patient, just another patient. I no longer had his attention; it was lost among his various other patients. I was annoyed with the doctor.

The next morning, the doctor took me to meet Pooja Malhotra. We stopped near Mrs Malhotra's window; she was combing her long hair, looking at the mirror. He said,

'This woman, too, is suffering from the mind's disease, just like you. Your mind cracked a little, her mind cracked into many pieces. Her family members hid her disease. People try to cover up the diseases of the mind. They are afraid of what others would say. They are reluctant to face the society. They think that it is something to be ashamed of.'

Mrs Malhotra was tying her hair and opening it; she kept doing the same thing over and over again.

'Do you know, Sontara? This beautiful woman is a murderess; she killed her own child,' the doctor said, still looking at her.

'Her own child?' I was shocked.

Mrs Malhotra turned around hearing my voice.

'Let us go, Sontara. The woman becomes fearful when agitated. She was brought very late to us. Her disease had become quite old and chronic. Do you know, Sontara? When the first symptoms appeared, she was confined to a room by her family members. Her husband brought other women to the house. Now the husband has remarried. The man sends a heavy amount of money for her treatment and considers himself free of any bindings towards her. Oh God! Help this sad soul!'

'What was her fault?' I asked, staring in disbelief.

'Her disease.

When Mrs Malhotra was brought to us for the first time, she used to laugh a lot and then, tears would flow down her eyes. She smiled because she killed the child of the man who hated her; cried because she killed her own flesh and blood. It was the result of a very old disease!' said the doctor.

I must have pressed Dr Joseph's hand, 'Doctor! Things like this happen, people do become like this?'

Dr Joseph looked at me, his blue eyes fixed on me. So cool and tough his voice was. 'Do you not love your child?'

I must have become hysterical while replying, 'Why are you asking me this? Sonmoni is my life, not only my child. For the sake of Sonmoni only, I have denied him, my love …'

The doctor's voice was unaffected, 'You have misunderstood me. You are wrong. To be a normal mother, to give love to your child, you must be happy. A mother with a cracked mind cannot offer love to her child; she kills her child, just like Mrs Malhotra did.'

'But Sonmoni went away on the red bicycle. He was wearing the red vest with the words LOVE ME written on it. Sonmoni assaulted him. I have not seen Sonmoni after that. My son hates me. He has become a part of Santanu Chaliha's family. Sonmoni asked me to marry him and then leave the house. He does not want me any more. They have taken him away.'

The doctor continued, 'These are your wrong notions; misconceptions of a diseased mind. Don't be weak, Sontara. Your son has come many times to meet you. You either run away when he comes or turn aggressive. Once he brought you flowers on your birthday, but you ran away. Sonmoni cried, striking his head on the wall. You smiled seeing his bleeding forehead.'

'Lies ...' I ran away from the doctor.

Lying down on the bed, I wept. Dr Joseph said, 'Weep, weep my child!'

The lines I drew on the canvas which was lying in my suitcase were that of the room in Sibsagar—Sonmoni the premature baby lying amidst cotton wool. The quietness after the sindur was rubbed off from my forehead was broken by the cries of Sonmoni. Gradually, the colours and lines brought me closer to Sonmoni. I was drenched in the memories of Sonmoni—putting Sonmoni to sleep in my arms; the soft touch of baby Sonmoni; the smile he brought to my face while trying to turn on his back all by himself; Sonmoni smiling with his two teeth; Sonmoni learning to utter a few words; Sonmoni pressing my forehead till his little fingers hurt when I suffered from migraine.

Where was he now? The school teachers said they had a lot of expectation from Sonmoni. Sonmoni asked me to write something in English. Sometimes, he complained of a pain in the area where he was hit by a ball while playing cricket. A good doctor has to be consulted.

Sonmoni! I slapped you. There was the mark of my four fingers on his cheeks. In this society, where murders are committed on the basis of differences of religious faith and where people's lives are played with in order to fulfill one's selfish interest, Sonmoni was so inexperienced and naive.

I sketched upon Sonmoni's little rose-coloured lips an indistinct smile—the mysterious and wonderful smile.

My Life

In the morning, Ram Ratan handed me a piece of paper. Somebody from Assam was coming over to meet me that afternoon.

Who could it be? Who had so much time? If he comes … Sister Mariam told that a tall man often came visiting with a boy of 10–11 years. The doctor did not permit me to meet anyone. A tall man and a boy of about 10 or 12 … Was it Sonmoni and he? But Sonmoni asked him not to come to our house. Sonmoni started hating him. The slips of money orders sent to me lay on my table. They had the signatures of my father, brother and brothers-in-law. Were they coming? The tall man could be my brother.

I waited with bated breath for the afternoon. I was excited. I washed my hair. After lunch, I took off my loose gown and wore a neat pair of *mekhela-chador*. After what felt like forever, I applied kohl on my eyes and coloured my lips, matching it with the coloured border of my chador. There was an unopened perfume bottle in the corner of my suitcase; I immersed myself in the floral scent. I forgot everything else—my disease, my distress. I simply wanted to be like a flower—beautiful and fragrant.

From far, I saw him standing in the visiting room—his head lowered. The hair covered half of his face. Ram Ratan gave me a piece of paper with his name written on it. Clasping the paper in my hand, I looked at the sky; the light clouds looked like cotton against the blue backdrop. The sun was about to set. The winter evening's sunrays seemed to stop amidst the rows of devdaru trees. I walked through the beautiful garden thriving under the gardener's care. A cold breeze blew. I had no warm clothes on me. Will he ask: 'Why have you not put on warm clothes? You will feel cold'?

A mild fragrance erupted as I walked by. Do flowers smell like this? Was it the scent of the devdaru trees? Was it the scent of the blue sky or the soft sunrays? Was it the scent of the wind? On reaching near him, I remembered that I sprayed the perfume on abundantly at noon. It was me wearing the scent and I had been searching all around for its source. Smiling to myself, I stopped near him. So thin he had become, the under-eyes were dark and his clothes hung loose on him.

My first words to him were, 'Have you suffered from any disease?'

'Why do you ask, Sontara?'

'You look unwell.'

He simply laughed—a pale laugh.

'Your health was also bad, Sontara. You had become frail and your hair was beginning to fall. But now you've recovered a lot.'

'I have recovered fully now,' I said, reassuringly.

He stared at my face—that intolerable gaze that pierced into my heart.

'Then my health too will improve, Sontara.'

'Do you know about my Sonmoni?'

He was still looking at me. Maybe he lost track of Sonmoni. Sonmoni told him that day …

'Sonmoni stays with me, Sontara.'

'What?' I was shocked.

The wind blew many devdaru leaves around.

He continued, 'After you were brought here by your brother and brothers-in-law, Sonmoni went to stay with your family. I saw him a couple of times while he was on his way to school. He always kept his head lowered. I too did not call him. One night, he threw his plate of rice at his aunt and came to me. He cried the whole night with his head on my chest.'

Sonmoni threw his plate of rice at his aunt? Did his aunt, who disliked cooking, say something to Sonmoni? He hates it when someone says anything to him while he is eating.

He said, 'Sonmoni's uncle, grandparents, aunt, all came to take him away from my place. He was supposed to be admitted in a school in Darjeeling. All the arrangements were made. But nobody could take him away from me. Once, your brothers-in-law, fed up of convincing him to go, angrily called him a headache. Sonmoni shivered with anger.'

His eyes seemed moist, 'I am greatly worried for Sonmoni. He keeps scolding everybody: "Why did you tell me to scold my mother? It is because of me that my mother has become like this." Sonmoni is suffering from severe self-repentance.'

His face turned red with anger, 'Sontara, your brother is constructing a new house. One of your brothers-in-law is going to America.' He suddenly became excited, 'This society can only break one's life, never mend one's.'

I know this angry face. It calms my heart.

'Why did you not bring Sonmoni today?'

'The doctor has not given permission yet. Whenever you see him, you act strange. Once, seeing Sonmoni, you ran as if you had seen a ghost. He struck his head on the wall.'

'Does Sonmoni not give you any trouble? He has many likes and dislikes,' my eyes filled with tears.

He smiled, recalling, 'He has read many books. His poems have a distressing note. He also knows to cook. One day we cooked chicken. It was very tasty. But when we were about to cook the rice, we found out there was no rice. So, we had bread instead—English style.'

His smile was like that of a small boy; eyes closed and head raised.

'Sonmoni is with you, but your family, your society …'

'Do you know that Sonmoni is like a shield for me, Sontara?'

'Battle shield?'

'My mother, sister-in-law, sisters are all frantic about getting me married.'

'Yes,' I was unable to speak; as if something was choking me.

'Whenever the news of Sonmoni living with me reaches the ears of my prospective brides, immediately the power of my family is vanquished.'

'I shall join my duties next month. Nothing is wrong with me. I am totally normal.'

'Certainly, Sontara!'

'I want to be a happy mother to Sonmoni. You have looked after Sonmoni with so much love. I know not how to thank you. Next month I shall bring Sonmoni. After all you have your responsibility towards the society.'

'Sontara! Do you not have any responsibility towards me? For the last one year, I am neither able to eat nor sleep. After bringing you here, I have lost my peace of mind. How long will you live in fear? How long will you make me suffer? I am a man of flesh and blood, Sontara!'

I pressed his hand. I went on holding the sweaty hand.

The visiting hour was coming to an end. I did not let go off him. Sister Dorothy reminded me of the rules and regulations in a harsh tone. I was angry at her. The woman was like a machine.

I could neither eat nor sleep that night. I stuck my head between my knees and went on sitting. Sister Dorothy's curtness,

Sonmoni's sadness, his darkening face—I felt my head grow heavy with a burden. Tears soaked my thighs through my silk *mekhela.*

Sister Dorothy, who was on her night shift, silently handed me the night dress and a blue tablet—a sleeping pill. Changing into the night dress, I kept sitting like before; the blue tablet held tightly in my palm. Sister Dorothy tucked in my mosquito net. The moonlight entering through the windows made her white hair look even fairer.

She kept her hand on my head and sang softly, 'The lord is my shepherd, I shall not wait ...' It could have been Psalm 23. Towards the end, Sister Dorothy's voice became deeper and deeper like the growing night, 'Surely goodness and mercy shall follow me all the days of my life; And I shall dwell in the house of the Lord forever.'

Sister Dorothy laid the blanket on me and left. In the moonlight, she looked like a lively young girl. What kept Sister Dorothy so lively; she who had no one but only two cats and a dog in this big world?

Was it faith that kept her going? I, too, closed my eyes and tried to sing from the Bible's Psalm 23: 'Surely goodness and mercy ...' It, indeed, was faith that kept Sister Dorothy alive. I was sleepy; the tablet fell off from my hand onto the floor. The next day, the sweeper swept away the tablet; its soft blue colour shone in the heap of garbage.

The whole day I went on playing with the smile on Sonmoni's lips. Once I made his lips darker, once I lightened it, once I made the smile more prominent.

He came in the afternoon. Sister Mariam tied my hair neatly in a bun and stuck a white rose in it. I did not stop her. While putting on the white dress, I had a strong desire to turn my clothes red; red like the flowers in the garden. The blue sky, the deep green of the devdaru trees, the yellow of the chrysanthemums, the red of the dahlias, the rosy hue of the roses, the soft green of the grasses—I longed for all the colours.

Unable to control my desire for these shades, I coloured my lips pink—the deep pink of a half-blooming flower. Looking at my pink lips in the mirror, I felt a wave rising in my body. As if somewhere there was lightning, there was thunder; it rained on the parched earth.

Without any introduction, I told him, 'Yesterday you told me about my responsibility towards you. That responsibility for me is a blessing. But ...' I stopped.

'But what, Sontara?'

'I am a widow, I have a child, I am getting old, I suffer from a serious disease. Mrs Malhotra was kept imprisoned by her family members. Her husband ...' I wanted to tell him the story of Mrs Malhotra that Dr Joseph told me.

'Tell me about yourself! What need is there to know about who did what to Mrs Malhotra?'

'Your parents, your friends, the society ...'

'In this social system where it is difficult for a man to live, how can one satisfy everyone?'

That sharp intolerable, unmoving look, 'I need you, Sontara, to live.'

'What do I have to offer? I know once I was beautiful. People told that I looked like a Goddess.'

'See, Sontara! You are still beautiful. You have traversed life's sadness and suffering. There is more to you than meets the eye. But I am not trying to make you mine for your beauty alone.'

'Then?'

'When I developed a relationship with you, my family members said that you have fooled me with your beauty. My sisters tried desperately to find a beautiful girl for me.' He smiled like a small boy.

'You saw the girl named Rupjyoti.'

'Yes, she was enchantingly beautiful.'

'My parents thought I was trying to seek beauty in my partner. They thought that my need was confined to physical beauty only, like all other men. One cannot live with the flesh for long. The addiction to flesh is temporary. I need a partner to live with; a beautiful mind is what I need.'

'Do you really think I can be your partner? Even now, after all I have been through? With this mind and body struck by the storm?'

He simply smiled a little.

I tried to check my flowing tears, but failed, 'If I would have met you before meeting Santanu Chaliha, I would have had no complaints.'

'Then I would have not liked you, because then like Rupjyoti the beautiful girl, you would simply be a person of flesh and blood. Now, you are a complete woman. Your distress, your disease, your motherhood, your faith have made you a complete woman, Sontara.'

We went across the flowers and sat under the row of devdaru trees. He caught hold of my hand. My whole body was pervaded by a shower, a sky with lightning.

'Dr Joseph told me that my mind has become like a schist.'

'That cracking stone is no more there in your heart, Sontara.'

'This is possible because of you, Aditya.' Suddenly, addressing him by his first name, I felt embarrassed. I forgot the whole world around me.

'No, Sontara! You, all by yourself is complete. I and Sonmoni are only an extension of your personality.'

He pointed at the line of mountains leaning upon the sky.

'Those mountains have hard rocks. If there were no stones, the mountains would not have been so proud of its height. Like the trees on the mountains, Sonmoni and I will live on the basis of the faith in your heart.'

He took my hand to his lips; a fully grown pair of lips crawled on my fingers for some time.

'Sontara! Your long and delicate fingers are beautiful, like the champa flower. No man would like to give them away. But do you know why I like your fingers? Your fingers know how to speak; they are a medium of self expression. These fingers know to talk about life.

I will come tomorrow with Sonmoni. Dr Joseph told me that you may be released in a couple of days.'

He kissed my fingers and I was again soaked in that shower. My blood cried with the lightning sky, my ears seemed deaf from the thundering.

I sketched a picture that day when my blood was filled with that lightning—a string of mountains in close view, trees full of flowers in those mountains, and a portion of the earth falling down the slopes and revealing the stones that lay beneath. I slept with my hands covered with colours. Sister Dorothy woke me for dinner,

'My child!' She looked at my drawing for a long time.

I woke up with the first rays of the morning sun. Sonmoni was coming to see me. I went on reciting: 'Sonmoni! My Sonmoni! Sonmoni!' My mind shivered like the first time I saw Sonmoni—happiness, fear, a strange feeling. As if I was pregnant again; I was going to be a mother.

How long I have not heard the word "Ma". I brought sweets and fruits for Sonmoni. He loves to eat. Ram Ratan brought them for me. I felt a strong desire to cook something for Sonmoni and him. He said that he could not eat or sleep from the time I came here. Sonmoni may not have eaten properly for a long time.

I took my bath, combed my hair, arranged the fruits and sweets, decorated the flowers given by the gardener on my bedside table, stuck the incense sticks on the wall. And all that while, I felt as if my body was heavy with the blessing of motherhood. Thinking of my unborn child, I was stitching dresses secretly, knitting small sweaters, secretly looking at the tiny clothes at night and smiling to myself.

I saw Sonmoni and him coming. Sonmoni was wearing a readymade coffee-coloured sweater.

Aditya may have purchased it for him. They came up the stairs. Sonmoni had grown very tall. Everybody said that he looked like me. He came forward and embraced me, 'Ma!'

He looked at the picture that I had drawn of the baby Sonmoni with a smile on his lips. He said, 'Ma! You have not named the picture?'

I took the black paint and wrote at the bottom of the painting a few words from a poem: 'Be near me when the light is low …'

Sonmoni laughed, 'What can this baby of skin and bones give to others? He will break at the mere touch, like the yolk of an egg. What baby monkey have you drawn?

Is this me? Oh no!' Sonmoni looked at himself in the mirror.

This time Sonmoni looked at the picture of the mountain, and said, 'It is very beautiful. It really is, Ma! The mountains look so real! The rain seems to have stopped just some time back. The drops of water are still sparkling on those trees.'

Sonmoni went to him with a jump, 'We shall hold an exhibition of Ma's paintings. Just you wait and see what craze it will create! Everyone will be asking: "Who is this young artist?" There will be headlines in the newspapers, Ma's photo …'

Sonmoni sprang and came towards me. He was again looking at the picture, 'Ma! In this painting, the earth is falling down the slopes, revealing the stones. There are so many flowers and so much greenery in the midst of this rough earth. Look how beautiful it looks!'

Sonmoni broke a pomegranate which was kept on a plate nearby, 'If there are no stones, there won't be any mountain, any trees, any flowers, any greenery.'

He gave a title to the picture—The Proud Hills: The pride of the mountain.

The pomegranate fell from his unsteady hands while trying to break it and the bright red seeds of the fruit fell onto the floor. Guilty, Sonmoni looked at me once, and then at him.

The table, the floor, the room, the sky, the air, the whole world seemed to be filled with those pomegranate seeds—sweet, crystal-clear, and red like rubies.

Doiboki's Day

'Take it, babu, take it. Give me ₹20 and take it. How long can I keep sitting over just one fish?'

Tying up the roe-filled kurhi fish with the tender bamboo strips, Doiboki wound up her makeshift shop with swift hands.

She gave a shout towards Monu and the others sitting at the other end of the market, 'Hie, Monu.'

There was no reply. They must have already left. It had become dark now, and she was the only one left. But how could she have given away such fine fish for nothing?

The traders, till recently, had been paying the correct price. But suddenly, they had become stingy, and for some time now, when it came to paying up, were behaving as if they were parting with their own flesh. They had to fork out a whole lot of money to someone, or something like that, she had heard.

Doiboki stuffed a *tamul* into her mouth, 'These good-for-nothing phlegm-eaters, *mekhela*-wearers; they want the fish for free! Bloody cursed race, doomed to be eaten by vultures.' After loudly mouthing the abuses, she felt a little better and settled down.

Here and there, small lamps and candles had started glowing. Next to her, Roghubir stuck two candles on top of his onions and potatoes heaped into pointed piles.

Looking towards the candles, Roghubir joined his hands in prayer, then looked at Doiboki, 'What happened, Doiboki Bai? Aren't you going home today?'

Slapping her thigh, Doiboki snapped back, 'What should I do? Keep looking at your beautiful face instead?'

Joduram was neatly arranging his greens and vegetables, and scattering water on them. It was time for his buyers, the babus from the city, to come. Gonesh, who usually sat between Roghubir and Joduram with his makeshift shop of spices, did not come today; Joduram spread out his shop wider, arranging his limes and lemons according to their colour and shape. Joduram's work, arranging the piles of green vegetables the whole day, looked like child's play to Doiboki.

Just about to say something mocking, she asked instead, 'What happened to Gonesh today, ha?'

Joduram fixed the pile of ribbed-gourds and spoke in a whisper, 'How could he come? After they blew up the bridge with a bomb and killed the military men, it has become impossible for anyone to stay in Gonesh's village. The whole village is being trampled under the military.'

Even Doiboki had heard of the incidents. A shudder ran through her body suddenly.

The darkness was getting thicker. A feeling of unease began to grow inside Doiboki's chest. If only she had given the basket of fish to the trader, she would have had dinner by now and lying on her mat. Monu and the others had also suggested so; it was she who had dug in her heels for a few rupees more.

Luckily, she had not made a loss today; even after buying rations, she would still have some money left in her hands. She had to save just a little more and then she would break into her savings. If she could get her old mother-in-law's cataract removed at the hospital in town, she would be free from a big worry.

Seeing her getting late today, the old woman must be groping about at home, trying to get dinner ready. Since her daughter had grown a little older, she was able to help her grandmother out with chores around the house. The old woman enjoyed eating a boiled potato mashed with salt and oil along with her rice. Doiboki bought half-a-kilo of potatoes. Anyway, how often did she buy potatoes? She just happened to get lucky today. She bought two kilos of rice as well. There should be three–four kilos at home already. The boy had probably got some fish also.

Carrying her bundle of rice and potatoes, Doiboki left the market. Taking out the money from inside the tucked-in knot of her *mekhela*, she thrust it inside her blouse. Then she started walking fast, taking long strides. The old lady must be worrying, asking the children again and again, 'Has your mother come or not? God only knows where she has gone to die—that woman from a cholera-ridden race.'

The children troubled their old grandmother quite a bit too. Thinking about her, Doiboki's mind started getting anxious and restless, much like a bunch of kawoi fish that had been emptied onto the ground from a *khaloi*, and was thrashing around.

The streetlights had been on for a long while now. The shops were all ablaze with lights. Coming from the market, lit dimly with the flickering light of lamps, into this glare of lights, Doiboki now felt naked and exposed.

The last two buttons on her blouse were missing and the *mekhela* she had tied on without a petticoat underneath barely covered her calves. The narrow chador seemed to expose her buttonless blouse again and again as she moved.

Doiboki felt that everyone on the road was leering at her; someone was even whistling at her now. She shifted the basket she was holding pressed under her armpits onto her head, along with the bundle of rice and potatoes. Hiding in the darkness under the basket, head bent, she started walking faster, her *mekhela* making a loud flapping noise as she went.

Doiboki stepped onto the unpaved road to the village, which lay towards the southern corner of the city, on the banks of a river. There were fewer people and lights now. The rice fields on both sides of the road were filled to the brim with wet darkness; like small darikana fish moving in clusters, bunches of fireflies glimmered here and there. Somewhere, a pack of jackals started howling. A young rickshawallah crossed her, singing as he clanged along noisily, cycling the empty rickshaw towards town.

Doiboki glanced up at the sky; like a river all swollen up with rains during peak monsoon, it was overflowing with darkness. Not a pinpoint of light anywhere. It was getting unbearably hot and sultry. Stopping, she pulled open the blouse from her body; soaked with sweat, it tore with a ripping noise. Throwing the blouse into the basket, she pulled up her *mekhela* and tied it over her breasts. The cold wind cooled her body down. Now she tucked the money, which she had put inside her blouse, into the knot of her *mekhela*.

Normally, no cars or vehicles plied on this road at night. Just a little further down was the *naamghar*. Doiboki had seen the *naamghar* from the days when she was a child and ran around naked.

The *naamghar* was in the middle of a compound that was quite large, with two vast ponds, Ganga and Jamuna, in the front.

Winter or summer, the water in the ponds never dried up. People came from far away to take water from them in bottles to place near their altars. Bang in the middle of the compound was a huge banyan tree. The shade from the banyan tree fell on Ganga-Jamuna, giving them a green tint.

In the green waters of the pond lived two huge moss-covered turtles, Doiboki and Jashoda. If anyone threw a handful of anything, and called out, 'Doiboki, Jashoda, come,' the turtles would immediately appear near the platform on the pond.

She had only heard of them, never seen them. How would she? The dark-as-plum people who went about carrying the smell of fish on them were forbidden to enter the *naamghar*. Did her mother name her after the turtle whose name she had heard every day? When she was young, her friends used to make fun of her, calling her "big pond turtle".

Right next to the sharp bend in the river—just beyond the *naamghar*—was the bridge that led to the village, with its nets billowing and making waves in the wind, and reeking of fish. When they were kids, Doiboki and her friends would come to the *naamghar* at least once in the day; the people would sometimes offer the bunch of kids scampering around, a banana leaf with the prasad of sprouts. But it wasn't just the prasad that lured them here, they were curious. What lay inside the big building, surrounded by trees and ponds, to which every passerby bowed his head in veneration?

Doiboki quickened her pace. Once she crossed the *naamghar* and set foot on the bridge, Doiboki didn't have to worry. There would be her village resounding with its quarrels, the roars of its drunkards, cries of the children and the curses of the women whose husbands had showered blows on their backs.

Across the dark sky flashed a creeper of lightning. In the light that lasted for just a second, she saw a black-and-yellow striped snake slowly crossing the road. The darkness was suddenly dispersed by three loaded military vehicles. Doiboki stepped onto one side of the road. She saw clearly the back wheels of the middle truck crush the snake under it. The thunder boomed noisily, lightning flashed again and again. Seeing the snake that had been flattened, in the flash of lightning, she felt a sharp stab inside her, as if she had been stung by a singi fish.

The woman, a stranger to any kind of fear, started shivering with a strange terror. If her man was here today, would she have had to work like this, far into the night? Remembering the sturdy man who had passed away after a week of fever and diarrhea, two hot rivers of tears flowed down her cheeks, like water slipping down the slippery surface of a magur fish.

The *naamghar*'s compound was vast. On one side was the *naamghar*, on the other sides were huge fields. Passing this place, even in broad daylight, a faint-hearted person would find his heart pounding. Usually by the time Doiboki and her friends neared the *naamghar*, the ladies would be singing their *naam* in the open area outside it. Women were not allowed to set foot in the *naamghar*; they kneeled in prayer on the steps itself.

In the summer, Doiboki and her friends often took a break under the banyan tree, stretching out there for a short while. Sometimes, one of the ladies after finishing prayers and crossing from that side would hand them a banana leaf filled with sprouts. Or even call out and inquire about the fish, 'Doiboki, my daughter and son-in-law have come. So, give us some good fish.' As Doiboki and the others crossed the bridge, these dark women glistened like ripe blackberries in the rays of the setting sun.

Now, as she stepped onto the threshold of the *naamghar*, even the lights flickering here and there from the lamps of the small huts in the distance died down; all around silent darkness. Doiboki took out a *paan-tamul* and put it into her mouth.

She was never out this late before. The traders had also been giving her the money. It was not exactly their fault either. But the measly amount they were handing out for those fish, so fresh they were still thrashing about, and filled with roe too, her head had heated up. Spitting out some abuses in her mind, and about to spit out the juice of her chewed betel nut, Doiboki stopped in her tracks.

In the field opposite the *naamghar*, some sharp beams of light were bobbing up and down, like kandhuli fish flopping around in shallow waters. She sank to the ground, on the small bamboo bridge leading to the *naamghar*.

The thunder and lightning grew fiercer. Looking towards the *naamghar*, she folded her hands in prayer, 'Lord, what have I got myself into today?' She kept sitting there on the bridge.

In the flash of lightning, Doiboki saw clearly the troop of military men wading in the water as a single bodily form, like villagers entrapping fish with their equipment. In their midst, a great borali fish seemed to be thrashing about. Doiboki heard some sounds, as if someone was being stabbed, tortured, silenced. She started shivering violently. The beams of lights started jumping around wildly like kandhuli fish, again.

The body of the military troop now broke up. Doiboki placed her hands on the gate of the *naamghar*. They were coming; in the darkness, the military guys were coming onto the road. About to open the gate, she shuddered suddenly. What was she thinking of doing? Was she really going to go inside the Lord's *naamghar*?

The bamboo fence in front of her seemed like a stone wall. It seemed, often at night, a golden boat floated up on the Ganga-Jamuna. Whoever saw the boat vomited blood and died. If anything were to happen to her, the blind old woman and her two children … she pushed open the gate and stepped in. Almost running, she went towards the banyan tree and sat down under it.

The military men were now on the road. A bright flash of light licked her.

Immediately, a harsh, hard voice floated down, 'Kaun hai?'

Doiboki crawled into the hollow of the banyan tree. The stomping of boots … Almost together, the trucks roared to life. Briefly lighting up the whole place so it seemed like daytime, the vehicles went away towards the town.

There was an anthill inside the hollow. Her presence disturbed the anthill, and a few ants started crawling out and climbing up her body. They started biting her. She couldn't see them but knew they were black ants. The smell of the nest and eggs filled her nose. She came out of the hollow.

In the flashes of lightning, the water of the ponds glistened now and again. Doiboki threw away the chador from her body; sweating in the boiling heat, she felt like a fish being roasted on coals. Her throat was drying up with thirst. If she didn't get a drop of water soon, her chest would burst. Could she drink a drop of water from Ganga-Jamuna? Slowly, she crept nearer towards the ponds.

Doiboki heard a noise in the water—a clear rustling noise from the bank of the Jamuna, then the noise in the water disappeared. Her heart started palpitating. Once, Podu's brother, it seems, while returning to the village at night and hearing the two turtles, Doiboki and Jashoda, splashing about, had come inside the *naamghar* to get a look at them. A moonlit night, Doiboki-Jashoda came up to the bridge as soon as he called out. As he was throwing a handful of the fried gram that he had been carrying and that had got soggy on the way, towards them, the one coiled around Lord Shiva's neck struck him, turning him blue.

The rustling sound had disappeared into the banyan's hollow. What had this one gone searching for there, where she had left behind her smell of fish mixed with the smell of the black ants' nest?

The people had apparently been too scared to even touch Podu's brother's body. What then had happened to it? She had never got around to asking anybody. Had the vultures and crows fed on that decaying corpse?

She felt her own body, all soaked and sticky with perspiration. She wiped her face with her palm, reeking strongly of the roe-filled kurhi fish. Carrying this stench, how could she … She licked her parched and hardened lips. She couldn't carry on; she needed a drop of water. Going down on to the bridge on Ganga-Jamuna, she stooped to scoop out a handful of water, but couldn't, and stopped. With these hands that were still slimy with the stench of fish, she couldn't …

Doiboki sat down on the bridge, her feet touching the cold water around the bamboo platform. Her hands suddenly sprang out, like sang fish that had jumped free of a fishing rod, and fallen into the water. She brought up a palmful, then gulped down several handfuls, even threw some over her head, 'Lord, forgive me if I have sinned.'

She stood up, with the intention of coming up from the bridge. Her feet formed two thin rippling lines on the water. Not a sound anywhere. The thunder had stopped; the sky was pitch black, like the colour of her own body. The trees and leaves were all still. Then suddenly, there was a splashing sound in the water. She stood still, listening to the sound. This was not the familiar sound of a fish flapping its fins in water. A sudden chill ran through her veins.

Who had told her? Where had she heard? Sometimes at midnight, a golden boat floated up in the waters of Ganga-

Jamuna. The two big moss-covered turtles stood like guardians on either side of the boat. People said that the way her strong and sturdy husband had died, from just two days of fever and diarrhea, was mysterious. The fields in front of the *naamghar* had been inundated with kawoi fish. On that moonless night, lightly drenched in a drizzle, that rash man, not heeding anyone's warning, had gone out of the house. When he returned in the morning, he had a *khaloi* full of fresh, red kawoi fish—each the size of a palm. The man had shat blood non-stop after that. People had started talking in whispers: 'The man had seen the golden boat.' Otherwise how a man who was absolutely hale and hearty be reduced to this state overnight?

Seeing the clots of blood in the courtyard, her mother-in-law had beaten her chest, and cried, 'Consumed by greed! A moonless night, and on top of that it was the day his father had died. Oh, why did he go to catch fish in that haunted field? So what if it had been full of kawoi fish? Greed! Sheer greed!' After that the mother-in-law hurled abuses at her. Doiboki could hear clearly, even in that silence, her voice distorted by grief and anger, 'Greed! Sheer greed!'

And now, she had been consumed by greed, too. The notes tucked into her *mekhela* were burning like live coals, stinging like nettles.

The noise in the water was getting louder, drops of water splashed onto her feet. Her eyes had grown accustomed to the dark by now, and she clearly saw a huge turtle had come and was waiting near the bridge. Like a kawoi fish jumping free of a fishing line, Doiboki sprang on to the ground. Trembling, she kneeled down, her eyes on the pond. The turtle continued to wait in the ankle-deep waters of the bridge. Tears were rolling down from Doiboki's eyes, she was afraid to look towards the pond.

Anytime now, there would float up near the bridge a golden boat, a golden boat floating around all by itself, a boat possessed by an evil spirit that whoever saw, vomited blood and died. Yet again that splashing noise in the water. Guarding the golden boat would be two huge moss-covered turtles.

She ran for her life, from the banks of the pond towards the *naamghar*, not looking back even once. She halted in front of the door. This was where all the ladies sang their prayers from—the ladies who were as perfectly beautiful as the puthi fish, with skin as fair and smooth as that of pabho fish; the women who wore clothes that shone like the scales of a mirika fish. Hadn't Doiboki seen it since she was a child?

Doiboki sat down there, her head buried between her knees. The noise in the water had disappeared; telling herself she wouldn't look, no, she wouldn't, she glanced towards the inside of the *naamghar*; a flock of fireflies were flickering in the dark. She bowed towards the *naamghar* once more.

Gradually, she took a few steps, intending to get out of the *naamghar*. All of a sudden the trees, all still till now, started heaving in the wind that was pushing and pulling them. The rain, threatening to come down all this time, poured down now. About to come away, she had to retrace her steps. She stood there, where the ladies chanted prayers, getting soaked to the skin. Then, there was the sound of something hard striking the roof of the *naamghar*, again and again. Hailstones, the size of small round lemons each, started pelting Doiboki. Only the *naamghar*'s sanctum sanctorum, the dome-shaped sacred room where the altar was raised, was kept locked; the prayer area outside it was always open. Doiboki stood holding onto the door of the *naamghar* for a while. She couldn't bear the assault of the hailstorm any more. She stepped in.

Taking one step in, she came out again. Once again she was thrashed by the hailstorm. Her exhausted body couldn't take it anymore. Slowly, she went into the *naamghar*; it was dry inside and the air refreshingly cool. A shiver ran through her as the cold air touched her wet clothes. She squeezed the water out of her clothes. A smell of raw fish spread all over the place. Then, she heard that rustling sound again; it seemed to be coming from inside the sanctum sanctorum. It must be still looking for her.

She stared fixedly at the sanctum sanctorum. There was a huge lock on the iron grills. Through the grill she spied the floral *gamosa* upon the altar. On the stand for the earthen lamps, two lamps were still burning, probably from the afternoon. In the tiny firefly-like glow of the two flickering lights, she noticed the many gold and silver flowers in different shapes and sizes placed on the *gamosa*. Looking towards the sanctum sanctorum, she kneeled down. A single lamp that was glowing on the raised bed of earth outside the sanctum sanctorum, suddenly got extinguished. Something jumped from the tin roof of the *naamghar* onto the big kettle-drum in the corner; there was a small sound. Doiboki started shivering.

She could hear the thing again, moving around near the drum. The smells inside the *naamghar*—of mild incense and resin, of mustard oil and cotton wicks, of sprouts, the earthy smell of the neatly wiped floor—overpowering all these and filling up the entire area was the strong smell of raw fish. The rain had soaked the basket in which she carried her fish every day, making the stench stronger. Doiboki felt panic-stricken.

What had she done? She had smeared the great *naamghar* with her stench of fish, the great *naamghar* where even those women with skin as fair and sweet-smelling as jasmine flowers were not allowed in.

Like a magur fish on which salt had been sprinkled, she became agitated. Her head felt light and giddy. She had left at the crack of dawn, eating only a handful of the leftover rice kept soaked in water overnight. Doiboki now felt a twisting sensation in her belly, as if her insides would come out, and threw up loudly. With her chador, she quickly wiped up all the slimy, sour-smelling vomit from the floor. She was afraid to even glance at her chador, sure there was blood on it, clots of blood, yes, it was certainly blood.

Slowly, she lowered her body onto the floor of the *naamghar*. In her half-conscious mind, she heard the rustling of the long one, the moss-covered turtles coming nosily up the slope, the golden boat floating up. Then, everything became indistinct. Just a chador completely soaked in blood, slimy clots of blood.

'Still breathing.'

'She's moving, she's moving.'

'Not dead, she's not dead.'

'She's getting up, sitting; the woman is getting up, sitting.'

Doiboki sat up to the tumult of a crowd of women. Rubbing her eyes, she looked all around. She seemed to be sitting inside the great *naamghar*; outside, a crowd of women. The hailstones that had struck her were no longer there. Where was the blood-soaked chador? She looked at her useless chador; it was stained with yellow patches of dried vomit all over. The golden boat? The pair of giant turtles? The long one moving around, making a rustling sound? The golden and silver flowers glowing in the flickering, dying light of the lamps?

Rubbing her eyes, she peered inside the sanctum sanctorum. The golden-silver flowers, the lamp-stand, the large bell-metal *xorais* were now shining brightly in the daylight. Doiboki fell onto her knees and said a prayer of thanks; then she fixed her chador and came out of the *naamghar*. Her head felt giddy. She took a few unsteady steps, then collapsed and sat down at the spot.

'Isn't that Doiboki, the fisherwoman?' spoke out one of the ladies who were waiting under the banyan tree and who looked as beautiful as the crimson-coloured puthi fish.

The ladies had come at dawn to sing their prayers, as later in the afternoon the men were meeting there for discussions. Just as they were bowing down from their designated spot, before starting their songs, there rose a huge commotion. There was a woman lying just outside the sanctum sanctorum. The person in charge of the *naamghar* stayed a little further away, it took him some time to reach. How could they, who were born as women, step inside the *naamghar*? The in-charge was informed. In a moment, the news spread all over—a low-caste fisherwoman had entered the hallowed *naamghar*. People started rushing towards the *naamghar* from all directions to witness this.

It was true, there was indeed a fisherwoman sitting with her head between her knees at the entrance to the *naamghar*.

'I often buy fish from this woman,' said a woman standing nearby.

'She lives in that village over there,' someone pointed to the village across the bridge.

'How did she get inside the *naamghar*?' Many people were asking the same question, worded differently.

'Now our country's sure to burn. A fisherwoman has entered the sacred abode of God,' someone spoke in a loud voice.

'Something bad is bound to happen, the country will burn for sure,' said old Bonmali Sarma, beating his chest.

'Such a sacred place, even our wives are not allowed in, and, you, the daughter of a fisherwoman dared to ...' Krishna Mahanta started bristling.

'Were you not afraid of entering the *naamghar* with the unclean body of a woman?' Mrs Barua's voice was really trembling with an unknown fear.

'She will die, she will vomit blood and die,' Mrs Saikia cracked her knuckles and cursed her.

Doiboki tried to get up, but sat down again. Her head started to spin. She felt the bile rising inside her empty stomach. Holding her forehead with one hand, she vomited. The place became wet with the foul-smelling, yellow vomit. The sharp pain in her belly abated, her body felt lighter. She stood up now.

Looking towards the crowd, she folded her hands and tried to say something, '... military, hailstorm ...'

While she was getting up, a hundred rupee note, a fifty rupee note and some ten rupee notes fell out of the knot in her *mekhela*.

'Where did she get so much money?' Mahanta's wife, who had never in her life had a hundred rupees of her own to spend, who had never earned a rupee in her life, shouted out.

'She must have stolen it, then gone into the *naamghar*.'

'Who knows, maybe, the silver, golden flowers inside the *naamghar* ...'

'Better go and check if anything is missing inside.'

'How can you trust these low-caste people? She must have entered the *naamghar* with some ulterior motive.'

The crowd started to heckle. Doiboki picked up her money.

'Ladies, why don't you frisk her body once, who knows what she has hidden where?' someone remarked in a slightly jesting tone. A sound of tittering laughter rose up in the gathering.

The men were eyeing Doiboki, licking her with their glances as she stood unsteadily there, her dark, full body, luscious as a mature magur fish, showing through her inadequate *mekhela-chador*.

Barua's wife, flat-as-a-bamboo strip on a weaving loom, suddenly noticed her husband staring, without blinking once, at her full, blouseless body. She pounced on Doiboki and shook her by the hair, 'How can you trust a woman who doesn't wear conch bangles or sindur? She must have come in here with some lover.'

'Indeed! For whatever reasons she came in, she must surely have had someone with her.'

'Who was with you?'

'Where has he gone?'

The abuses and reproaches were injuring Doiboki more than the lemon-sized hailstones had. The sharp-tongued, quarrelsome fisherwoman had become speechless now. Suddenly, she spied on the bamboo bridge in front of the *naamghar*'s entrance a small dark boy. Seeing the strong-limbed boy, she felt her heart about to burst. Everyone said he had got his father's looks. The boy glanced at her once, then ran away along the bridge.

One of the ladies held her nose with one hand and with the other groped Doiboki's bundle of rice and potatoes.

'What do you have here?'

Doiboki's head heated up instantly. These people were calling her a thief, tainting her hard-earned money, and accusing her of having stolen the potatoes she had bought for her blind, old mother-in-law! She stretched out her hands like the sharp stingers of a magur fish about to be caught, her dark body bristling with the poison of singi fish. She gave a push to the woman who was pressing her bundle of rice.

Suddenly, Doiboki caught a familiar scent in the air. Everyone had turned their heads and was now looking towards the bridge. A crowd of people, their dark skins glistening in the sun, was striding down the bridge in a great hurry towards the *naamghar*. They were coming in one big group, like a great shoal of goroi fish.

Doiboki glanced towards them once, then she slapped her thighs in a confident gesture, 'Yes, I am a woman. I am impure. I've carried a child in my womb. I am a fisherwoman. I eke out a living by catching fish. I have sinned by entering the great *naamghar*. But I am not a thief. Last night, because I was afraid of the military, the hailstorm …'

She could not finish her sentence. From all sides, slaps and blows rained down on her. She became engulfed in the shadow of the people who cribbed when even her shadow fell on the grains of rice laid out in the ground to dry under the sun.

A small, dark and sturdy boy came into the *naamghar* shouting, 'Ma, Ma.' Someone gave him a shove as well.

From the midst of the darkness of the crowd, Doiboki gave a terrifying scream, 'Don't kill me, my two kids are alone with the blind old lady …'

Her scream fell, like a bait into a nest of goroi fish, amidst the crowd of dark-skinned people standing on the bridge at the *naamghar*'s entrance. The crowd roused itself. Like tiny kawoi fish being emptied out onto the ground from a *sepa*, it spilled out onto the *naamghar*, where none of them had ever dared to set foot before, from the time of their forefathers.

The blind old lady, holding onto this one, that one, came groping towards where she had heard Doiboki's scream coming from.

'Doiboki, oi, let's see who dares do anything to you! You are my child, my blood. This blind old lady who in her prime could nab a ripe rohu with one throw of the pole, is not dead yet! The old lady is not dead yet, Doiboki.'

The Midget

The boy was surely 21 or 22 years old. Anyway, was there any way to know his real age? His father caught in a maze of alcohol, the battle between irregular and uncertain daily labour and the responsibility of feeding seven hungry souls at home, and a stabbing pain that grew worse every day—was Abhimanyu caught in the middle of a Chakravyahu. It was one month today since the mother died. Who was there to tell how old he was? He himself had lost count of how many years he had spent fishing, playing football with a pomello fruit, climbing trees, and plucking betel nut and coconut for people at times. After his mother's death, he came to understand how unbearable hunger was. And there was only thing he knew to do for that fistful of rice—climb betel and coconut trees.

That boy had now become a man of 40, almost old, doing just that. And on this skill, now ran his household of four children and wife. Actually, their daily fistful of rice came from the rent of one room of the small row house built on land grabbed from the railway. Early morning, he left with his *da*, to roam the streets of the town, crying out melodiously, 'Clean coconut trees.' A few coconut groves had come up in this town. He got some work there, too.

He had put his eldest son Putu in school. He would never allow Putu to do this work. He didn't have to get a job in some office after he finished his studies; it would be enough, good enough, if like the other graduates, he started a small coconut grove. But study, he definitely would. Study, graduate from college; the government would give him money, and he would start his own coconut grove. And then, he himself would clean the trees in his son's grove. Anyway, was there any other person as skilled as him in the job in the whole town?

After he cleared away the cobwebs and rubbish, hacked away the dried-up fronds, put salt in between the leaves, dug a groove all around the plant and put in the pesticide, the trees would bear fruit in bountiful bunches, so that everyone was forced to remark, that that was how a job was done.

It would happen of course, why wouldn't it? Putu studied so hard. Even the master said the boy had brains. Whatever he did, he put his mind to it, was quick to learn a job, and also did it well, in a neat and orderly manner.

His small dream for his son kept growing straight and tall like a coconut tree. One day, he had caught sight of Putu clambering up a coconut tree. He was on his way back after clearing Headmaster Gagan Sarma's trees, 10 of them, at the northern end of the town. He caught sight of Putu atop their neighbour Nabin Hazarika's coconut tree. Putu was dropping coconuts from the top; Hazarika was counting them and gathering them in. He gave his son a good thrashing that day. He was already in a disturbed state of mind because of another instance. Raghu, who like him also cleared coconut trees, had got electrocuted by a loose wire while trying to clean the trees on the street outside Dr Bordoloi's house.

Exactly eight days after that incident, Putu's father went to Bongaon. After signing a contract to clear eight trees, he was able to do only two. It had taken a lot of time. No one had lain a hand on the trees since they were planted; cobwebs that had hardened in between the fronds, ant hills, bird nests—it was a whole dirty mess. By the time he cleared two of them, the sun was already overhead. His body was burning from the heat, the ant bites. Climbing up the third tree, he had just put in his hand on the mass of cobwebs which encircled the tree like a sack, when a snake struck him on his forehead. Putu's father did not fall down from the tree like Raghu had. But after climbing down, he lost consciousness, and never regained it.

Putu's father always folded his hands in prayer before climbing a tree, as Raghu did too, just like before entering a temple. After his work was done, he would touch the tree base again in respect. Coming down from the last tree that day, he hadn't been able to do it.

And Putu? Putu, who could learn a job so fast, could do it so well and who the master said had brains? None of his grandparents, or anyone, had left anything for Putu. Two generations of despair, want and hardship—that was his past and legacy. And what about the country Putu lived in? Could it have any responsibility towards this 10-year-old child? No, he would not get a grain of rice from anyone. Standing in the midst of this desert of absolute nothingness, with his siblings—three of them—and a mother immobilised by illness, was Putu. At any moment Putu, his brother, his sisters and mother could die of hunger, freeze from the cold, be forced to lie on the streets.

The only thing he owned was a pair of small hands. His legs were also still small; they had not yet grown long enough for him to be able to cycle and do some "line". Most of the people on their row of houses did some line. Putu felt angry with his small legs. He could also have piled up stuff on his bicycle and gone out every morning to do line work. So many things: biscuits, sweets, clothes, mosquito nets, peanuts, fried munchies. He could have gone from village to village with his cycle all loaded up. He could have been a handyman like Puna and the others. 'Empty bus, get on! Guwahati!' he, too, would have shouted, half-leaning out of the bus. What could he do with his two short legs?

After his father died, the sprouts-rice-greens given by this family and that family made up at least one meal a day; they survived on that. But with each passing day, Putu saw only darkness. What could he do? What could he do with his tiny hands, his small legs? His mother worked for a day in the fields or in the rice mill or in someone's house and then would be bedridden the next three days. The landlord had threatened to throw them out if he didn't pay the rent by next month. He had left going to school altogether.

At the end of the line of houses where Putu stayed, lived Rani didi, Rambha jethai and Sumati mahi. Their children and families lived in the village. Renting one room in the town, all three worked in a hotel. Rani didi ground masala, starting with black dal, and also chopped vegetables; Rambha jethai cooked all the vegetarian food; Sumati mahi was responsible for the rotis. On their efficient hands depended the hotel Relish-a-Meal. The owner also, if possible, avoided displeasing them. He knew that the amount of work these three women did for the money he paid them, he would not get even if he spent three times that. Of the line of houses, these three were the only ones who made a regular income. The three women maintained their three respective families in the village.

Rani didi was not married. Her father had been a bus-driver. Once when driving the bus on a day of a bandh, a stone that was hurled had broken the glass, and a piece had got into his right eye.

His other eye also gradually became useless. Together with his four children and wife, he waited for the money sent by Rani at the beginning of every month. Rambha jethai's husband had long ago married another and moved out. Her son was an alcoholic; he was good at carpentry, but what use was it? Whatever he earned, he blew away on drinks. The daughter-in-law with her small babies waited for her mother-in-law's money to arrive. Sumati's husband had left her and disappeared a long time ago. Leaving her two sons at her mother's, she lived here, making rotis.

With their work-roughened hands, these three women, three fairies, embraced Putu. For Putu, they were indeed fairies. They bought him a new pair of shirt-pant with their own money, bought him lozenges on the roadside and took him to Relish-a-Meal.

The whole day he looked after the customers, brought black dal-gourd fry to them, placed steaming hot rotis and rasogollas on their plates.

In the afternoon, he would sit down with Rambha jethai and the others, and himself have rice-dal with them. He would have a roti, too. He felt all strange while eating. How heavenly it was to mix the rice with dal and subzi and put it into his mouth, to have a proper and filling meal. You could forget all your troubles on earth for a moment. As he put the first fistful of rice in his mouth and it touched his tongue, he forgot everything else and felt a wonderful kind of happiness overcome him, such as he had never experienced in his life ever before. One ball of rice mixed with dal, with it the jeera-pepper soya bean-pumpkin curry cooked by Rambha jethai.

When the fire in his stomach was quenched, all that wonderful happiness turned into a lump of sorrow and now stuck in his throat. He suddenly and achingly remembered his mother, brother and sisters.

Before he left for home, the owner asked Rani didi to pack a few leftover rotis and some subzi into a polythene packet for Putu. Returning home now, packet in hand, Putu felt as if he was flying, not walking. His short legs had grown wings. It was not the packet of stale, slightly spoiling roti-subzi he spread before his family, but gold and riches gathered by seven generations of kings. He hadn't returned from a hotel named Relish-a-Meal with its wooden benches and where food was put out in aluminum dishes. He had returned home from victory. He was a general back with the spoils of war.

Smearing the rotis with subzi, chewing on them, his brother and sisters watched him with awe. So did his mother. In front of their eyes, Putu's eyes closed shut and he was tilting in sleep where he was sitting. He moaned the whole night in his sleep. His child's pair of small arms and legs was aching. Throughout that night as he groaned and moaned, he dreamed of the school he had given up the day his father died.

Gradually, his feet stopped aching. His eyes no longer closed shut on reaching home. He had a new name now, "little one". He learnt the art of carrying six tea glasses in one hand, could clean the table top in one sweep, then place the roti-subzi with a confident thud on the table, could take customers' order, relay the order inside and inform the owner of the bill amount—all in one breath. He no longer looked like a skeleton. With the money he brought in at month-end and with the leftovers he brought home every day, their household kept running. Slowly, he stopped dreaming about his school.

That day, his owner had sent him to Hotel Tajmahal. Putu and the others knew that the owner sometimes borrowed money from Hotel Tajmahal, sometimes got stuff on loan too. Hotel Tajmahal was the biggest hotel in the town. Stepping in,

Putu was awestruck. Where was their hotel, where was Hotel Tajmahal! The food, the drinks! Paneer, chicken, malai-curry, roll! Those plates and bowls with small white floral designs, the lights everywhere, the beautiful floor, one could go on looking at the paintings on the walls! The small chaps like him had such beautiful uniforms on. He was stunned for a few moments. The owner was wearing such a grand pyjama-kurta, and he smelt of attar. He spoke kindly to him, took from his hands the money sent from Relish-a-Meal. He beckoned a boy, fed him paneer and puri. Thinking of his own mean owner, he felt bitter. What a miser! Even the garam masala and lemons were kept inside locked boxes. God forbid anyone broke a glass; it would surely be deducted from their salary. If Rambha jethai happened to put in more soya bean in the curry, he cribbed and cribbed. The owner himself measured out the mustard oil, as if it was not oil but gold. He did not even feel any embarrassment.

He went to Hotel Tajmahal many times after that. For a few days now, the owner had been buying sweets, flour and oil in small amounts from Hotel Tajmahal. That miserable miser! Not one rupee could slip through his fingers.

Day by day, Hotel Tajmahal started glowing in his eyes, Relish-a-Meal started looking shabbier, darker. He couldn't stand the sight of the owner, with his slightly jutting teeth. What a bad tempered fellow, how he cribbed and complained. The other day, a plate fell from his hands and got dented, and the owner gave him a resounding slap. The plates and dishes, bought who knows how many ages ago, had anyway become thin as paper, and were bound to get dented if they fell! That ugly, miserly creep ...

Rambha jethai and the others said he was good-hearted; that time when Rani fell ill, he went out of his way, and even when aunt had a toothache, he spent money. Good-hearted? Putu bristled whenever he heard that. He gave them a couple of rupees, and they all melted. How that miserly creep counted his money! Let them go and have a look at Hotel Tajmahal, go and see the owner, they would understand what generous-hearted meant. He hadn't told anybody, but from the first, he would be donning a new uniform with the words "Hotel Tajmahal" written on it. If that miser even heard about his salary, his head would spin.

And from the first of June, Putu did, indeed, start sporting a Hotel Tajmahal uniform. And how the red-yellow uniform suited the fair Putu, with his skin all made smooth now by Rambha jethai's roti-subzi. Putu melted in with the paneer-malai-puri-pulao-chicken-ice cream. What tasty food all around. And his generous boss ... When he thought about his master, Putu's heart melted like an ice cream.

One night, the generous master told him to stay over at the hotel. Since a few days now, customers were coming to stay at the new building constructed behind Hotel Tajmahal. The owner stayed one floor above. He kept back a couple of them by turns to look after the guests. That day was his turn. When they heard about it, the other workers started giggling, a couple of them even whistled, 'Oho he's going to be a bride today.' Putu hadn't understood anything.

That night, in the beautifully decorated room of his large-hearted master, Putu had a terrifying experience. Under the crush of the inebriated and attar-smelling owner's weight, small Putu fell unconscious at one time. When he came to his senses, he saw that he wasn't in that room, but in the dark room where their charpoys were kept. He woke up and left Hotel Tajmahal, it was dawn. He couldn't walk. He was groaning under the pain. That day, limping along the half-dark, half-lit road, Putu remembered his father after a long time. Thinking of his father lying blue under the coconut tree, Putu's eyes welled up again and again that day.

Once again those fairies, with their work-roughend hands and masala-smells, engulfed him in their embrace. Yes, indeed they were fairies. They got him back once again to Relish-a-Meal. God only knows what went though Putu's mind when he saw that cranky, miserly old owner, when he touched the plates and dishes that had become paper-thin with time.

When he had finished sweeping and swiping that damp and dull floor, Putu sat down on a rickety wooden bench and started howling. What heart-rending cries! He hadn't cried like that even when his father died. A crowd slowly gathered around him. A little while later, he calmed down by himself.

Putu set up the stove in the verandah of the hotel and started making chow mein and potato chops every evening; rolls soon followed. He pestered the owner to replace the aluminium dishes with plastic plates with floral designs. In the evenings, Putu flew around—tomato sauce for the rolls, chopped cabbage-onions with the chops, fried eggs with chow mein. It was an elaborate affair. An extra ₹100 per month started slipping out of the miserly owner's hands for Putu. Rice at ₹3 per kg, the school lunch; Putu's family was getting along.

Exactly around that time, some 10–15 days after Putu started the rolls, there was excited talk all around—something about a Child Labour Act. Their whole world of roti-subzi, rolls, rice, soya bean, pumpkin, turned topsy-turvy. The police started raiding hotels at any odd time. Children under 14 years of age could not be employed at work. The never-before heard words "child labour" was now on everyone's lips. All the little fellows started disappearing. No one had ever known that so many little ones were working here and there. What a confusion it created! The garages almost closed down. There was panic in the gas agencies, the ice cream factory, the bakery, the sweets factory—all were going to be locked down anytime.

Those tiny legs had been supporting so much weight. Everything was all shaky now. Putu's world of roti-subzi, chow mein-rolls was not only wobbling, but was about to topple over. Many hotel owners were arrested. At Hotel Parijat, the bother-in-law had gone home in the afternoon. Sitting on the owner's chair in the hotel was the college-going nephew, who had come to visit his elder sister during the holidays. There were five or six little ones working at the hotel. This was an open-and-shut case. The police picked up the college-going boy. The news had reached that the owner of Hotel Tajmahal had also been arrested. Money, connections, nothing worked. Putu had to leave Relish-a-Meal within an hour. Everything was left as it was. The buzz of activity in the evenings outside the hotel vanished. There was an eerie stillness all around.

Even quieter grew Putu's household, which could no longer run on the ₹3 rice and school lunch. Putu had just taken out and started sharpening his father's old *da*, used to clean the coconut trees. Just then, Rambha jethai and the owner arrived at his house.

After that, everything was spoken in whispers—as if hell would break loose if they spoke just a little louder. Just one certificate was needed to be issued, and Putu would become a young man, all in the blink of an eye. A young man of 20–23 years of age ... Yet, this person would remain the same—the same small legs, the small hands with the tiny fingers. He would still look like any other small, stocky 10-year-old. There would be no changes in him, but the certificate would make him a 22-year-old! Magic ... What else is it if not magic? That piece of paper certainly was magic. The 10-year-old boy would become 22 in one day; his age would be more, but his body would be the same. What, then, would this magical piece of paper do? A small boy, small hands, small legs, small face, yet he would be 22 years old. What was the paper going to do to Putu? Make him into a dwarf? Yes, a dwarf, of course!

So, Putu became a midget. The village headman put a government seal on the paper, and Putu became a 22-year-old midget. The owner locked it away in his box. No matter how many times the police came, that piece of paper settled everything.

In the two months since Putu left Relish-a-Meal, was caught by the child labour laws, and became a midget with the headman's papers, so much had changed. His mother's stomach ache had worsened; earlier, the pain would come every three–four months, but last month it came twice. The doctor said if that thing inside was not operated and taken out, it would burst inside one day. That would be too late then to do anything. Putu had saved some money; he would take his mother to a hospital in Guwahati. He was going to borrow some more from the master, and from Rambha jethai and the others.

That day, Hotel Tajmahal's owner had said he would bear his mother's entire expense ... Just remembering the smell of attar mixed with sweat and alcohol made him want to puke. He started to sweat rivers. Whenever he remembered that smell, he would shake his head at once, 'no, impossible!' Today also, he shook his head and spoke out aloud, 'No, never! Bloody dog! He doesn't know what i can do.'

Rambha jethai and the rest were working nearby, but when Putu spoke out those words in the midst of making rotis, they didn't ask him anything. Whenever they remembered the heart-rending cries that day, his head on the rickety bench, they felt afraid.

Putu walked slowly towards the hotel's verandah and leaned against a pillar. His uniform took on a green hue; the rain was making puddles in places. The bricks were getting exposed. He and Mitharam had made that stove with a lot of effort, fetching potter's clay from the river bank and mixing it with the husk of paddy. What tact was needed to take out the money for expenses from the miserly master's pocket! If even a single rupee escaped his clutches, it was as if he was parting with his life …

But if he wanted to make money, he would have to put in money. Staring at the moss-covered stove, Putu fell drowning into a sea of worries. How could he start his chow mein-roll-chops again? These days, the master was less interested in running the hotel than in getting name-fame. If the hotel closed down, what difference would it make to the master? He had fields, houses on rent, a son who had a job. The hotel was just time-pass.

Putu and the others knew that he wouldn't put in even a paisa more. In this fast-growing city, the hotel would not run on Rani didi's plain rotis and Rambha jethai's pumpkin-soy bean curry. But if one said anything to him, the master retorted angrily, 'I will sell it off, you see! It's a burden. Buyers are already there.'

If Relish-a-Meal closed down, it would be only their end. Yes, it would have to run like this; else the master would just give it up. Will that miser, that miserable stingy man put money into the hotel?

Remembering his mother—his mother all doubled up in pain—his heart ached. In the last two months, he had used up everything he had. The master had also stopped giving him that extra ₹100. And how could he say anything? After all, hadn't he done enough already by getting him that certificate from the village headman? His sisters and brother were also growing up. Rice for ₹3 and the school lunch were not enough any more.

Putu's body felt like it had lost all its strength. He held onto the pillar gingerly, leaning his head against it. Resting his whole body weight onto the post, his knees buckled under, he kept staring at the moss-stained stove of Relish-a-Meal.

Those small pair of legs and the little pair of hands, and stuck atop that small 10-year-old body was the face of an adult—grave and thoughtful. His forehead creased with worry; Putu, indeed, looked like a midget.

Wednesday Market's Virgin Mary

When I go to drop Junmoni off at school, I keep some time at hand. Crossing the big gate and walking down the red-bricked road, I stop awhile under the row of deodar trees by the pond. Each day, I am charmed anew. Every inch of the spacious school grounds bears the touch of loving hands. Under the gulmohur tree, encircled by the red, white, orange and yellow rose bushes, the statue of the Virgin Mary snatches a glance from everyone, even if for a second—the pointed nose on her fair, round, beautiful face, and in her lap the plump-limbed infant Jesus. The baby clutched to her breast, the Virgin Mary wears a calm, quiet and happy expression. Face to face with this extraordinary calm, I forget, even if for an instant, the distress and cries of turmoil clutching at my heart.

The statue of the Virgin Mary in Junmoni's school, seen through the screen of the slender gulmohur leaves, awakens glimpses of my own youth. The soft green leaves of the gulmohur rouses in my heart the image of another Virgin Mary, standing with her pink-and-gold, smooth-as-petals cheeks and mouth. The same sharp nose on her fair, round face, the curly locks on her forehead, and infant Jesus in her lap. The bunch of girls playing noisily on the merry-go-round runs hastily to assemble in the long verandah near the chapel hall as soon as they spy through the hostel gates the golden-brown Alsatian come running with the basket in its mouth. The pony-sized dog with its red tongue hanging out usually meant that Sister Miriam was close behind, and Sister Miriam meant strict rules. Following a few steps behind are Sister Maria, Sister Louisa and Sister Eliza.

The pale rays of the setting sun fall on the Virgin Mary's statue. The bell rings at the end of the day at Junmoni's school. Through the noise and clamour of the crowd of unruly girls and boys, and the sounds of the rickshaws, scooters and cars that have come to pick them up, comes floating to my ears the sombre sound of another bell ringing. It is the ringing of a prayer bell; the long line of chattering students falls silent.

On the rickshaw with Junmoni, once again my eyes fall on the Virgin Mary's serene and happy face shining amid the crowd of girls and boys running around. I see clearly before my eyes, Sister Miriam's wrinkled face with her short hair, which has turned the colour of a ripe betel nut bark. Sister Miriam is standing on the stage. Hymn book in our hands, we enter the chapel. Avanti's dull eyes are hidden by the row of girls standing and singing hymns. At the end of the song, when we sit down on the carpet, Avanti's pale face becomes visible. Sister Miriam is telling a story—The Virgin Mary and the shabby maidservant. Her voice is very soft, 'Once upon a time …'

Once upon a time, there was a maid, dirty and shabby, and shunned by everyone. One day, going to the market to shop for household things, the maid sees the statue of the Virgin Mary in the market church, and stops, astounded. She is captivated by the beauty of the statue. She goes home, and after finishing her work that day, gives herself a good scrub. She washes and cleans her dirty, oil-spattered dress. Every day, she goes to the market, and every day, she is entranced by the Virgin Mary's beauty. Her desire to look beautiful grows day by day, and soon, her face begins to reflect the beauty and serenity of the Virgin Mary. One day, the bishop greets her, and says, 'You are as beautiful as the Virgin Mary.'

Ending her story, Sister Miriam gazes towards Avanti, 'Avanti! You have been cursed with a disability. But if that girl could become as beautiful as the Virgin Mary, you can also. Pray to God.' For an instant, a rush of blood colours the face of the ninth-standard Avanti, left a cripple by typhoid. Sister Miriam's words keep ringing in our ears, 'Keep faith in God.'

We, the ninth-standard girls, stop going to the playground during play-periods. We begin playing throw-ball with Avanti as her doctor has advised, and she slowly starts hitting the ball back with her hands and legs. Slowly, walking with halting steps, she starts playing games such as handkerchief-thief with us. We help her to do the various exercises which the doctor has shown—for one whole year. Then, when Avanti walked by herself to her new class, Sister Miriam crossed herself and smiled, looking at her. Looking at Sister Miriam's blue eyes in her smooth-as-wax face, we were smiling as well. And so was Avanti.

The story of the Virgin Mary and the maid and Avanti's freedom from her disability had left a deep impress on my tender mind. I told my father, and brought and hung a big picture of Virgin Mary by my study table.

Granny had been angry, 'The girl goes to a Christian school and has become a Christian.'

Deuta had laughed, indulgently.

The image of the Virgin Mary with infant Jesus clutched to her bosom, and the boundless happiness and peace on her face had become engraved in a corner of my heart, since my childhood.

I couldn't be wrong. Seeing the woman seated in the market in her makeshift shop—some bunches of greens, a couple of raw mangoes, banana flowers, and a few clutches of bananas spread out in front of her—I was startled. What a strange likeness. The same nose, the same mouth, the same curly locks on her forehead, that same beautiful plump child in her lap, and above all, the same, exactly same, profoundly serene expression over her eyes and mouth; as if she had discovered the source of eternal happiness.

Unable to stop my excitement, I whispered urgently to my husband, who was in the midst of haggling over the price of gourd, 'Just look over there! That woman with the child! Doesn't her face resemble the Virgin Mary's?'

Not replying, he simply squinted at me.

As soon as we got onto the rickshaw, he rebuked me, 'Here I am thinking how to keep the bag at Sarma's shop and make it to the honours class on time. And there she is, caught by the ghost of poetry in the middle of the market.'

I laugh.

He is still ranting, 'She herself complains that she doesn't want to step into the kitchen if the vegetable shopping is not done on the market day. But what does she look for in the market? Not vegetables, but the Virgin Mary. Height of fantasy!'

His taunts couldn't erase the picture of the woman from my mind.

One day, we were looking at some cloth in a shop. My Virgin Mary, with infant Jesus in her lap, walks into the shop with a group of chattering girls and ladies. The quiet shop is filled with the echoes of loud laughter. Virgin Mary had closely examined some skeins of thread, touching it, turning it again and again in her hands. Perhaps I had been staring at her for too long. She had become nervous. After buying a few small things, the group of girls and ladies went away. It felt like a bubbly spring had suddenly dried up.

Virgin Mary came back in again, she had left the packet of thread behind. Casting a hesitant glance towards me, she got ready to leave. I looked in her direction and smiled.

'Left something behind, did you?'

Lowering her childlike eyes, she nodded in consent.

'What will you weave?'

'A *gamosa*.'

She moves her baby onto the other lap. There is a smile on the baby's tiny pink lips. Moving his arms and legs and stretching out, he keeps leaning towards me, trying to grab my bag again and again. An intense desire to know about the woman's life overcomes me. I leave my husband's side to touch the baby's soft cheeks.

'Where do you live?'

The baby grabs one of my fingers.

'Near Chompa Oil mills.'

Like the baby's touch, her voice is also soft and warm.

'What does his father do?'

'He is a rickshaw puller.'

'Do you have a house of your own?'

'Yes, just a roof over our head; it is from my father-in-law's days.'

She is very hesitant. The baby is trying to grab my white bag.

Laughing, I put the bag in his hands. The woman is startled, as if the child has touched a piece of live coal. She snatches the bag from the child's hand and returns it to me.

'I have mm … money … dear child,' the woman stammers feeling guilty.

Shifting the crying baby with a jerk to the other side, she leaves the shop.

My husband had mocked me, like he usually did, 'It's the same thing; saying that you like the monsoon in the villages of Assam after reading Rabindranath's poems, and finding the Virgin Mary in the weekly market after reading Howard Frost—an acquired feeling. Awkward sensibility!'

As usual, I also digested his taunts with laughter.

What had she said when she was leaving? She would weave on the loom; start making a *gamosa.* In my mind, Virgin Mary was swirling around like a dream. She finishes clearing up the hearth, smoothens her hair with a comb, puts on a sindur bindi on her forehead; seating the boy on a sack cloth with a few grains of puffed rice in a bowl, she sits herself down by the loom. Bihu was already around the corner, her well-shaped hand is moving fast. The boy, intently engaged in putting the puffed rice into his mouth one at a time, gives a loud shriek of joy when he hears the ringing of the rickshaw bell at the bamboo gate. In his excitement, he even takes a faltering step or two. Leaving the rickshaw under the jackfruit tree, a strong, well-built man comes and stands by the loom; the child climbs onto his lap and is gurgling and laughing. Virgin Mary gets up from her loom. On the red floor wiped clean, she lays out his meal and hands out the *gamosa* to the man just back from a bath. On her face, covered with beads of perspiration, is an uncommon serenity, a soothing reflection of a happiness born from love.

Amidst the knotted eyebrows, the sullen faces, the angry and sunken eyes of the people around me, my Virgin Mary's serenity completely overwhelmed me, filling me with a secret intoxication, like the heady fragrance of the sewali flower, which blooms at midnight. Absorbing it drop by drop into my heart, I wanted to become immersed in that potent feeling. Drunk on it, I wanted to forget the piled-up mountain of pain and despair in my heart which was inflicted by this uncaring, despicable world every day.

Taking refuge in Virgin Mary's tranquil and happy face, covered with beads of perspiration, I repeated like a prayer those words engraved in St Paul's cathedral: 'Even in the midst of all the falsehood, destruction and broken dreams, the world is a happy place. Try to be happy.' Even in the midst of falsehood, destruction and broken dreams she lives peacefully and happily; the peace and happiness that mankind always longs for, really does exist. In that desolate mountain in my heart, a single tiny flower starts blooming.

One of our colleagues, Biren Barua, had bought a piece of land on the outskirts of the city, built a house, and had shifted there from the house next to ours. He had invited us to see his house. Stepping into his threshold, I felt soothed and heartened. The house was incomplete, only two rooms had been built, no floor, no ceiling yet. But, under the touch of his hard-working hands, there had already sprung up on that piece of brittle land a grove with mango, jackfruit, betel nut, coconut and banana trees, and also a garden with roses, sewali and champa flowers.

Sitting in that neat and clean courtyard, we ate the bananas and papayas. It was a rustic setting—a herd of cows returning home; an oxen cart with its bells jingling as it moved; nearby, a shy young girl with a pot come to fetch water; small thatched houses. In the setting sun's rays, everything had acquired a golden glow momentarily.

Suddenly I noticed, entering the courtyard of the house in front of Barua's house with a *jakoi* was she, my Wednesday Market's Virgin Mary. The wet clothes clung to her supple body. Seeing the fish jump on the floor, where she had poured them out onto from her *khaloi*, the little boy squealed with laughter.

Standing next to him and looking at him, she too started to laugh, making the world a beautiful place immediately.

Barua was talking about the loans he had acquired while building the house. My husband was trying to prove with the help of examples how difficult it is to build a house in this society with honest earnings. My own middle-class desire to live peacefully in a house of my own, which had been lying dormant in a corner of my mind, while admitting its impossibility, completely consumed me. She is smiling, in her damp clothes, in the light of the waning sun.

The wall made of betel nut fronds, the hut with a leaking roof could not fade out her smile. Virgin Mary's smile merged with the rosy glow of the sun. The white flower which has sprung up in my arid hills spreads its fragrance through my veins. The roots of the flowering tree have broken through my bare hill and are spreading deep inside.

Following my fixed gaze, Barua sees her, and asks, 'What are you looking at, Mrs Kalita? Are you looking at that woman? A rickshawallah's wife, she helps out my wife now and then, she is very skilled, you know. She has planted so many things on this small plot of land.'

In the descending darkness, my Virgin Mary got lost.

I saw her once again at Barua's son's *annaprasan*. She was frying *luchi*s, washing dishes, cutting betel nut, and the little boy following her, whining. Seeing her I froze, like a snake that had been beaten numb by a stick. A ruthless hand had wiped away that serene and happy expression from her face. That supple body, damp and glistening in the setting sun, had now withered away. The child's plump hands and feet were now thin as reed. His belly was protruding. Her harshness as she gave the child a jerk, saying, 'Why don't you die of cholera, you cursed one,' uprooted the lone flower which had started to bloom in the barren mountain of desolation in my heart.

In the real world, the beauty and tranquility of the Virgin Mary and infant Jesus are just an artist's creation. In the real world, no mother with a child on her lap can keep the smile on her face forever. A mother's smile, as she clasps her child to her breast, is simply a poet's imagination, an artist's creation. Virgin Mary's face sinks into the familiar whirlpool of agitation inside my heart.

Asking her to cut a betel nut, Mrs Barua looked towards her and gave a sigh. Seeing my questioning glance, Mrs Barua told me, 'Her husband has fallen ill. How much can she do with her two hands? I help as much as I can. I am myself trapped in a cage.'

I didn't say anything.

An ordinary occurrence … A totally ordinary occurrence … The death of a woman's smile—an extremely ordinary thing. It happens every day. Every moment, the smiles on people's faces are being wiped away by riots, floods, famine, want.

I had almost quite forgotten Wednesday Market's Virgin Mary.

Barua's family came over to visit us, and on seeing the lady who helped me with the chores in the house cleaning fish in the verandah, Mrs Barua remarked, 'The lady you saw?'

I swallowed. 'What happened to her?'

Mrs Barua had taken a betel nut from the tray, put it inside her mouth, and sighed. 'We explained so many times to her, she didn't listen. She sold off the house and land, and went off to Guwahati with her husband. According to her, when her husband recovers, they will get their house, their land back.'

'What happened to the husband?'

Within, the turmoil raged in my barren mountain. A little laughter, a little peace, a little happiness—why was it so rare?

'Some unknown illness ... Could be a tumour in the stomach, says my husband. The doctors are saying to operate.'

For a long time afterwards, Virgin Mary had followed me everywhere. Her face, drowning in the whirlpool of her turmoil, rises to the surface now and again ... She is sitting leaning against the wall next to her husband, who had been lain on the verandah. The child lies lifeless on a *gamosa* nearby ... All around Virgin Mary, flies and mosquitoes, dirt and despair ... Her husband is groaning in pain. Sitting nearby, a dried-up teat thrust into the child's mouth, is Virgin Mary. In her dull eyes and mouth, only struggle and suffering ... Standing in the middle of the road, in a violent fit of agitation, she tears up the piece of paper with the doctor's prescription ... She goes to ask at a big building if they will keep a maid, but the dogs and the chowkidar chase her away and she has to flee. For the sake of her husband's treatment and her child's meals, she enters an infamous alley. In the midst of the knotted foreheads and pale faces, my Wednesday Market's Virgin Mary disappears and is lost.

Gradually, her memory becomes grey. Perhaps, it would have disappeared into darkness one day. But it didn't. My last encounter with her had left my Virgin Mary embedded like a thorn in my heart; a thorn which couldn't be plucked out.

It was during the Puja holidays. Free from my regular routine for some time, I had come to stay in Guwahati for two–three days. Whenever I go to Guwahati from elsewhere, a feeling of homecoming envelops me. Cotton College, my days as a Gauhati University student, my sisters, and the many friends who live there ... The city lures me in spite of it being dirty and disorderly. It did so, that time too.

That day we had been invited to a friend's house. We were supposed to do some shopping at Fancy Bazaar, on our way back.

We spent considerable time gossiping at our friend's. My literary friend and his witty wife praised some stories I had written on women's problems, pointed out a few negative things, too. We were returning from Jalukbari. In the midst of the crowd, I was all the time conscious of my purse slung over my shoulder. There was almost ₹2,000 in it. There were no suspicious people around me, only a few women.

Just about to get down at Fancy Bazaar, I realised my big Shantiniketan bag was missing from my shoulder. The woman who had taken it had not been able to hide it. Holding the child in one hand and the bag in the other, she was hurriedly trying to get down from the bus. Hearing my shouts, several men grabbed and held onto her. In the blink of an eye, there was an uproar. People from the bus and others who had joined in to see the fun surrounded the woman. The crowd was pushing and slapping her. Someone returned the bag, everything was intact. Seeing the crowd some policemen had also come, had given her a couple of slaps, too. The sudden turn of events had me confused.

Getting down from the bus with trembling legs and catching sight of the woman, standing still as a statue amid the slapping and obscene abuses and curses, my blood froze. My Wednesday Market's Virgin Mary—the Virgin Mary who had made that lone white flower of hope bloom secretly in my heart and who had stood glistening in the setting sun's rays in her wet clothes.

She was standing immobile in the middle of the crowd. Grey hair covered both sides of her middle parting. The boy in her lap was crying. The boy's hands and legs were thin like dried twigs, his stomach bloated and his head unnaturally large. On her face, which was starting to turn black and swollen in places, there was no trace of the tranquility, no beauty, not even an iota of happiness; only a terrible suffering, a dreadful manifestation of dire poverty.

The swollen and blood-smeared face of this woman standing mutely, holding the crying, malnourished child in her lap, was not the face of the Virgin Mary with her purity, serenity and eternal happiness. It was the face of a miserable, hapless mother, born to the sufferings and trials of abject poverty.

Seeing my Wednesday Market's Virgin Mary standing on the footpath of Fancy Bazaar, inhaling the poisonous polluted air all around and trapped in misery, it occurred to me that this wretched woman with her puffed-up, bloody face was the genuine Virgin Mary. The Virgin Mary of my youth, smiling with an expression of everlasting happiness, was merely an artist's imagination and fancy. Only this wretched and pitiful mother would be able to tear her dear son away from her breast to suffer the agonies of the cross. Because she wanted a world where one could live.

I grabbed her rough hand as limping and moving slowly, she tried to get away from there. As I held her hand, I knew that I had found the real Virgin Mary, born to suffering and one who could sacrifice her own son for the salvation of the entire human race.

Cultivated feelings? Awkward sensibility? Perhaps ...

Glossary

Aarnai: shawl

Aita: grandmother

Akhoi: puffed rice

Annaprasan: a ceremony where an infant is fed rice or cereal for the first time

Bao dhan: a variety of rice

Bhado: the fifth month of the Assamese calendar

Bhogi: The king selected a healthy and young man to be sacrificed at the altar of the Goddess for the welfare of the king and his kingdom. The young man was known as a bhogi. He would live life at his will till the day of the sacrifice.

Bhotbhoti: motorboat

Bohag: the first month of the Assamese calendar, beginning mid-April

Bohag Bihu: the festival celebrating spring

Bota: bell-metal tray on a stand, used to serve paan-betel nut, or offerings to deities

Bothi: knife with a stand that is placed on the floor. It is mostly used to cut fish and vegetables

Da: machette

Dao: machette

Deuta: Father

Dokhona: a piece of garment

Dambaru: a drum

Gamosa: a piece of woven cloth with floral designs used as a towel

Gurguri: used for tobacco smoking, like a hookah

Jakoi: a triangular bamboo scoop for fishing

Japi: a hat made with thin bamboo strips, used in the fields

Jeth: the second month of the Assamese calendar, mid-May

Jethai: aunt, mother's or father's elder sister

Juroon: the ceremony in which the bride is presented the bridal trousseau from her husband's family

Kati Bihu: one of the three Bihu festivals, observed in mid-October

Khaloi: creel, a basket made of bamboo strips to hold small fish

Khar: a form of alkali derived from the banana tree and also a typical Assamese dish made with it

Koka: Grandfather

Koli-joha: a variety of rice which is blackish in colour

Lau-pani: a local alcoholic drink made from fermented rice

Luchi: puri

Magh: the tenth month of the Assamese calendar, mid-January

Mahi: aunt

Mekhela: the bottom half of the two-piece mekhela-chador, the traditional dress of Assamese women

Mekhela-chador: traditional Assamese two-piece attire

Murha: a stool made with fine bamboo sticks

Naam: prayers

Naamghar: community prayer hall

Namghosa: a religious book

Paan-tamul: a mixture of betel leaf and betel nut

Pisi: paternal aunt, also called Pehi in Assamese

Pitha: rice cake

Saun: the fourth month of the Assamese calendar

Sepa: basket

Tekeli-pitha: a delicacy prepared from rice powder in an earthen pot

Than: shrine

Uroni: head-cover

Xorai: a tray on stands, made of brass or bell-metal, used for offerings in worship

Arupa Patangia Kalita is one of the most accomplished and refined writers of Assam. She has to her credit over 19 publications (some of which have been adapted as films and tele-films). She has been conferred a number of awards for her contribution to the realm of Assamese literature—the Bharatiya Bhasha Parishad Literary Award (1995), the Katha Award (1998), the Sahitya Akademi Award (2014) and the Assam Valley Literary Award (2017).

A number of short stories written by Arupa Patangia Kalita have been translated into English, Bengali and Hindi. Her works are used extensively for research by MPhil and PhD students. Some of her stories have been prescribed as texts for universities, including the Gauhati University.